PRAIS.

M000043361

Havana Odyssey: Chasing Ochoa's Ghost

"Having visited Cuba often since 1994, I credit the author for spotlighting the multiple levels of Cuban society, including its shadowy security forces. Beware the enigmatic Priest, the ravishing Eloisa, and the determined Inspector hunting down Professor Luke Shannon. *Havana Odyssey* is a compelling read."

—**Professor Jose Antonio Echenique,** senior fellow and dean emeritus, *la Facultad de Contabilidad y Administración, la Universidad Nacional Autónima de México* (UNAM). Author, *Ética Práctica,* several academic articles.

"*Havana Odyssey* takes the reader on a wild ride through the corridors of power in Cuba, where the ghosts of Ochoa, Che and Cienfuegos still roam. As a professor, I empathize with the main character trying to open dialogue with academics. First, Luke Shannon must survive inspectors and deans of unknown loyalties, making the reader ask in whom one can place trust."

—**Professor Eduardo Gamarra,** director, Latino Public Opinion Forum, School of International and Public Affairs, Florida International University. Author, *Bolivia on the Brink;* member Bolivia's Academy of Science.

"One of the best compliments I give a book is that it makes me turn the page. *Havana Odyssey: Chasing Ochoa's Ghost* delivers this excitement and a history lesson. Cuba, only 90 miles from the United States, is inscrutable for most of us. The book peels away layers of the shroud and gives us a riveting look inside."

—**Jim Hessler,** author, *Land on Your Feet, Not on Your Face;* President, Path Forward LLC

"In *Havana Odyssey* Stephen Murphy has put together all the elements we want from a story of intrigue and romance, all taking place in contemporary Cuba, beyond tourist eyes."

—**Stephen W. Holgate,** author of *Tangier, Madagascar* and *Sri Lanka*

"I have followed the author's vocation to build bridges between all people of the Americas. Havana Odyssey reveals a professor's attempts to do so in authoritarian Cuba. The author pays special attention to cultural details that pull the reader in beyond the façade. Captivating and thrilling!"

—**John McPhail,** President and CEO,
Partners of the Americas Inc. (Washington, D.C.)

"When the Iron Curtain fell on Eastern Europe and the Soviet Union, it also shrouded events that took place on an island 90 miles south of Key West, FL. Havana Odyssey reveals unique parts of that history, weaving it into a story of a young man fulfilling a pledge to his lost love. It's a journey worth taking."

—**Gary Schwartz,** author, *The King of Average;*
Director, Improv Theater Group

"As a fan of the author's activities with Hollywood studios and Rio's street kids, I am happy to provide entrée to Cuba's film school in San Antonio de los Baños. Despite trying circumstances, the author interviewed Habaneros from all walks of life. *Havana Odyssey: Chasing Ochoa's Ghost* captures this drama in 2020."

—**Steve Solot,** manager, Netflix Production Policy, Latin America,
Editor, *Current Mechanisms for Financing Audiovisual Content in Latin America,* Former Senior Vice President, Motion Picture Association
(Rio de Janeiro, Brazil)

"*Havana Odyssey: Chasing Ochoa's Ghost* is an insightful look at modern-day Cuba. The book is sympathetic to the Cuban people yet critical of the inner workings of the authoritarian state. This historical novel reads well, offering romance, treachery, and personal redemption. I like it."

—**Dr. Jaime Suchlicki,** Director, The Cuban Studies Institute
(Coral Gables, FL). Author, *Cuba: From Columbus to Castro and Beyond, Breve Historia de Cuba, University Students and Revolution in Cuba.*

ANOTHER BOOK BY STEPHEN E. MURPHY

On the Edge: an Odyssey

HAVANA ODYSSEY

HAVANA ODYSSEY

Chasing Ochoa's Ghost

STEPHEN E. MURPHY

Odyssey Chapters
Seattle, Washington

bookhouse
PUBLISHING

2950 Newmarket St., Suite 101-358 | Bellingham, WA 98226
www.bookhouserules.com

Printed in the United States of America

Library of Congress Control Number: 2020913352

ISBN: 978-1-952483-12-7 (Paperback)
ISBN: 978-1-952483-13-4 (eBook)

Cover design: JD Fuller

Odyssey Chapters, P.O. Box 15155, Seattle, WA 98115
www.stephenemurphyauthor.com

To Ana Maria

CONTENTS

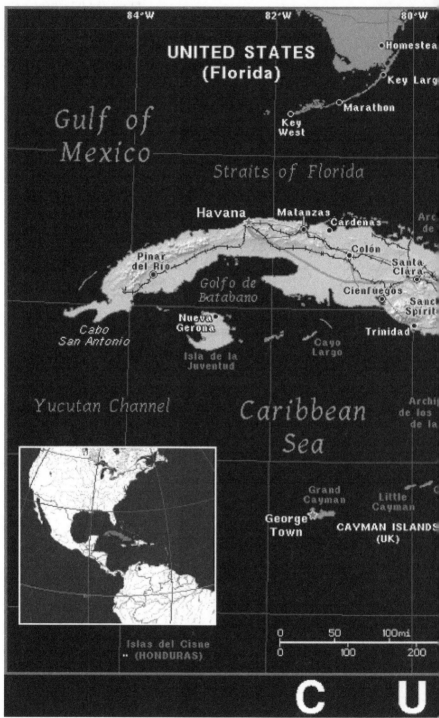

FOREWORD

Baracoa base, west of Havana, July 13, 1989, at dawn

THE MOTORCADE RUMBLED DOWN FIFTH AVENUE, past embassies and classic homes. The soldiers and officers inside the jeeps looked straight ahead. All wore somber looks. One master sergeant could not control the tears running down his weathered face.

The convoy turned into the military base for "Special Troops" in Baracoa. It passed soldiers at port arms and made its way toward a narrow beach.

In darkness, four prisoners exited the jeeps. Soldiers surrounded them on either side, marching to the infamous wall. Its courtyard overshadowed a spit of sand.

The tallest of the four senior officers asked that no blindfold be placed over his eyes. Instead, he extended his arms and forgave the six soldiers with rifles raised.

"You're doing your duty," someone heard him say.

Six shots rang out, startling the seagulls perched nearby. Theirs were the sole laments heard that morning in behalf of Cuba's Hero of the Republic.

General Arnaldo Ochoa Sanchez and three officers lay dead, crumpled on the sand.

THE FIRST JOURNEY

*"The mystery of human existence lies not in just staying alive,
but in finding something to live for."*

The Brothers Karamazov
—Fyodor Dostoyevsky

CHAPTER 1

Washington, D.C., December, 1989

OUTSIDE, DECEMBER'S WIND HOWLED DOWN PENNSYLVANIA Avenue. Inside the TV studio, Luke Shannon stood in front of a monitor, reviewing a program edited by Cuban exiles for rebroadcast to Havana. The documentary questioned how Cuba was dealing with Soviet President Gorbachev's initiative for openness in government.

The Castros were pushing back. Now, without Russia's support, daily life got more difficult for the Cuban people. To keep them in check, Castro's secret police clamped down on any and all dissent.

A six-foot-tall, youngish-looking man followed the filming, offering an occasional pointer about the camera angle. He'd only spent a year and a half at the TV station, but his politically connected boss helped him secure this position when George H. W. Bush was elected president. As the cameraman and a production assistant looked back at him, he seemed lost in reflection. He toyed with his reddish-brown hair, a habit he couldn't break when deep in thought.

Luke Shannon pondered how the year unfolded. Despite Gorbachev's *"perestroika,"* the Soviet bloc was fraying at the seams. Reagan's call for liberation resonated when the Berlin Wall came tumbling down.

Students rebelled around the world. As the new director of Worldnet TV, Luke had witnessed these events from studios in Washington, D.C. The documentary on Cuba would capture this upheaval.

He raised his tall frame and gave the producer a thumbs up. It was her final cut and the documentary was "tight." A side door sprang open, letting in a winter blast. Luke shivered, reminding himself how much he detested the cold. If only he could return to the Caribbean, where he'd won that trip from the TV station. He recalled swimming in the crystalline waters and diving under rolling waves. He closed the door and refocused on the present.

Suddenly, all conversation stopped. CNN's satellite feed showed one student facing down a Chinese tank. The student moved right, then left, to protect his classmates in Tiananmen Square. Gazing in horror, they saw the young man offer his body in sacrifice.

At the back of the studio, Luke heard a muffled cry. He turned and saw a striking woman wipe her tears away. He walked back to her and stood nearby.

"This student breaks my heart. What will happen to him? At least the world has seen him stand up for freedom," she said, tears rolling down her cheeks. She brushed back her chestnut hair and shook her head.

"But how many know of the sacrifice of Cuba's beloved 'Hero of the Republic,' sent by the Castros to a firing squad this very July? Despite serving his country with courage in Angola, the authorities cut his life short. Now, they are sweeping his memory away. It's like General Arnaldo Ochoa never existed. What injustice!" she exclaimed. Her eyes flashed and she clenched her fists. Electricity seemed to flow from her.

Luke was moved. He was also attracted to her ardor. What was driving her—family, politics, or maybe a lover? How on point she was to recount the Cuban general's demise. Wasn't Luke's responsibility to uncover the truth and share it with international audiences? "Perhaps a documentary would remind journalists about his tragic death, señorita. People seeking liberty would take note."

"*Señor Director*, please tell his story to the world. He was a beloved figure who aspired to bring hope to the Cuban people. For doing so, his sole reward was a bullet. Would you tell your viewers what happened to him?"

"I promise to do my best," Luke replied, touched by her words and her passion.

Her eyes gleamed in expectation. She introduced herself as a "relative" of Cuba's deceased hero. Her name was Ana.

Luke stepped back to admire this five-foot-nine dynamo, whose gray-green eyes locked onto his. She wanted action. Maybe he did, too. If only more people in the world were like her.

Ana was visiting a friend who worked in the studio. Luke felt drawn to her. He debated whether he should ask her out. His heartbeat rose as he heard himself say, "Could we meet another time, Ana?"

Ana opened her fist, dried her eyes, and bobbed her head.

Luke met her late that afternoon at the classic Willard Hotel, not far from the White House. He led Ana by the polished-mahogany bar through a klatch of lobbyists and politicos trading gossip. Luke loved this iconic watering hole with sketches of notables like Mark Twain hanging on forest-green walls. A corner table opened up, and Luke secured it before a young congressional staffer could. He pulled out the chair to seat her, as his mom taught him to do.

When their hands touched, Luke's heart rate rocketed. Over Cuba Libres, they shared the ups and downs of their young lives—hers more dramatic in Havana than in his hometown Seattle. Holiday spirit loosened their tongues, and emotions bubbled over in that quaint lounge. One gesture led to another. Luke and Ana left arm-in-arm into the light snow falling on the nation's capital.

Romance bloomed that cold winter night and lingered through the spring.

* * *

One damp morning, Luke awoke and gazed at Meridian Park, down 16th Street Northwest to the White House. Ana was hugging a pillow, her eyelids fluttering. Her joie-de-vivre had lit his fires throughout the long winter. She had opened a little crack into Luke's interior door. As an introvert, he usually kept it shut. She also made him feel whole. As long as Ana was present, he didn't mind the cold.

Ana's drive for justice in behalf of her slain uncle and the Cuban people resonated with Luke. "Who else can we call?" she beguiled, prompting him to work the phones on her behalf. She never gave up and knocked on many doors to raise her *cause celebre*. Unfortunately, the TV program he tried to film about her famous uncle got sidetracked by budget cuts. Rumblings about a war in Iraq made his boss take pause. Still, he loved Ana's "fighting Irish" spirit, even though she was a native of Cuba.

The sun broke through the clouds. He saw tulips in the park's gardens and maple trees budding green. Ana's eyes flickered open and caught a ray of light. He never tired of looking into her enchanting gray-green eyes. If only this moment could last forever.

"Ana, would you like to be a part of the capital's ritual of spring? Let's take a walk under the cherry blossoms. Sunshine is making its appearance. What do you say?"

She radiated that special smile, which melted Luke's heart, "Let's go, Lucas!" Soon, they were strolling hand-in-hand down 16th Street, past the White House to the Tidal Basin. At the Jefferson Memorial, they joined thousands of pedestrians admiring the blossoms and relishing the springtime air.

Luke and Ana kept a brisk pace with the multitude circling the pool. Kenyans in red-and-brown Dashiki's were shouting in Swahili to family members. Middle-Eastern women in colored scarves chatted in Arabic while slyly glancing at younger men. Latinos of all generations spilled over the sidewalks, dazzled by this explosion of spring. Luke felt at one with the world.

Falling blossoms grazed Luke and Ana's cheeks. The sun played peekaboo with the clouds. Luke closed his eyes. A warmth surged through him. Love was in the air.

Without warning, Luke heard a loud cry coming from behind. He opened his eyes, pivoting to avoid a scuffle among five Latino men. They threw punches back and forth and cursed *en español*. Luke tried to avoid them but sustained a glancing blow. Their aggression broke the springtime spell. Luke prepared to defend himself. Ana moved away with others to avoid the fight.

One man began swinging at Luke and missed by an inch. Another fighter shouted to someone outside the circle. Luke didn't know what was going on. Why he was being targeted? He heard the tallest fighter whistle between two fingers. Was it a signal? The others began drifting back over the grass, two of them staring at Luke. The one who swung at him sneered, spun around, and quickly disappeared into the crowd.

By the time Luke turned toward the Tidal Basin, he'd lost sight of Ana. Where had she gone? Luke moved through the throngs, startling walkers, "Ana, Ana!" The fighters had vanished into the surging mass. Luke feared that this fight had been staged, covering an action to take Ana away.

Luke hurried along the walkway and circled back to where they had begun their stroll. No Ana, anywhere. He jogged around the Tidal Basin, searching frantically right and left. He ran into a National Park Service officer and asked if he'd seen a Latina appearing lost. The officer promised to keep an eye out for her. If not, he recommended filing a missing-person report at the D.C. precinct, not far from the National Mall.

Cherry blossoms continued fluttering down. To Luke, they'd lost their charm. They were saying *adiós*. Ana had disappeared into the springtime mist. Luke feared more than foul play.

That afternoon, he filed the missing-person report and queried D.C. police throughout the week. They had not discovered any sign of Ana. At the TV studio, he asked Ana's friends if they'd seen her. They only responded with a shrug. One male colleague finally said, "We thought she was living with you." Luke didn't know what to do.

In 1989, diplomatic relations between Cuba and the U.S. were nonexistent. It was almost impossible to ascertain the whereabouts of anyone inside Cuba. Desperate, Luke spoke with a friend in the U.S. State Department. The diplomat promised to check on Ana with a Swiss acquaintance in Havana. At the time, the Swiss embassy housed a small, "American Interests" section. Days, then months passed, without word. His friend at the State Department concluded, "Sorry, Luke. If Cuban intelligence had a hand in this, it'd be impossible to find her anyway. They imprison dissidents in remote compounds, beyond the public eye. Government agents are cracking down harder now. As you know, Cuba is a police state."

Distraught, Luke tried to refocus on work. He asked colleagues again about doing a story on Ochoa. They didn't think it would make a big splash. Besides, they had their weekly teleconferences that took their time, energy, and budget. War was threatening in the Middle East, demanding Worldnet TV coverage and expense.

Luke let the idea go, but he never stopped thinking about Ana or the promise he'd made to her.

* * *

Life relentlessly moved on. When President George H.W. Bush was defeated in 1992, Luke lost his job. He left Washington, D.C., for "the Crossroads of the Americas," closer to Havana. In Miami, he consulted for a Latin American TV group and volunteered to teach basic economics at an inner-city school. He asked around the Cuban American communities but heard nothing about Ana. It was the "special period" in Cuba, without Soviet support to keep its economy afloat. It was dicey to get any kind of news from the Castro regime. Luke began to lose hope that he'd ever find Ana again.

After a few years, he accepted an offer of an international bank, which relocated him to Rio de Janeiro. He filled his days meeting with clients and credit analysts, usually staying late at the office. Afterwards, he often walked the streets, following base desire if not common sense. He behaved like a kid in a candy store, seduced by Brazilian beauty and *bossa nova*. His personal life became a roller coaster of impromptu affairs. He tried to forget the past. Still a certain word or inflection brought back memories of Ana. No one could hold a candle to what he'd felt for her.

Luke went through the motions without romance. Sometimes, he even sought solace with prostitutes but usually departed lonelier than before. Haltingly, he pushed himself to open up, and he had a fling with a dazzling Afro-Brazilian actress. Though the sex was exhilarating, he sensed she had another motive. He held back. She called him shy. When he learned that she'd left Brazil with a German TV producer, he pulled up his inner bridge, locked the door, and threw away the key. He asked himself if he wasn't destined to a life of solitude.

Y2K came and went, and a new decade lurked around the corner. What was he to do with the rest of his life? He finished his M.B.A. online for one little victory.

He eventually found his way back to hometown Seattle. He tried to settle down but hated returning to an empty apartment. Luke adopted "Buddy" from the rescue shelter. Two lonely souls, they took to one another. The cocker spaniel also gave him a reason to get up in the morning.

He accepted an adjunct post at Seattle University and began teaching courses about Latin America. Occasionally, Luke went out on dates. But no one seemed to turn on the switch. He was drifting through middle age and considered entering the Peace Corps. Instead, he joined the University Rotarians to fill his time. At the Chieftain Irish pub, just across from campus, he rarely declined the barkeep's offer, "Another Cuba Libre, professor?" Then he'd stumble up Capitol Hill and get a lift from Buddy's licks, before flopping into bed.

Yet, in the quiet hours of night and occasionally in his dreams, Ana returned to him. Though her face was indistinct, Luke sensed her presence and passion. Luke often woke up panting and searching the bedroom for her. Just like at the Tidal Basin, Ana had vanished without a trace.

But late one spring morning, he received an unexpected report. His life was about to take a startling turn.

CHAPTER 2

Miami en route to Havana, Saturday in July

Luke looked out the window and spied the Gulfstream below, skirting Andros Island in the Bahamas. As the plane headed south, the aquamarine waters flowed into the Florida Straits, suggesting hope. It had been 30 years since he'd last seen Ana—if only he could arrive in time.

When he attended a university debate on Cuba, he met a Cuban dissident who mentioned the Ochoa family. When sparks flew between the Cuban exile and Cuba's second secretary of its embassy, Luke got involved in the debate. To those in the audience, the Cold War had blown in from the Caribbean.

During the recess, Luke met the exile again. He was connected with Miami's Cuban American National Foundation. Luke confessed his unkept promise made to the deceased general's niece. The exile advised that Ana recently was living in Ochoa's hometown but was in failing health. If Luke wanted to see her again, he needed to go to Cuba as soon as possible. Luke looked over his shoulder and saw the second secretary monitoring their conversation.

Astonishment and hope seized Luke. Ana was alive! He thanked the exile for the good news and knocked on the dean's door that very day. He pleaded to represent Seattle U. on an educational mission to the University of Havana.

When the dean approved his trip to Cuba, Luke sensed an invisible hand drawing him there. Though 30 years late, maybe he could honor his promise to Ana. After his scheduled call on academia, Luke would search for his long-lost lover. He sensed a renewed purpose in life.

As the current administration tightened the screws on Cuban travel, it had become dicey to visit. Fortunately, Luke secured the last seat on a charter flight from Miami to Havana.

Since Ochoa's name was suspect in Cuba, he'd have to meet discreetly with the exile's friends. He had to find Ana without raising alarm. Luke hoped such "friends" would not be spies for the state. He pondered the dean's parting words at Sea-Tac Airport, "Be safe." Luke wondered where this journey might lead and how it might end.

A flight attendant recommended a mojito to steady his nerves. Luke enjoyed the mix of lime juice, mint leaves, sugar, and rum. When he lived in Miami, he'd downed not a few mojitos with Cuban Americans along *Calle Ocho*. The concoction loosened him up, releasing him to sleep. He dreamed that he was swimming in choppy waters, striving to reach a distant shore. He kept up his strokes but didn't make headway. A gust kicked up and breakers pounded over him. Salt water entered his mouth, stoking fear that he was drowning.

He jerked awake to a shaking plane dodging a towering thunderhead. Perspiration ran down his cheek. The plane fluttered over the turquoise water, aiming for the metropolis stretching along Cuba's northwestern shore. *Cubana Aviación's* 737 bounced off the airstrip once and slogged toward Havana's José Martí Airport.

Luke came down the plane's steps to a broiling tarmac. A Cuban flag flapped in the wind. Luke saw the red triangle with a star and three horizontal blue stripes. He recalled that the Puerto Rican flag reversed the colors. The flags' designs reflected America's historical sway on both islands.

Luke exited with the Vietnamese diplomat, with whom he'd sat and talked inflight. Mr. Dong had a sister in Seattle who needed help with U.S. Immigration. Luke promised to connect her with a Seattle U. law professor. The diplomat gave Luke his card in Havana. They followed plainclothes men and women to the door marked "*Imigración*." There, armed guards roamed inside, and Customs officials dressed in khaki waited behind a 40-foot counter painted red.

The Vietnamese diplomat shook Luke's hand and said goodbye. He was whisked through the counter marked for "Official Visitors." Luke's group lined up behind the "Visitors" sign. Many chatted about "fun in the sun and Cuba Libres at the Tropicana."

"Do you have anything to declare?" a uniformed woman in Afro inquired, no nonsense in her voice. A supervisor stood behind and looked over tinted glasses at Luke's passport. He examined its entry and exit stamps with care.

"I'm bringing in $7,000, small gifts for friends, and books for professors at the University of Havana." Luke had learned that Cuba allowed tourists to bring up to $10,000 in foreign currency but no "objectionable" media. He'd drained his savings account to pay for this trip.

"Don't forget to exchange your dollars into 'Convertible Units of Currency,' or '*CUCs*,'" she commanded. "You should pay for services in CUCs—do you understand? Don't lose your copy of the tourist visa. It's required to leave Cuba," she warned.

The supervisor moved forward and asked: "What is your profession? I notice that you've traveled to several Latin American countries."

"I teach courses in Latin American business and do consulting in Brazil. But this is my first time in Cuba," Luke replied, wiping damp palms on his pants.

The man pushed the tinted glasses up his immense nose and looked intently at Luke. He checked his computer screen for several minutes. "Follow me, señor," he ordered brusquely.

He directed Luke to an empty room on the left. With the agent following closely behind, Luke entered a dimly lit space, covered by gray acoustic tiles. It smelled of disinfectant and sweat. The supervisor pointed to the sole table and chair: "I will retain your passport and will retrieve your luggage. Please wait in this room." He closed the door.

Luke's anxiety rose with the room's temperature. Time moved slowly. His throat was parched and no water was in sight. The stuffy room unleashed memories of the cross-examination he suffered at the hands of military intelligence years ago. Unease penetrated Luke's secret place, where he'd tried to lock up his miseries from the past.

The door finally opened and the agent stepped aside, letting a tall, thin man breeze by. He wore a beige *guayabera*, a shirt typical of the tropics, loosely covering his dark trouser tops. He held Luke's passport in his hand, tapping it back and forth.

"Buenas tardes, señor. What is the purpose of your trip to our Republic?" the inspector inquired. He stood six-foot-three and his frame was slight. His eyes hid behind dark glasses above a hooked nose.

"I'm here for educational purposes. I'm bringing letters and books from Seattle University for instructors at the University of Havana," Luke replied. Outside, he saw others in the tour passing through Customs without a query.

The inspector closed the door.

"Yes, I see you checked 'Education' on the visa. You cannot teach in any classroom or conduct research in Cuba without explicit permission from the Ministry of Education. Open the larger suit case and let's see what's inside. You stated that you have 'nothing to declare,'" he said with a sardonic smile.

The inspector patted down the outside pockets of Luke's Air Force cargo bag and pored through shirts, small gifts, and books. He pulled out two books and asked: "What are these about, professor?"

"That book is about finance," Luke replied, "to support the university's small-business program on campus. The director requested this textbook for her students."

"And *Our Man in Havana*—is this also a textbook for the director?" he inquired with a smirk, eyeing Luke over Ray-Ban sunglasses. The inspector seemed to enjoy flipping through the book's pages.

"That book is for my personal reading pleasure. Graham Greene is a renowned author from England and wrote about Havana in the 1950s. Are you familiar with his work?"

"No. Maybe another time. I do know the works of Hemmingway. He remains popular in Cuba and spent time on our island. *Habla español?*"

"Sí *señor*," Luke responded, keeping his answer brief. He yearned to escape the stuffy room and probing questions. He rested his elbows on the table, feeling light-headed.

The inspector said nothing for a minute, fraying Luke's nerves. What would happen next?

"OK, professor. Remember—no teaching in classes or conferences without permission. You are dismissed." Luke shouldered his backpack and struggled forward with his heavy bag. He followed the immigration agent out an unmarked door.

Luke looked back once and saw the tall inspector monitor his retreat. Their eyes met briefly, a silent reminder that Luke was on his turf now. Luke no longer enjoyed the sanctuary of academic freedom nor access to America's Bill of Rights. Instead, he had entered a new world of tropical heat, interrogation rooms, and arrogant inspectors behind dark glasses.

Outside, Luke sought out the *Cubatur* van scheduled to take his group to the Hotel Nacional. He asked a roving guide. "That tour left 20 minutes ago. Maybe I can be of assistance?" Luke declined his offer. Sweat pouring through his North Face jersey, Luke wrestled the bag across the inner island. An assortment of classic cabs whizzed by. Ladas from Soviet days and Chevy Impalas of the '50s fought for space. Farther on the horizon, clouds were gathering, and a lone seagull circled in the breeze.

Suddenly, a bright-yellow Packard convertible swerved ahead of official-looking Lada cabs. It stopped in front of Luke. "Can I take you somewhere, señor? My brother and I have an American car, especially for American visitors." He extended his large, brown arm toward the red-leather seats. It was a welcoming sight.

Luke mulled over his offer and answered *en español*: "Do you have an official license, as the cabbie behind seems unhappy?"

"No worry, we'll take care of him—he's a friend," he said airily. "We're happy to show you Havana. Help us out, *Americano*. We are the face of the 'new Cuba,'" he announced, smiling with pride. His lighter-skinned "brother," wearing a Panama hat, enthused in English, "We like *Americanos*."

Luke looked at the other cabbie, who shrugged. He approached the aggressive impresario, "As an entrepreneur of the 'new Cuba', how much do you charge to the Hotel Nacional in the Vedado neighbor-hood?" In his rush from the airport, he'd forgotten to exchange dol-lars into CUCs. After some back-and-forth, they agreed on $25 and were off. Casting a quick view back at the airport, Luke observed a tall man in *guayabera* standing in the shadows, staring his way.

The brothers seemed to take the scenic route, skirting Havana's worker suburbs of faded homes. Luke saw boys in threadbare shirts driving donkey carts on bumpy surfaces. In the town square, an immense tree provided a canopy for residents escaping the afternoon sun.

"That's the Ceiba, the sacred tree of Cuba. Rites of *Santeria* are performed under its broad boughs. Best to avoid, señor," warned the brother.

The driver passed a military barracks with neatly trimmed lawns and uniformed soldiers. He made a quick right turn off the highway and parked at a turnabout without exit. "I have to make a brief stop to retrieve some 'unofficial' motor oil. But not to worry, it won't take long."

An austere compound loomed at the end of the street. Over a barbed-wire fence, Luke spied a blockhouse and ochre-colored buildings extending deep inside. Luke cast a worried look at the driver's brother. "You don't want to end up there, *Americano*. That's *Villa Marista*, where they detain political prisoners, both foreign and domestic. I've been told that inmates have no idea whether it's day or night inside. It's best to stay put in Vedado."

His brother lugged back five cans of Pemex oil. "He owes me CUCs but pays me in motor oil. He's a chauffeur for the state and 'borrows' from the motor pool."

The driver doubled back to the main highway and passed a billboard chastising the U.S. embargo. Luke translated the words underneath, "The biggest genocide in history." A rope surrounded the "O" in "embargo," showing the island of Cuba caught inside.

The driver angled onto a seaside boulevard. "Welcome to Havana's famous *Malecón*. It runs five miles along the sea." He pointed to couples strolling along the wide esplanade, dodging surf splashing over the wall. A few fishermen were casting lines in between the waves.

"Let's hope that no hurricane hits this year. Irma was terrifying, crashing over this bulkhead. Irma swept people out to sea and inundated their homes."

Luke watched gulls glide by and inhaled the salt air. He turned toward the sea and shut his eyes. The trade winds rolled over his face. At last, he let his shoulders relax. Little by little, the tropical scene lightened his mood.

They sped by a tall, non-descript building, flying an American flag. "That's your embassy in front of the Anti-Imperialism Plaza. There are no more lines for a visa now. If we secure a passport—no easy task—we have to go to Panama or Santo Domingo. We spend scarce dollars and wait in long lines," complained the driver. He mirrored Che Guevarra's scowl from an adjacent mural.

Luke took in another deep breath. To his right stood an imposing building on a promontory. "This place looks familiar—are we almost there?" he asked wearily.

"That is the Hotel Nacional, built upon the Santa Bárbara battery, dating way back to 1797. The guns kept English pirates at bay. Citibank financed the hotel in 1932. It became the residence of President Roosevelt's emissary when Batista took power. Since the Revolution, Hotel Nacional is our 'go to' place to commemorate Cuba's heroes." The Packard belched smoke and accelerated up an incline. The hotel resembled an architectural mélange of Art Deco, Roman and Moorish design.

They entered a U-shape driveway, passing well-kept gardens and vintage automobiles. The brothers stopped before a smiling doorman with gray, kinky hair. He wished Luke, "Buenas tardes," and retrieved his heavy bag. Luke paid the brothers, who offered their card. "You never know when you might need our services, *Señor Americano*. We know how to navigate Cuba's ever-changing currents. Call us," bid the husky driver. He waved a smartphone in the air, his armament in the "new Cuba."

The brothers drove down the lane bordered by date palms, classic Cadillacs, and Oldsmobiles. They exchanged banter with other drivers, checking out their competition for tourist dollars, CUCs, or Euros.

At the reception desk, the clerk informed Luke that since he hadn't arrived with the rest of the tour, his reservation was canceled: "I'm sorry to say that the hotel is overbooked."

"What! So, what do I do now?" Luke queried, his voice and pulse rate rising. Why was this happening to him, an emissary of goodwill?

"Why don't you have a mojito in the bar, and I'll ask around. Would you mind staying in a private residence? I know a place not far from here with a guestroom. The family is known to me."

"As long as it's clean and a legal residence. I don't want to get into trouble," Luke rejoined, his North Face shirt dripping sweat onto the polished floor.

He checked his bag with the reception clerk and exchanged $100 into Convertible Units of Currency. Counting the CUCs, Luke found only 90 and turned toward the teller. "Yes, there is a 10 percent tax on U.S. dollars. If you had exchanged Euros, Mexican pesos, or Canadian dollars, there would be no charge. Some call it our 'gringo tax,'" he explained, shaking his head.

* * *

SETTING FOOT IN THE GARDEN BAR, Luke marveled that he'd entered a Hollywood set. Coconut palms were rippling overhead, and an upscale clientele spoke in conspiratorial tones. Some leaned back in their wicker chairs and observed Luke trudging along. A steady wind blew off of the Florida Straits.

It reminded Luke of the New Year scene in *Godfather II*. He could almost picture Michael Corleone and mafiosos sharing mojitos while bombs sounded off outside. When word arrived that President Batista had fled Cuba, everyone had to find a way out. On January 1, 1959, Castro was marching on Havana and guerrillas were hunting down sympathizers of *l'ancien regime*. Hopefully, Luke would not have to beat a hasty retreat.

He walked cautiously by two sturdy men in *guayaberas,* eyeing every visitor of the vast open-air bar. Under his damp American shirt and shifting pack, he felt out of place. The Vietnamese diplomat he'd met on the plane sat in a far corner. He was alone under a coconut palm. Luke moseyed in his direction.

"Professor Shannon, our emissary from Seattle, what a pleasant surprise. Please join me. You look like you could use a drink," invited Dong in a friendly manner. "Waiter, another mojito, please."

Luke exhaled in relief. As Dong seemed happy to see him, Luke sat at his table, letting his backpack slip to the floor.

"You look a bit bedraggled, professor. Did Customs not treat you well?" Dong asked, lowering his voice.

Luke looked closely at him again, wondering if the diplomat was psychic or truly concerned. On the plane, Luke had agreed to seek immigration help for Dong's sister in Seattle. As fellow Catholics, they seemed to connect. Luke hoped he could trust him. But again, this was Cuba.

"You are correct, Mr. Dong. I was interrogated at the airport by a senior inspector. It was an unpleasant experience. I missed the tour bus and hired a gypsy cab. My reservation was canceled at this hotel— not a great beginning for my goodwill visit. A mojito sounds great."

"Hmm, that seems out of the ordinary. Have you upset any Cuban official or have reason to be flagged by Customs?" Dong inquired.

"I attended a Cuba seminar at my university and directed questions to the visiting second secretary from Cuba's embassy. Maybe he didn't like what I asked. Have you ever encountered him? I also spoke with the other panelist, a well-known Cuban exile from Miami, with ties to the Cuban American National Foundation. The secretary watched us closely."

"Hmm," said Dong, looking around the neighboring tables. "Yes, I have met the second secretary. He's an outspoken advocate for the Revolution, a true believer."

Two Asians dressed in seersucker suits approached Dong at a measured pace. The diplomat stood up. "Let me present you to my colleagues from our embassy, Messieurs Tran and Nguyen. Gentlemen, Professor Shannon is from Seattle University, on mission to Havana University. Waiter, two more mojitos, please."

"My pleasure, gentlemen," Luke replied to the diplomats, whose ages were hard to determine. "Yes, I look forward to helping the university's new small-business program. We would like to open a dialogue between our institutions."

Dong's colleagues smiled agreeably but offered no words. Filling the silence, Luke continued: "As a former employee, I've also been tasked to ferret out the old Bank of Boston building, an important institution years ago. Have you seen it in Old Havana?"

Dong translated Luke's comments to his colleagues, who maintained their silence. From a table overlooking the water, they heard "*Viva!*" A boisterous group of men with short, clipped hair stood toasting the short, stocky man in the center. He wore a dark-blue *guayabera* and commanded attention. Luke frowned and turned to Dong.

"That's the most powerful general in Cuba, with close links to the Family. You don't want to cross him, professor. He directs many soldiers, agents, and police. Here in Cuba, the armed forces control most hotels, including the Hotel Nacional and joint-ventures with European chains. But the army calls the shots through its state holding company, GAESA. The General runs that organization."

"Hmm," Luke said with irony, "Maybe he could confirm my reservation at this hotel?"

As if on cue, the front-desk attendant wound his way toward him. "Good news, Professor Shannon. I found you a place to stay. Please follow me."

As Luke was about to rise, he saw a beautiful woman with sun-bleached hair streaming down a shapely back. She approached the group with nonchalance. Her ivory teeth contrasted nicely against her dark tan. She looked stunning in her red, silk dress. She said "*Hola*," to the General, giving him a familiar peck on the cheek. She stood taller than the General and caused heads to turn. The men around the table stopped talking and addressed her more formally, "*Buenas tardes, señorita.*"

Dong anticipated Luke's questioning look and whispered, "She's the General's current lover. She also has a special history linking her to the celebrated but disgraced military general, Arnaldo Ochoa."

Luke tensed at the mention of Ochoa. "I once met Ochoa's niece, Ana, in Washington, D.C. many years ago. I made a promise to her. I haven't kept my promise yet but hope to do so on this trip. Once my university business is concluded, I plan to seek her out and pay my respects. She was seen living near her uncle's hometown."

"Thank you again for the mojito, Mr. Dong. Your counsel is always welcome." Luke turned and bowed formally toward the diplomat's colleagues.

"Professor Shannon, you have my card. Let me know if I can be of service while in Cuba. Be careful on your other mission. The authorities avoid uttering Ochoa's name. As the economic situation worsens, the government is trying to keep a lid on the growing unrest. They don't want Ochoa's specter to upset the troops or the veterans of the African wars. Take care.

"And let me know if you can't find a room or have more problems during your stay."

Luke fingered the diplomat's card in his pocket, making sure it was there. He followed the clerk out of the garden bar and heard more "*Vivas!*" coming from the General's table. He looked back at the statuesque beauty. The way she carried herself reminded him of Ana. She radiated that special spark of life.

The reception clerk, Arturo, introduced Luke to a young man with a hungry look in his eye. "Your room is arranged in a private home, not far away. Pedro will take you there."

Luke thanked Arturo and tipped him 10 CUCs. He followed the guide through the hotel's main entrance. Beaten down by the day's events, he yearned simply for respite and a soft bed. The elderly doorman sensed Luke's distress and nodded sadly as he left.

Rain clouds swept in from the northeast, and a pelican marked time before the breeze. Night was falling on Havana, and Luke followed the young man down the driveway, away from the sea. In dimming light, he stumbled in a pothole and almost lost his balance. He was exhausted but walked on. At least the guide was carrying his cargo bag. He began counting his steps, which he often did to relieve boredom or stress.

He dodged a pack of wild dogs flashing their canines. Luke thought about his own cocker spaniel, probably playing with the neighbor's Lhasa apso this very night. What a great life they had in Seattle, compared with these curs prowling Havana's streets.

Night fell quickly in the tropics. Luke felt unmoored and unsteady. He was falling behind the young guide, who turned down a side street. A gaggle of teens hung out on the corner and looked Luke up and down. They soon lost interest and turned back to their smartphones and private jokes.

The guide rounded another corner and led Luke into a dead-end street. He stopped in front of a shabby, four-story building. Its front door was ajar, and voices cascaded down the stairs. The scent of garlic and mold wafted through the air. The guide pointed Luke upstairs, saying, "After you, *Señor Americano.*"

Luke stepped into the dank hall, his hand feeling the way forward. He grabbed the railing going up. He was so tired that he'd lost all concern of what lay ahead. He just wanted this day to end. He'd lost count at 300 paces from the hotel.

Luke kept climbing the wobbly stairs. He arrived at the third floor and let his backpack slide to the floor. The guide gave Luke a quick look and knocked three times on the thin, wooden door.

The doorway scraped open. Luke peered into a darkened room, hoping for the best.

CHAPTER 3

Vedado, Havana, Sunday, 8 a.m.

T*HE* INSPECTOR ADMONISHED *HIM,* "*You're here without permission. I warned you to follow our rules, you troublemaker. Now it's time for a different brand of tourism, inside a Cuban jail.*"

Luke awoke in a sweat, looking around a room measuring 10-by-10 feet. He lay on a narrow bed against a wall, atop a pink spread. Odd, he thought. He hobbled toward the small window and smelled salt air. Was that the sound of surf?

Slowly, Luke regained consciousness, taking in his surroundings. He'd just had a bad dream. This should be the room arranged by the hotel clerk. He could hardly remember how he'd arrived after leaving the Hotel Nacional. He saw his bag and backpack sprawled on the floor. He said aloud to reassure himself, "They don't allow personal effects in prison." A gecko, high on the wall, stared down at him without blinking an eye.

On the other side of the door, he heard someone moving about. His throat was parched and needed water. He cracked the door and saw an older man at a table playing solitaire.

"Buenos dias, señor. Do you have any water?"

"Buenos dias, señor," the man replied and opened a squat refrigerator. "You look much better this morning. You seemed very tired last night, so I helped you to your room. Here's a glass of filtered water from our cistern at home. It's best to avoid normal tap water in Havana. Our plumbing, you see, is a few years old."

"Excuse me, but what day is it today? I've lost my bearing since arriving here. Yesterday was very long," said Luke, piecing together how he'd made it to this apartment.

"Yes, travel always is tiring. It's Sunday. As your host, let me introduce myself again, I am José." His smile broadened over a mouth of uneven teeth. His brown eyes exuded warmth on a wizened face. What a contrast to the airport inspector, whose dour look sent a chill through Luke.

"My name is Professor Lucas. Thank you for your hospitality. I was at my wits' end yesterday. Do you know what time mass is held at the Cathedral? Perhaps I should say a prayer to improve my luck in Cuba."

"Yes, every little bit of help is welcome, including that from above. The most popular mass is at 10:30 a.m. today, and the Cathedral is beautiful. Are you Catholic, professor?"

"Some might refer to me a 'zigzag' Catholic, as I've had several ups and downs in faith. It'd be good to attend mass this morning."

"Life is not easy and often leads us in unexpected directions. Please have a little *café cubano* with me," the old man offered, pouring sweetened coffee with a touch of cinnamon into two small cups. They sat savoring espresso in companionable silence.

Carrying his pack, Luke tiptoed by his host's "living room," where a woman snuggled under covers and two teenage boys tossed and turned on a trundle bed. He walked carefully down the unlit stairway into the dazzling sun. He wandered down the street until he spied a sign for "Old Havana." Luke enjoyed watching the city wake up. He picked up his pace, trying to sweep yesterday's memories away.

He turned a corner and smelled the aroma of hot bread. A queue of women and young boys shuffled their feet, their coupon books in hand. Two scrawny cats policed the locked bakery from their perch above. Luke's stomach sounded off.

Luke scoured the street for a café and passed the sign for "Centro." Coffee odors grabbed his attention. He followed his nose through a gray building to an inner courtyard. He paused briefly to adjust his eyes and headed for the wooden counter. A muscular man followed Luke's entry while wiping down glasses at the bar. Three older men looked up from a metal table, balancing a bottle of Havana Club.

The bartender raised his chin and Luke ordered toasted bread and another *café cubano*. The other men stopped their conversation. When Luke began eating, they resumed muttering to one another. They kept an eye on Luke and complained about rising prices, power outages, and unfaithful wives.

The bartender broached a grin when Luke left him three CUCs. Maybe he had over-tipped?

Tourist map in hand, he pointed himself toward Old Havana, feeling a thrill to wander its streets. He spotted clothes hung on window sills of colonial-era buildings and heard residents' staccato Spanish, ricocheting off peeling walls. He wiped his brow, wishing he'd worn a cap to protect his thinning hair from the blazing sun.

He wasn't paying attention to the cobblestones, lost his balance, and barely caught his fall. With his luck so far, he'd be fortunate to avoid injury. He could almost hear a critic's remark back at school: "Yes, Professor Shannon slipped on a banana peel and cracked his shin, ignominiously ending his short-lived mission to Cuba."

Luke carefully crossed a viaduct over a roadway into a maze of weathered buildings. As the sun rose higher, residents spilled into the streets and shot curious looks at him. Turning right, he followed others into a large plaza with a Beaux Arts pool and swaying palms.

Newly painted colonial buildings surrounded a lush park and a replica of the U.S. Capitol loomed through the boughs. Luke read "*Parque Central*" on the sign and stood before a marble statue of José Martí, whose finger pointed outward.

Admiring the cast figure of Cuba's national hero, Luke noticed a group of youngsters sitting on the steps, checking him out. "*Que pasa?*" a lanky adolescent asked, examining Luke's pack. "Hey, gringo, what's your name? Can you fit me into your backpack and take me to America?"

"My name is Professor Lucas, and yours?" Luke hadn't read about street crime in Havana and didn't sense danger from this gaggle of youth.

The teen's white teeth contrasted with his chocolate-brown face. He stood almost six feet, wearing a stud in his left ear and a chain of red and white beads around his neck. His eyes danced as he spoke: "I am Johnny." Pointing to five other youths of varying ages and colors, he continued, "Here is my family on the loose. Maybe we can become friends? Where are you from in America?" His young friends bobbed their heads in unison.

"Yes, I'm an American from Seattle, where they make jet airplanes. Let me give you a postcard from my hometown," Luke volunteered. "As this is my first visit to your lovely country, do you have any recommendations?"

"Lovely, nothing, *Americano*. We have a hard time surviving out and about. Thanks for the postcard, but could you spare some CUCs as well?"

"How about a couple dollars, Johnny? I don't have any small CUC bills."

"Great, but large bills are cool, too." The teen added brightly, "Maybe you need a guide to show you around Havana? I know people of all walks of life who can do small favors for a few CUCs. Here's my new card and my cell number."

"Thank you. By the way, I'm heading to the cathedral in Old Havana—would you like to join me at mass?" Luke asked, noting 10:15 on the clock.

"Maybe another time, *Americano.* The church and me, you see, we don't get along too well. My friends and I often spend time around the *Parque Central.* I hope to see you," he exclaimed and gave Luke a tight hug. Johnny's friends hollered, "*Adiós, Americano.*"

Luke hurried through Old Havana's narrow streets, asking directions along the way. A pedicab driver pitched a ride in his oversized tricycle, but Luke declined. He eyed two towers of uneven height rising from a cobblestone plaza. He admired the baroque façade of the Cathedral of the Virgin Mary of the Immaculate Conception. A procession was gathering outside. Luke heard the bell toll once.

He pulled open the tall, heavy door and crossed himself. He sat toward the back of the long rectangular nave of a half-filled church. He inhaled the incense-filled air and relaxed. Despite his vagaries in faith, Luke felt at peace inside. He also felt safe.

The lights grew brighter and the altar reflected shades of gold. Three older men in scarlet vestments proceeded down the aisle, led by a young acolyte carrying Jesus on a cross. The cathedral included older ladies holding rosaries and tourists snapping photos and selfies. Luke put $10 in the collection plate and said the Lord's Prayer in quiet English. He took communion from a tall, slender priest, who looked quizzically at him. Luke decided to seek him out after mass. As he exited, he noticed fossils of flora and fauna on the cathedral's beige stones. A parishioner told him that the stones were cut centuries ago from sea coral and hauled to this site by slaves.

"*Buenos Dias, Padre.* Do you know Father Sebastian? I am Professor Shannon, a friend of a Cuban exile in Seattle. He suggested that I call on him."

The priest's eyes narrowed. "Professor Shannon, I am he." He paused, perusing Luke like a book. "Please come by the rectory down the street at noon and we can speak more privately. I am here in Havana only this month, but I'm free this afternoon." Luke thanked the priest and watched him turn to a couple wanting him to baptize their baby son.

* * *

At noon, Luke rang the bell outside the two-story rectory in faded ochre. After a minute, the tall priest opened the heavy, grated door. "Buenas tardes, professor." He gave Luke a loose hug, a typical greeting in Cuba. "Any place you'd like to visit in Old Havana, Professor Shannon?"

"Padre Sebastian, please call me Lucas. Let me invite you to lunch at a place of your choosing. Is there a bistro of Cuban cuisine that you'd recommend?"

The priest led them through a warren of neoclassical buildings in various stages of repair. He stopped in front of a sandy-colored low-rise with "*Paladar Mercaderes*" inscribed over the door. "This is a privately owned restaurant, or a '*paladar*', named after the bistro featured in a Brazilian telenovela. *Paladares* number a thousand in Havana and serve tastier food. They are usually run by families but are having a tough time surviving now. The government is cracking down on owners, requiring more fees and inspections. There are fewer tourists now."

A mustached man in a black jacket and bow tie, greeted them at the door: "Buenas tardes, señores. May I offer you a corner table?" The maître d' added, "Our chicken soup and *ropa vieja* are freshly made."

Luke gazed at the cream-colored walls and dark cabinets. Red-and-white-linen cloths covered carved wooden tables, suggesting elegance. "This *paladar* has the feel of a fine Spanish *taberna*, padre."

"Yes, this is a respected *paladar*, serving both Spanish and Cuban dishes. It can fill up after 1 p.m., so we may wish to order. Would chicken soup be acceptable to you? It's their house specialty."

"Two chicken soups, please," Luke said to a young waiter, whose worn tuxedo was a couple sizes too big. He bobbed his head enthusiastically. He turned to greet two muscular men waiting at the bistro's entrance.

The priest shifted in his seat. He remained silent for a moment but quietly asked Luke about his life in Seattle. He told Luke that his family had come from Spain during the Batista regime, but that he was born in Cuba in 1959, the year Castro came to power. His family resided in Santiago in Eastern Cuba, known for its sugarcane. He visited Havana in the summer and served as a substitute priest.

Luke admired the cleric's manner. The priest listened attentively and paused before offering a reply. Luke added, "I once considered becoming a priest, padre, but wasn't sure I could honor the vow of celibacy."

"Yes, it's a vow not to be taken lightly, given recent events. The church in Cuba also has difficulty finding priests for our parishes in the interior. We have several clerics from Spain." They finished their chicken soup, and the priest asked softly. "Now, please tell me more about how you met Señor Sanchez in Seattle and why you've come to Cuba."

Luke recounted how he'd met Sanchez at a conference and that he'd learned that an Ochoa relative, Ana, had returned to Cuba. He described how he'd met her 30 years ago in Washington, D.C. and promised her to tell the world what had really happened to her famous uncle, General Ochoa. Luke acknowledged that he'd not kept his promise and felt ashamed. The exile had suggested that he meet Fr. Sebastian to ascertain Ana's whereabouts. After his official university visit, Luke yearned to visit her.

On hearing Ana's and Ochoa's names, the priest's eyes narrowed again. He glanced toward the door, where the two men sat facing them. "Lucas, would you mind if we had our coffee elsewhere—maybe in a calmer place?" The *paladar's* tables were filling up, and a line began forming at the door.

Luke paid the bill and walked by the two men in *guayaberas*, following the priest outside. Fr. Sebastian strode briskly along the cobblestones and angled through a narrow street. He entered a youth hostel and greeted the young receptionist. She opened French doors to an inner courtyard. They ducked under the arch and sat at a table near a mosaic fountain, sputtering into a large sandstone basin. Luke heard the sound of crickets chirping among the potted palms.

"We can converse more discreetly here," the priest said, pouring each of them a watered-down coffee from a cracked urn. "Please, continue your story, Lucas. One never knows who's listening in public places."

"I have a meeting with the dean of the University of Havana's business school to deliver books and a letter from Seattle University. I've asked them for advice on how to investigate the archives about the former Hero of the Republic but haven't heard back. It seems that Ochoa remains a sensitive subject here."

The tall priest paused, gazing intently at Luke. "I'm not sure how straight forward the dean may be for your purposes. As you know, the university is controlled by the Ministry of Education, with close ties to the Party. Its rector is a known Marxist.

"You intimated that you met Ana several years ago. This May, she was involved in an accident along the *Carretera Central,* the main East-West highway. She was in and out of a coma for several weeks.

"I am sorry to be the one to bear this sad news to you. Ana passed away at the end of June. She was interred last week in a cemetery in Holguin. The police report has not yet been released." After a pause, the priest crossed himself, "May Ana's soul rest in peace."

Luke sat up straight, not wanting to believe the priest's words. After expectations raised by the exile, he'd looked forward to seeing Ana after all these years. He longed to embrace her and to spend time with her, trying to reconnect. But it was not to be. He found himself without words or hope, only budding tears. His secret devils came back to haunt him, drawing him closer to the abyss.

After a minute, he forced himself to say, "Years ago, I met Ana and spent time with her when she visited Washington, D.C. She mysteriously disappeared one spring day. I filed a missing person report and asked the Department of State for news about her in Cuba. I never received word. Your friend Sanchez said that she had returned to Holguin. I wanted so much to see her again and honor my promise to her. But now you say that she is dead?"

The priest touched Luke's shoulder, which began to tremble. Tears rolled down his cheeks, as they had on Ana's years ago. "I'm sorry, padre, but this is shocking news. What am I to do?" Luke muttered, his confidence fading. Lulled by the bubbling water, he feared that he was just chasing a dream. Tossed about so far in Havana, what was his purpose now? Beyond the fountain's mist, the image of Our Lady of Charity loomed in sorrow.

"Lucas, again I regret to share this tragic news. It seems that you had special feelings for her. If you'd like, I could communicate with a trusted friend in Holguin. He knows Ana's relatives in the province and could help you to fulfill your promise. Her grave is near his parish.

"One can't utter Ochoa's name in public. However, her distant cousin, Eloisa, has a relationship with a powerful general. He seems to enjoy flaunting her in public. Though married, he's a jealous lover and tries to keep her under wraps," the priest warned.

Luke tried to digest what the priest said. Half-heartedly he asked, "So, how could I conduct interviews without raising eyebrows?"

"Your tourist visa doesn't allow you to teach or conduct official research in the field. However, you may entertain private conversations with individuals, including 'friends of friends.' Perhaps acquaintances at the university may help out, if not the dean," the priest suggested.

Luke looked closely at this priest, hoping he could trust this man. Some clergy had cozy relations with security forces, but Father Sebastian's manner imparted peace. He took a chance to admit, "I've received mixed responses from the university so far. They've avoided my questions about Ochoa. What other course would you recommend?"

"Don't battle head on, Lucas. Be indirect in your approach. As the rector is a known Marxist, most professors and students are closed-mouthed on campus. Maybe invite them for a meal at a *paladar*. They don't have the budget to do so on their own. Professors don't earn much and must do other jobs to get by.

"Keep your eyes and ears open and pay attention to 'body language.' Remember that the Cuban worker averages a dollar a day. It's hard to gauge loyalties of a person with an empty stomach.

"If my friend is in town, I could send you word if it's safe to visit him. As long as you keep a tourist-like profile, he could take you to Ana's gravesite and to the countryside near Ochoa's village. They also practice *Santería* there. Are you familiar with this Afro-Cuban religion?"

Luke shook his head, his interest piqued.

"It means the 'worship of saints,' a 'syncretic' religion blending Yoruba gods from Africa with Catholic saints. It's commonplace in the countryside. The sessions can become scary when worshippers go into a trance—sometimes violently—and communicate with the spirits of the dead. Take special care."

"Any other advice on how to approach people met along the way?" Luke asked.

"Cubans do love baseball and follow the major leagues in America. Tell them about the Seattle Mariners. Play ball with them," he counseled, his eyes twinkling.

"And if the police show up, Father Sebastian, what then?"

"Whatever happens, never lose your temper, Lucas. And remember to smile, always smile, despite the situation," he counseled, his mouth turning up in suggestion.

"Let me know how to reach you and if you can visit my friend this weekend. He's likely saying mass at San Jose's parish in Holguín."

As an after-thought, the priest added, "Did you know that Ana had a son, who should be 29 this year? I have not met the young man, but my friend in Holguín baptized him. Ana was quite fond of him. The boy's father was not in the picture, so she raised him alone."

Luke gave the priest José's fixed phone number and received the rectory's in return. They exchanged light hugs and headed in different directions.

Luke meandered through the labyrinth of Old Havana, pondering the priest's words. His lovely Ana was no more—so how was he to honor her?

Another thought kept returning to him: Ana had a son.

CHAPTER 4

Ministry of Interior, Havana, Sunday, 2 p.m.

THE MAN STOOD SIX FEET TALL and weighed a solid 220 pounds. Had he been in America, he had the build to play an NFL linebacker. However, his sport was baseball, until he'd blown out his knee as a catcher in Cuba's youth leagues. As he approached the big "60," his face surrendered more creases, his hair more salt than pepper. He trained every morning at the police gymnasium to keep himself in shape. When he flexed his biceps, he liked the way people looked at him.

He continued walking toward a building concealed by trees and spotted kids kicking a frayed soccer ball. It soared over the sidewalk, landing at his feet. On instinct, he arrested the ball with his right instep and adroitly kicked it back, earning cheers. He realized again how much he missed his son.

Crossing the street, he confronted the mural relief of Che Guevara in beret frowning down from the immense sculpture. It was the Revolution's method to commemorate its iconoclastic hero. It stood guard over the '*MinInt*', as the Ministry of Interior was known. He looked at Che's image and his words etched in black. A pedicab driver rendered his translation to tourists, whose faces glowed a startling pink: "'Until Victory, Always!' That's what Che's words say." They looked up at the huge monument built of steel and concrete, shuddering under the Argentine's stare.

The driver moved aside to let the big man pass by. He continued up the gravel path toward the entrance of *MinInt,* a huge Cuban flag hanging from the top floor. A soldier with an AK-47 stood at attention while another opened the ministry's heavy door. The nine-story building was enshrouded by trees, maybe laurels? The big man entered the beige edifice and passed another soldier at port arms. He stepped into the open elevator and greeted, "Buenas tardes." The soldier looked apprehensive but pressed floor number two.

He swung right into the corridor and walked through the double doors to a large conference room. He acknowledged the vice admiral and current minister, who blinked over his glasses but offered no greeting. The big man sat in a large chair behind the long, rectangular table and listened to the murmuring of older hands. Against the back wall sat their underlings, ramrod straight and keeping quiet. A somber mood hung over this room without windows, shuttered by acoustic tiles.

The ministry's black-and-red emblem, surrounded by a pentagon inside a circle, hung on the far wall. Its motto stared out at everyone, "Our strength is the strength of the people."

Though this was a scheduled session of senior intelligence officials from the Armed Forces, the Party, and the Ministry, he sensed unease among grayer-haired attendees.

To lighten the mood, he asked a tall, thin man across the table:

"Hey, *Flaco,* how goes it? Any new guests inside your special suites, comrade?" He referred to the former Marist school outside Havana, taken over by the ministry to serve as prison for political dissidents.

The inspector, standing six feet three in a slight Caucasian frame, flinched on hearing his nickname, *Flaco.* "Thin man" also meant "weak" in Spanish. The inspector replied with irony: "Nobody of consequence, Big Man. How about you—any new blood for our illustrious General?"

It was his turn to draw back. He answered simply, "On occasion, *Flaco.*" He purposely sat up straighter to contrast his muscled frame to that of this pallid, thin man. "Big Man" preferred his nickname to José Antonio Sanchez, a common family name in Eastern Cuba. He sensed that his bulk gave him an edge among the barracudas circling in this room.

Though he'd known the inspector for 30 years, he'd never cottoned to his superior attitude. He preferred calling him the "thin man" and hardly recalled his Spanish name, Andrés Cristobal Quiroga. The inspector liked to wear sunglasses, he thought, so that no one would notice his shifty eyes. Big Man took care in his presence. The chief inspector of Havana retained hundreds of informants inside and out of government. He was rumored to kept archives online of thousands of people in Cuba's Revolutionary state.

Big Man smiled at a uniformed woman next to him. "It's good to see you, Morena, and find a soulmate in this august gathering." He adored her broad smile and coiffed afro. He respected her objectivity in sizing up others. As he gazed at the sea of white faces, only he and Morena represented the darker hues of the Revolution.

The thin man wore a sly look and spoke under his breath to a pudgy man in *guayabera.* Apparently, that operative still shared small talk with the inspector, unlike others of the métier. Though they feared the inspector's sources, most in this room avoided him in social settings. Big Man was aware that Andrés had denounced friends and relatives in the early days of the Revolution. Like hundreds of others condemned by the regime, a few members of Andrés' family faced the firing squads against *El Paredón,* the infamous wall.

Big Man had learned of Andrés' rise through the Young Pioneers where he impressed his handlers by ferreting out traitors. What a solitary life the "thin man" led, without family and friends. Like many Cubans during the "special period," the inspector suffered loss when his wife and son had fled by boat. She succumbed to sharks in the Florida Straits, though his son was recovered alive by the U.S. Coast Guard. Apparently, his estranged son led a gay lifestyle in Miami. Big Man wondered how the inspector spent his evenings and how he warded off the ghosts of victims past.

In 1988, they had traveled together to a counter-intelligence workshop in Moscow. Big Man was the only man of color and was proud when Russian generals praised General Ochoa's military victories in Ethiopia and Angola. At the time, Ochoa was held in high esteem by the Castros and Gorbachev's top brass for defeating "imperialist forces" in the field.

In the mid-eighties, Ochoa's senior officers had recognized Big Man as a young but loyal stalwart. Later, they selected him as their chief intelligence operative in Angola. Africans liked his manner, and Ochoa honored him for his bravery under fire. They did not look down their nose at him, a man of color, unlike some operatives in this august room. As the clock struck two, he discarded these memories and returned to the present.

"*Señores y señoras*, may this meeting come to order," said the minister, his white uniform parading three stars over a robust frame. The current minister had come to power thanks to Raul and curried favor with the new apparatchik president. "Maria, please read our agenda and take the official roll call."

Intelligence representatives from the Cuban Army, Navy, and Air Force, said "present," as did a special representative from the Central Bank. A gaunt agent from Maduro's regime fidgeted with his papers. Big Man had met him accompanying the General to Caracas and thought he looked like a weasel. He represented Venezuela's VP, in charge of its "pharmaceutical" and gold-export activities. Next to him sat his physical opposite, a grandiose visitor from Mexico with a handlebar mustache and an affable manner.

Alone at the end of the table was a man of Asian descent of indeterminate age. Big Man had met him once at a cross-intelligence gathering with Chinese, Russian, North Korean, and Vietnamese operatives. The admiral introduced him as "Mr. Dong of the Embassy of Vietnam." Dong bowed his head respectfully.

"Before we discuss internal financial issues, I'd like to present comrades Hector from Venezuela and Armando, a new observer from AMLO's administration in Mexico. Welcome gentlemen."

The Mexican representative seemed a throwback to Pancho Villa, carefully massaging his immense moustache. Big Man considered him a simpatico sort and appreciated his mestizo looks. He'd heard that Mexico's new president had encouraged non-Caucasians to take more power and responsibility. His political movement called *"Morena,"* or a "dark woman," had swept the last election. Big Man liked the sound of that.

"So, comrades of the Central Bank, how are our accounts faring?" inquired the minister, smiling at a 40-something woman. She sported close-cropped, blondish hair and wore a tight, blue halter and matching pants. She used to be a special friend of the General before he latched onto Eloisa. The assistant now captured the attention of the bank president, inside and out of official gatherings.

She was prone to smile, despite the hard numbers from her report: food imports were rising as Cuban agriculture had missed its Five-Year plan again. Tourism revenues were down as fewer foreign visitors were showing up. The "export" of medical and paramilitary advisors abroad was growing and had become Cuba's top source of hard currency. However, Brazil's president had curtailed that arrangement, sending back 7,000 doctors to Cuba. "A temporary setback," she advised. "Argentina and Mexico have expressed interest in our doctors to battle this unknown virus.

"We're looking to reintroduce 'dollar stores' of decades past. The worms from Miami have brought in many goods for their relatives. They go door-to-door selling their American merchandise for dollars. We're hoping that state stores may pull in the dollars and not these contraband artists.

"Our chief challenge remains finding oil at special prices. As you're aware, our comrades in Venezuela have curtailed their shipments of late," she intoned, looking pointedly at the Venezuelan visitor.

The spy shrank deeper into his chair. He crossed his leg twice before responding:

"Comrades, the lackeys of Yankee imperialism are making life difficult. They're causing power outages and have decreased our capacity to export oil. Through their courts, the gringos have gone after refineries in the Caribbean, curtailing petroleum at special prices. They've also frozen some accounts at international banks.

"But we're developing new sources of income. Russia and Iran are helping out. We also may trade gold via Turkey to secure scarce goods. When petrol prices rise again, we'll be happy to increase our assistance." He looked up briefly but returned to the security of his papers.

Big Man heard the inspector ask if there were any threats from the more than five million Venezuelans who had fled abroad.

"Perhaps in Cúcuta, where some Army deserters have gathered, egged on by Yankee and Colombian advisors. Our intelligence officers, with Cuban help, have infiltrated those groups. We're not too bothered at present."

Big Man credited the Venezuelan operative for keeping up his façade of "business as usual", despite thousands marching in the streets for food and medicine. He wondered what it'd be like in a country where daily life was more difficult than in Cuba. He'd heard that some intelligence and medical advisors were heading home, as they hadn't received pay from the ministries of the "Bolivarian Republic of Venezuela."

"And your other commercial activities?" probed the inspector. "Will they be able to subsidize your friends, who have stuck by you through thick and thin?"

The Venezuelan's face turned pink and his cheeks puckered as if sucking a lemon. He continued shuffling his papers. "Yes, that might be possible, but the gringo's Coast Guard has been vigilant of late. Perhaps our Mexican colleague has other petrol sources to offer up?" he pleaded, looking sideways at Pancho Villa.

The robust Mexican stopped twirling his mustache, looked up briefly and said: "Buenas tardes, señores. Pemex's production has trended down under previous capitalist regimes. We are confident that our new administration's actions against speculators, thieves, and political 'dinosaurs' will yield more gas in the not too distant future," he said airily, his thick arms opening as if seeking a hug. No one took him up, and the minister's eyes began to droop.

Blah, blah, blah, thought Big Man, as the Mexican went on and on. He heard the inspector clear his throat again and caught the minister's eye.

"Let's break for a *café cubano* with a little kick. After all, the sun is well past the yardarm," the admiral reminded. He rose from his oversized chair and pulled back the seat of the attractive Central Bank assistant. They led the procession to an anteroom decorated in Spanish tiles and lit by chandeliers. At the bar stood three waiters in crew cuts and white coats. They served the invited guests *café cubano* in demitasse and *añejo* rum in crystal snifters.

Big Man followed the inspector and his chubby colleague in line. He smiled as they spiked their coffee with ample shots of Havana

Club. The spies went to a far corner, standing at a table and speaking in hushed tones. Big Man brought his espresso to a counter two tables away, feigning indifference. Thanks to the ceramic tiles, he was able to listen to their conversation echoing off the walls.

"*Que pasa*, comrade? I see you brought a visitor from Mexico City. What's his story?" queried the inspector.

"Hola, Andrés, all is well? As to our new comrade from the United States of Mexico, we've been nurturing him for years, starting in Cancún at GAESA's hotel. He's a distant cousin of the new president, though not the brightest of bulbs. He does enjoy his fiestas and young girls but nothing like our infamous writer," he sneered.

Big Man presumed that they were talking about Fidel's Colombian friend, whom he'd chaperoned in Havana in the early '90s. The visitor preferred underage girls, some of whom ended up in emergency rooms. What he had to do to survive.

As the visitor secured funds for Fidel in international circles, Big Man bit his tongue as chaperon. After the USSR imploded on the world stage, Russia curtailed support to Cuba. The decade of the '90s was called the "special period" with scant food, medicine, and gasoline. Some of the hungry reverted to softening shoe leather in desperation. Big Man hoped he'd never have to face such a time again.

As "tourist guide," Big Man had to submit reports to the inspector, documenting the visitor's extracurricular activities. The thin man forwarded them and videotapes to Fidel for his private viewing pleasure.

"And who are your quarry now, Andrés—anyone special in town?" asked his collaborator, downing his rum and looking for more.

"Not much, except for an expatriate group from the Cuban American National Foundation, who brag about the good life in Miami. But we have informants within that group that keep us current.

"There's also an American professor who somehow ran afoul of the second secretary of our Embassy in Washington. He seems a bit naïve, but it's hard to figure out what's underneath his professorial façade. At the airport, he tried to discuss literature with me, including a book, *Our Man in Havana*. Have you ever read it?"

"I'm sorry, my colleague, but I prefer baseball to literature. I plan to take our Mexican visitor to a Matanzas exhibition game tonight, with special cheerleaders to amuse him afterwards. I wish you good hunting among the Cuban worms and your American prof."

Big Man frowned at the sound of the rival baseball team. He'd been loyal to the *Industriales*, the team of Havana's common people. He didn't cotton to other teams, especially those favored by "superior Revolutionaries," like the two snobs in the corner.

The Minister's attractive assistant rang the bell twice, ushering the intelligence professionals back for the late-afternoon session. As Big Man had little to report on behalf of the General, he daydreamed about baseball and what his wife might be preparing for dinner. Maybe she had secured a chicken from the private vendor she had dealt with for years. Though not authorized, he knew that the "parallel market" provided sustenance to them and others in Havana who paid in CUCs.

He decided to mention to the General that the inspector was keeping track of that group of Cuban expats from Miami and the American prof now visiting Havana.

CHAPTER 5

Vedado, Havana, Sunday, 7 p.m.

WIND RUSHED THROUGH A BROKEN PANE, and the surf crashed high against the seawall. Along the wide avenue, palm trees tilted like windmills before the gathering storm. In the twilight, vintage Oldsmobile, Buicks, and Chevrolets sputtered up and down the wide avenue, giving the Malecón a retro feel. Pedestrians deserted the sidewalk as rain began to fall and pennants whipped before the squall.

From the bedroom's window, he let his eyes wander to a nearby bar. At the open door stood a lady dressed in black, immobile, her long hair flying in the breeze. Luke marveled at her rapturous beauty as she regarded the breaking waves. At a distance, he imagined her as a Cuban version of Helen of Troy.

The room smelled stuffy, so Luke decided to get some air. He wished José and his wife "*hasta luego*." They looked up from the TV news from Venezuela. An angry Maduro was raising his fist to a red-shirted mob. Their teenage sons were hollering at each other as they played "*God of War*" on a worn PlayStation. They hardly noticed Luke slip out the door.

Outside, Luke picked up his pace against the gale. He headed for the bar surrounded by five-foot walls and latticework that reached a thin, tin roof. Its pink color seemed inviting and its shutters flapped in makeshift rhythm. The neon sign announced the "California Café," so Luke thought that maybe he'd find other Americans here.

"*Buenas noches, Cuba libre?*" Luke asked the bartender, who was trying to hold down coasters from the blustery wind.

"Where are you from in America?" the bartender inquired, glancing quickly at Luke. The sturdy man with curly hair poured triple shots of Havana Club into a glass, with a splash of Coke, from a bottle stamped "Made in Mexico."

"How can you tell as I do my best to speak Spanish correctly?"

"It's your clothes, comrade, and *Norteamericano* is written across your face," he said in a friendly manner. "Your countrymen are always welcome in my bar."

"Gracias. Do you know Vancouver?" Luke asked. Sometimes in tricky countries like Cuba, playing "Canadian" often made people relax.

"I do like Canada," he said, putting on a Toronto Blue Jays cap. "Cubans play on their team," he smiled between craggy teeth but frowned when the wind swept it off his head.

Luke tried to grab it but saw the cap land at the back table, where the statuesque woman sat gazing out the window.

"Pardon me," Luke remarked, as he gathered the cap at her feet.

She murmured, "It's nothing." She tossed back her sun-streaked hair and returned her gaze toward the Malecón.

"*Momento,*" Luke said, handing the cap to the bartender, whose eyes flashed a warning. He put an index finger under his right eye, the sign throughout Latin America to "take care."

Luke paused briefly but brought his drink to a table next to the beautiful woman staring out to sea. He hoped for another glimpse of her gray-green eyes, similar to Ana's look of years ago. Luke felt unencumbered in the tropical breeze and heard the pitter patter of rain. Dust, salty air and inexpensive perfume greeted his nostrils.

Without looking at him, she said: "Do you know that you speak Spanish with a Brazilian accent, despite your North American looks?"

She seemed to pay close attention to a man walking along the avenue, a cellphone to his ear.

"I spent some time in Rio," Luke continued, "the Marvelous City— have you ever visited? Your manner reminds me of Brazil."

She paused but then turned toward him, sending a charge up his spine. With a hint of nostalgia, she continued: "I visited Rio once. I love the Brazilian people and their joie de vivre. Did you learn how to dance the samba?"

Luke's heart was racing. "I learned a few steps. Perhaps we could try the samba at a club sometime? By the way, my name is Lucas."

"Lucas—my pleasure. I call myself Eloisa. Maybe another time. Are you staying nearby?"

"Yes, I'm staying in a private residence across the street. My reservation was canceled at the Hotel Nacional. Didn't I see you there, yesterday afternoon?"

The question hung in the air. She didn't answer but leaned forward, watching the cellphone man dodge cars to cross the Malecón. A black, 1955 Chevrolet then pulled up to California Café and three men jumped out, running through the rain. A large man led two buff cohorts up the path. They arrived in damp *guayaberas,* hiding something bulky underneath.

The cellphone man stood beneath an adjacent balcony peering inside the bar. The big man glanced briefly at the bartender but aimed for Eloisa, asking her: "*Que pasa,* my beautiful one?"

"Nothing much, my dear major. The night is young," she replied, tension rising in her voice.

"Well, you're quite popular with a certain person. He's asked for your presence again. So, let's drink up, my lovely one. It's time to face the music." He advanced and took her arm, lifting her slowly from the chair.

She broke eye contact with Luke and tried to pull her arm clear. She faltered and put a hand on Luke's table, causing it to wobble.

Luke's "Irish" blood boiled over. He stood and asked: "Can I be of assistance, señor?"

"My friend, what is it to you? Just sit down and enjoy your Cuba Libre. It's best not to involve yourself in the affairs of others," the man commanded between tight lips.

"We were just having a conversation without bothering anyone."

"You've had your talk—so now, sit down," the major ordered, pushing Luke toward the chair. Luke grabbed the table, which teetered and tipped over, landing him on the floor. "Gringo, don't put your nose in things you don't understand."

His henchmen stood over Luke and then backed out of the bar into the pouring rain. The big man led Eloisa by the elbow, opened the Chevy's back door and placed her inside.

The man riding shotgun gave Luke a smirk and pointed his finger like a trigger at him. The cellphone man had disappeared into the wind.

Eloisa glanced out the window, but the Chevy sprang forward, jerking her head back. The car sped down the Malecón, enveloped by the storm.

Stunned, Luke picked himself off the floor and saw the bartender shaking his head. The man's wrinkles grew deeper and the rain beat down harder. Again, he put his right index finger under his eye, repeating to Luke, "Be careful, comrade. You're in Cuba now. They play by different rules."

CHAPTER 6

Vedado, Havana, Monday, 9 a.m.

"GUANTANAMERA" RANG OUT FROM THE PHONE in the living room. The old man answered, saying: "Professor Shannon, it's for you."

Luke cleared his throat and said "*Bueno,*" wondering how someone had discovered this phone number. He heard crackling on the line, so he repeated his greeting.

"Professor Shannon, this is Gladys, assistant to the dean of the University of Havana. We've received your emails and telephoned the Hotel Nacional. The desk clerk said that you weren't there but gave me this number—are you well?" said a woman, who ended each sentence in a rising pitch.

"Yes, I am well, despite the mix up in reservations. The clerk arranged a private residence, not far from the University. I do hope to meet with the dean. I've brought books on small business, as she requested," Luke responded.

"Hmm. Professor Manela no longer occupies the position of dean, rather Professor Montejo, with a PhD in Economics. He asks if you can come today to our old office in front of Coppelia on L Street and

21ˢᵗ—would 3 p.m. be fine? Next week, we'll be moving to the university's main campus."

"With pleasure. I look forward to seeing you and the dean this afternoon," Luke replied loudly, his voice echoing on the line.

Luke fit the books into his backpack and thanked Jose. He decided to see more sights and walk to the University. He looked down 19ᵗʰ Street and ambled toward the Malecón, for a detour along the seaside promenade. He crossed the roadway's six lanes and absorbed the sunshine beating down. He'd forgotten to wear his cap again.

"*Maní?*" A vendor thrusted peanuts in a spiral cup toward him. Luke declined and avoided others selling knockoff watches. He saw younger men and women gazing toward the Florida Straits. A high-pitched cry shattered this pleasant scene: "Help!"

A young girl had just fallen over the wall into the rumbling surf. She'd tried to grab her scarf flying toward the open sea. Luke saw the current pull her farther out. Luke heard another weak cry but saw no life guard. Many people hollered, but no one ventured out to rescue her. Without a second thought, he tore off his clothes and shoes and dropped his pack.

The girl bobbed farther out to sea, struggling to stay afloat. She disappeared under a roller for several seconds. Luke jumped off the wall in an open stance into the choppy waters. He didn't submerge in order to keep the girl in sight. The rollers bounced off the seawall, creating a counter current that pushed Luke out to sea. He saw her surface again, fighting for breath.

Luke kept swimming, kicking as hard as he could. He reached the spot where he'd last seen the young girl submerge. Someone grabbed him around his neck, pulling him under. He let himself go down and her hands released their grip. The girl fought to reach the surface. Luke spun around and approached her from behind. He grasped her tightly around the chest and headed toward the shore. He swam on his right side, using a scissor kick, the girl bouncing off his left hip. He body-surfed an incoming wave, aiming for a crack in the seawall. His adrenalin kicked in.

An older fisherman thrust himself through the broken wall, a rope around his waist. Two wiry men held him from above. The man threw a small fishing net to Luke, who grabbed it with his right hand. The shore current recoiled from the barrier, taking them back to sea. Luke's hands slipped down the net, holding on by his fingertips. He kicked with all his might to catch the next wave in. The fishermen kept hauling in the net. While breakers pounded on Luke, he pushed the listless girl overhead to the fisherman's strong grip. The man grabbed her by the hair and passed her up to outreached hands.

Luke clung to the net and rode the next comber in. He gained a precarious foothold on the crevice, despite the surf crashing around him. His left hand grabbed a rock above, and his right released the net. He pulled himself up through the broken wall to the Malecón.

Pedestrians circled the girl lying on the ground. Luke wove through the crowd hollering, "Give her room." His Boy Scout training kicked in. He knelt and rolled her on her side, letting water pour out of her mouth. He checked that her tongue was free and turned her on her back. Her pulse was low, so he began CPR on her chest. He blew into her mouth, remembering to pinch her nose and release it, so she could exhale. "Breathe in, breathe out," he coaxed himself, continuing in rhythm and embrace.

Suddenly, her eyes popped open as she threw up seawater into Luke's face. He pivoted her on her side as more water flowed out. He lifted her up slowly, patting her on her back. Helped by Luke, she sat up on the sidewalk, throwing up more seawater and shaking her long black locks. She smiled. Up and down the Malecón, people cheered, "Bravo!"

Luke spoke to her softly, "You look much better, señorita. Keep letting the water out. Then inhale as deeply as you can." He heard a siren and saw people snapping photos of them on their smartphones. The ambulance pulled up on the Malecón's sidewalk, and two attendants plowed through the curiosity seekers. "Gracias, señor. We'll take her from here."

Luke looked at the young girl, whose teeth reflected rays from the afternoon sun. Luke lifted her gradually to her feet and opened his arms to receive her hug. They embraced—an old, white gringo and a dark, Cuban teen, provoking another "Bravo" from the crowd.

She looked at him and picked seaweed from his hair: "What is your name, señor?"

"I am Lucas, at your service. And you, señorita?" he asked, feeling a spark of life between them.

"I am Arlene," she said. "May this moment join us forever, señor. Muchas gracias." She let the attendants lead her away and looked back with a resplendent smile. That was plenty of thanks for Luke.

Conscious now of his appearance, he pulled up his shorts and looked around at smiling faces. Luke took a threadbare towel offered by the older fisherman. "You did well, *Americano*. We've kept your clothes and pack secure. We'd like to invite you to our home to freshen up. Maybe over a shot of rum?" The ambulance siren faded, as did the throng.

"That's very kind of you," Luke replied, wiping saltwater from his brow. They heard a seagull cry and saw it plunge into the sea, rising with a fish in its beak. "Bravo," they shouted along the Malecón.

They dodged traffic across the six-lane boulevard and heard auto horns beep. Luke thought they might be honking at the spectacle of the dripping-wet gringo in boxer shorts. The fishermen led him to a fading edifice with a neo-classical façade. They climbed the chipped stairs to an open door on the second floor. A husky woman embraced the slight fisherman, exclaiming, "Dearest Arnaldo—what happened to this poor man? Señor, please be welcome to our home. I am Maria, at your service."

He entered with Arnaldo and the other two fishermen, offering, "Buenas tardes, señora." Her husband retold how Luke had pulled the young girl from the ocean waves. Maria led him by the hand to a small bathroom. "A shower will do you good, and the power is still on. Engage the tap ever so slightly for warmer water."

Luke thanked her and walked carefully on the patched-up floor. He turned on the faucet and heard a low buzz from the electric shower-head. A thin stream of water flowed over him, and the surf resounded outside. The water lessened to a drizzle and slowly stopped. He shook himself, using the thin towel sparingly, not wanting to add a new hole.

Luke put on his long-sleeved shirt and tan slacks and looked into the mirror. A sun-burnt man with a Roman nose stared back at him. Gray was thrusting through waning auburn hair. A change of seasons was imminent, he feared. His aquamarine eyes stared back in hope. His six-foot body reflected that of an older swimmer in reasonable shape. He recalled his mother's mantra to "stand up straight," as he rejoined the family in the living room.

A faded photo hung on the beige wall. A young soldier stood grimly by an armored personnel carrier, a shattered baobab in the background. Luke walked closer for a better view and heard the fisherman mutter:

"That was my older brother, Luis, before the clash at Cuito Cuanavale in Angola. Like many Cubans, he suffered death in 1988, even though the battle was heralded 'a victory' in *Granma*'s newspaper."

"May he rest in peace," Luke said. "I've been told that General Ochoa led the Cuban forces against UNITA and South African guerrillas. Did your brother ever bring up his name or the ranking officers who led the troops?"

"Ochoa was popular among the rank-and-file because he led from the front. But woe be it to any infantryman who crossed him. My brother said he exercised judgement on the spot, with his .45-caliber pistol in hand. We Cubans provided the backbone for that war, partly financed by Russian allies.

"They also recruited Cubans of color to fill army ranks. Like me, my brother was mulatto, so he served as platoon lieutenant in the field. Cuban sergeants and officers led the undisciplined African rabble against the mercenaries. Many Cubans did not come back. If so, they often arrived maimed, both physically and mentally.

"You seem like a man of letters, señor. Have you read Padura's books, describing the hard life of returning veterans injured by the war?" asked the fisherman, his eyes downcast.

"I'd like to read his books. Despite their bravery, I understand that several veterans suffered when they came back to Cuba—even the Hero of the Republic."

"Yes, many paid with their lives, sometimes at our leader's hands. They avoid speaking about Angola, Ochoa, or the suffering veterans anymore. 'Out of sight, out of mind,'" lamented the fisherman. Another chimed in, "It's our national policy of oblivion."

"Enough of such morose, talk, Arnaldo and friends! Let us toast our new hero of el Malecón, in our own backyard! The fresh coffee and *quesitos* are getting cold and our *añejo* seeks a companion," bubbled Maria. She took Luke by the arm and led him to a worn, Formica table, covered by a large doily. The bouquet of guava and country cheese rose from puff-filled pastries. After the rescue, he realized how hungry he was. She poured him a *café cubano* and added the golden elixir of Havana Club.

They helped themselves to pastries and coffee and sat around the table, regarding Our Lady of Charity looking down from the wall. Across the room, the photo of the fisherman's brother hung alone. The fisherman followed Luke's gaze and then glanced at his wife, his eyes brimming.

Maria crossed herself before Our Lady's picture. She spontaneously began reciting the Rosary. Haltingly, the other fishermen joined *en español* and Luke in quiet English. Silently, Luke also prayed for Ana's soul, hoping that he could honor his promise made to her years ago.

He wondered what confrontations might lie ahead. Like the fisherman's brother, would *he* really be willing to pay the ultimate price?

CHAPTER 7

El Malecón, Havana, Monday, 2:20 p.m.

THROUGH HUGS AND TEARS, Luke said *adiós* to the fisherman's family. How open-hearted they seemed. despite their meager means. Most people he'd met so far had a friendly demeanor, except for those officials at the top. He hoped that the university encounter would prove positive and squinted at the clock. A seagull circled high above the Hotel Nacional.

"Professor Lucas, do you remember me?" said a voice from behind, startling Luke. There stood Johnny, whom he'd met at the Parque Central.

"Wow, you sure get around," Luke exclaimed, seeing the teen beaming in newly pressed clothes. "Are you going somewhere special—you looked dressed up?"

"Not really, *Americano*," he replied, looking right and left. "Just out and about. Maybe a tourist needs my help. How about yourself, are you trolling for action?"

"No, I'm supposed to visit the business school of the University of Havana, near Coppelia—do you know the building?"

"No problem, *Americano*, let me lead the way," said Johnny. A passerby cast Luke a baffled look.

A teenage student in uniform piped up from behind, "*Americano*— you're quite the swimmer! On behalf of us along the Malecón, we thank you for saving the girl's life. Most of us don't swim too well. Your swift action meant a lot to us. I wish you a safe stay in Cuba. "I am also a registered translator in Havana. Here's my card. Maybe you could use my services sometime?"

Luke thanked him but Johnny frowned, maybe fretting about a competitor for Luke's scarce CUCs. They climbed up the hill through the hotel's back gate, past a sleeping guard. Johnny peppered Luke with questions about his rescue of the young girl, asking, "Was she pretty?" Luke nodded, smiling, as they arrived at the grand entrance.

Johnny greeted the doorman, whom Luke had met upon his arrival. The teen whispered something into the older man's ear. The porter looked at Luke and gave a thumbs up. "Thank you for braving the surf and helping the Cuban girl. I am at your service." The doorman's eyes sparkled, mouthing the word "hero" to another hotel attendant.

"Buenas tardes, señor. Life is short, so we must do what we can. I'm happy to offer swimming lessons to the youth of Havana anytime."

"Maybe to us old folk, too?"

"Of course," Luke answered and then asked: "Perhaps you might give me advice on how to find the old Banco de Boston in Havana? Former colleagues asked if the building stands. It was nationalized by Castro in 1961."

"Yes, professor. My father had a savings account at the bank on Aguiar street in Old Havana. In 1962, the Central Bank took possession of the building for its administrative office. After my father passed, we had trouble withdrawing pesos from his account. As a young boy, I accompanied him to the bank. The tellers were simpatico and used to give me American Tootsie Rolls. I even saw the master writer himself, Señor Hemingway, in the lobby, to collect his pesos at the bank. I miss that time." His eyes looked far away.

Luke thanked the doorman and followed Johnny out the main entrance. He had an extra spring in his step. "You sure know your way around," Luke commented, amazed at how Johnny navigated different areas of Havana.

"I wasn't born with a silver spoon in my mouth, *Americano,* so I must fend for myself. My street friends are my family and keep me posted. That doorman is a savvy one. He was a young man when the Revolution came to town," he expounded, flirting with a bleached blonde in tight jeans. She gave Luke the once over.

Older women carried umbrellas to protect themselves from the broiling sun. People of all hues and ages cruised up and down the busy avenue. Luke winced at the claxon from an old Studebaker huffing uphill, spewing exhaust on everyone.

"23rd Street is also known as *la Rampa,* but we're going to 21st Street, closer to the university building." Johnny continued. He seemed to enjoy his role as guide.

"Here is Hotel Capri, favored by the American mafia before the Revolution. Now, it's a hub for foreign tourists. 'Ladies of the night' also frequent its hallways—any interest?" The teen eyed another girl with reddish hair and swaying hips.

"No thanks, Johnny. It's best for me not to stray too far off the path," Luke said, appreciating the kaleidoscope of people coming in and out of the hotel. He wiped his brow again. The sun radiated off the sidewalk, penetrating him from below.

"Are you OK, Americano? Coppelia is just around the corner." They turned onto "L" Street and aimed for a plaza overshadowed by many trees. A two-story, circular building stood at its center. They saw a red, triangular "*Coppelia Recreativa*" sign and joined others in line at the ice cream stand.

Copellia's blackboard menu advertised eight different flavors. Luke ordered a guava cup and treated Johnny to a coconut cone. They took refuge under the immense Ceiba tree and its welcoming shade. Nearby, university students were gossiping about their teachers and classmates. They gave Luke and Johnny a quick look and began speaking in English, "How are you. my friend?" Luke replied, "So far, so good." The students wore clothes with designer labels, in contrast to Johnny's plain shirt.

Johnny changed the conversation, asking Luke: "Do you know how Copellia began, *Americano?*"

Without waiting for an answer, he continued, "In the '60s, Commander Fidel got personally involved in order to provide Cubans with more ice cream flavors than those available in America," he explained, puffing up his chest again. "They also shot scenes of *"Strawberry and Chocolate"* here. Have you seen the movie?"

Luke observed smirks from the university students. They directed the question to Johnny, "Do you speak English, my friend?" Luke responded instead, "Yes I do, how about you? Did you learn English in the classroom, or have you visited America?"

The students said that they had relatives in Florida and liked to practice English with tourists. They excused themselves and left for class. It was almost 3 p.m.

"Johnny, I have to go to the Business School. Thanks for guiding me. Here's another 'three-note' to help out," Luke said.

The teen flashed a quick grin. "Thanks. I'll see you around," he said casually, fingering the beads around his neck. He greeted two girls of color under milky white parasols and began chatting them up.

Luke said adiós, trying to understand the interaction between the lightly complected students entering the university high-rise and his darker guide carousing the plaza.

In the lobby, the porter directed Luke to the thirteenth floor. He followed students into an elevator that groaned at every level. He exited on floor 13 and entered the Office of the Dean. Gladys greeted him in the anteroom with her sing-song Spanish. She asked him to wait and disappeared into an inner office.

Luke walked about and examined the bookcase nearby. He admired editions by Jose Martí, Ernest Hemingway, Salvador and Isabel Allende, and even *Das Kapital* in German. A large photo of Fidel in khakis presided above the assistant's desk. The commander's eyes seemed to follow Luke around the room.

After 10 minutes, Gladys opened the door and motioned Luke to enter the spacious office. A long conference table with a dozen armed chairs filled the room. A large, mahogany desk presided at the table's end. There sat a jowly man fingering a black Montblanc pen. He rose slowly, offering Luke a limp handshake. The blinds were drawn, and the Chinese A/C wheezed lukewarm air. A huge photo of Fidel stared straight at Luke.

"Professor Shannon, thank you for coming. I presume that these are the books from your university," said the expressionless man, over brown-rimmed glasses. He was shorter than Luke and sat on a festooned chair with extra cushions. He received the books about small business without enthusiasm but did finger through a few pages.

"Your request, however, to conduct research about General Ochoa is another matter. As you must be aware, he was convicted of treason at a precarious moment in Cuba's history. It would not be prudent to ask around in a public manner."

"Thanks for your efforts, dean. I just hope to check the University of Havana or National Archives about the 1989 trial. As you know, they're difficult to access from abroad."

"I'm sorry to say that you need a special permit to investigate those archives; they're considered 'confidential,'" said the dean, twirling his pen through stubby fingers.

"So, what must I do to secure this permit? I'd just need an hour or so."

Luke noted that the dean cast a quick look over his shoulder at Castro's photo, before replying:

"Well, if you insist, professor. You could go to the National Revolutionary Police office, which processes special requests for our university. However, it may prove difficult, because it requires the Ministry of Interior's concurrence. Do you really want to go that route?"

Luke hesitated but recalled his unfulfilled vow to Ana. He heard himself say, "Several years ago, I promised a relative of the general that I'd uncover information about the trial that led to his death. Since I'm in your country now, I'd like to honor my pledge. Any assistance you could offer would be welcome."

"As you wish, professor. I'll ask around and leave word at the residence where you're staying. Again, I counsel caution in this delicate matter." He glanced at his watch.

"Thank you for coming, professor. I wish you a nice stay in Havana." The dean stood and shook hands. He rendered no light hug, commonplace in Cuba. He blinked at his assistant, who ushered Luke out.

Luke exited the dean's lukewarm office into the hot anteroom. Perspiration resumed its course down his face. He thanked Gladys and looked back through the dean's door. He was speaking on the fixed-line phone, twirling his pen non-stop. The commander's eyes maintained their vigil on Luke's back as he left. The wall clock read 3:25. That 15-minute appointment was the briefest Luke had ever had with a university counterpart in Latin America.

"That really went well," he mused at the elevator door. Suddenly, gears screeched inside the shaft. The hall lights dimmed and then went out. Luke heard students shout, "The power said *adiós* again. Help get us out!" Emergency lights blinked on and off, and Luke sought a handrail to the stairs.

Despite his curt visit with the dean, Luke, the ever optimist, thought that his luck may have turned. At least he hadn't gotten trapped inside the antique elevator. He descended the stairs in intermittent light.

In between floors, he glimpsed a young couple necking in the stairwell. The students conceded a meek look before embracing again with fervor. Luke said aloud to them but more to himself, "Onward" or "*Adelante*" *en español.*

Luke felt upbeat, whistling as he walked down the flight of stairs. He passed other shadows in the corners until he reached the dank ground floor.

He returned outside under the brilliant sun and shaded his eyes. The contrast with the dark interior made him blink. It also made him ask himself how he could deal with the constant change of pace, illumination, and sounds he'd so far encountered in Havana.

His self-confidence hung in the balance.

CHAPTER 8

Vedado, Havana, Monday, 5 p.m.

AT JOSE'S EMPTY APARTMENT, Luke decided to take a siesta, a habit he'd adopted on slow afternoons. He fell asleep, glad that the inspector did not hijack his dreams. Pleasantly, the young girl, whom he'd just rescued, pointed to the bar. There, Eloisa stood gazing out to sea. Luke hoped that she'd glance back at him with her gray-green eyes. He wondered what she was looking at. A shadow drifted over the Malecón, covering both women in fog. Luke heard their words seep through, "Maybe another time?"

A knock on the door woke him up. A familiar voice, announced, "Professor? You have another call."

Luke stepped out of the dream and rose from the sweat-drenched bed. Twilight was falling outside, and the surf maintained its constant rhythm. Jose pointed him to the fixed-line phone in the living room, where his wife was stitching a shirt on an old Singer machine.

"*Bueno,*" Luke spoke into the phone, repeating his greeting when no one answered.

"Professor, this is Gladys, from the University of Havana. The dean followed through with your request. He said that you may visit the

Castle of the National Revolutionary Police tomorrow in Old Havana and solicit permission with the detective in charge. Go to the main information desk anytime from nine to noon. The old fort is located on Cuba street between Chacón and Tacón. Do you think you can find it?" she asked, her voice rising again.

"Muchas gracias, Gladys. I see it on my tourist map and will go there tomorrow morning. Please give my regards to the dean," Luke said, pleasantly surprised.

Luke thanked Jose and moved quickly into the small bathroom ahead of his sons. They had just returned from a baseball game. Through the thin door, Luke heard them banter about their rival teams. He took pleasure under the lukewarm water gurgling from the shower head. Water helped resuscitate him after the long day. He dried himself with a hand towel, but perspiration budded from the heavy, humid air.

Luke heard the teenagers shouting at each other, so decided to take a break outside. As the clubs were closed, most people stayed home Monday nights. Luke thought a low-key evening would be just right, maybe a mojito in an air-conditioned hotel?

He wished "Buenas noches" to Jose and his family and retraced his steps to the Hotel Nacional. The older porter was not at the entrance. The attendant, who had secured Luke a room, greeted him. "I heard about your heroic act this morning. Muchas gracias. Do you think you could teach me how to swim, maybe at Varadero beach?"

"I've heard much about that beautiful beach. If there are any tours to Veradero, I'm happy to teach you the basics, Arturo. Have you learned how to float? It's my first lesson in learning to swim," pronounced Luke in an academic tone.

"Professor, I plan to join our hotel tour to Veradero this coming Sunday. We're scheduled to spend the day on the beach at the Meliá

Hotel. I'll get you a free passage for the tour. It's a way to say thanks for your bravery today. Maybe you could teach me how to float?"

"With pleasure, Arturo. I may be outside of Havana but could meet you at the Meliá. What time do you plan to depart Veradero on Sunday?

"We'll leave here at 9 a.m. and stay at the Meliá until the sun sets. I'll add your name to our list to ensure you a place on the bus."

"Thanks. Can you point me to the Internet room? I'd like to send an email to my university dean."

"Just upstairs and to the right, Professor Shannon. Please note that our WI-FI is a little slow. As to Varadero, I look forward to bobbing in the ocean. I'll leave word with José. *Hasta luego.*"

Under chandeliers and subdued lights, the hotel's lobby transported Luke to a world of Roman arches, inlaid with Spanish tiles. An older couple spoke French in an adjacent alcove, giving the corridor an Old-World feel. Luke continued up the marble staircase but stopped when he heard a familiar voice. In a nook below sat Johnny, speaking intently to a heavy-set man. Luke hurried to the mezzanine, not wanting to be seen.

He found the Business Center and paid six CUCs for 30 minutes on the old Lenovo computer. He squeezed into a booth and waited several minutes to gain access to Google's website. It took another minute to log onto his Hotmail account, then click on "Compose." The blank PC screen glared back at him. At last, he was able to type his brief message to the dean: "Arrived OK, staying in private home. Met new dean at UH and some students. Internet's slow. Email well received? Stay well, Luke."

After hitting "Send," he waited another minute for confirmation. He checked his Inbox and read a note from his neighbor that Buddy was anxious. He tried to respond, but his screen froze up.

In the remaining minutes, he left Hotmail to check the online news. On MSN.com, the president and the speaker were trading insults with each other. Major League Baseball owners and players were at loggerheads. Some new virus had shut down Wuhan, China and had traveled to Europe and the U.S with dire results.

He clicked on Cuba's Communist Party paper's website, *Granma*, for "official news." Cuba's new President Diaz-Canel decried smugglers, who were siphoning off thousands of gallons of diesel a day. Luke thought of the two brothers wheeling and dealing in "off market" motor oil. The Weather Channel named a new tropical depression brewing in the Gulf of Guinea, heading west. That was Luke's last glimpse of the internet—his 30 minutes were up.

He left the Center and walked along the mezzanine corridor. Luke heard Johnny raise his voice below. He and the man were arguing about money. Luke kept a steady pace to avoid any contact. He longed for a quiet night, not one of confrontation. He descended the back stairs and found the doorman resting on a sofa.

"Good evening, professor. It's good to see you again. I hope that your meeting went well at the university."

"Thank you, Señor Roberto. It was a short, if not sweet. I'm not sure that the dean was interested in my projects. But I possess stubborn Irish genes and do not easily give up."

"Yes, professor, we must be persistent in Cuba. To survive, we've also learned to keep our heads down," the man cautioned.

"Señor Roberto, does Johnny work at the Hotel Nacional? I see him around here more often than not."

"Ah, Johnny. He does not work here but always pops up when one least expects him. Like many in our country, he seeks out people who offer him advantages. It'd be prudent to take care in your dealings with him.

"Now, if you'd excuse me. My old legs must rise again to greet visitors to our beautiful hotel."

They gave each other a light hug. The doorman limped toward the main entrance, and Luke circled back to the garden bar.

* * *

Luke found a table toward the back, where he and the Vietnamese diplomats had enjoyed mojitos under palm trees. He tried to catch any waiter's eye to order a drink. They seemed disinterested and chatted with each other. Maybe no one wanted to serve the table of a solo gringo.

"Professor?" Luke turned to see Johnny under a Panama hat and broad grin. He was fondling that long necklace of beads again. His face glistened and wore an expectant look.

"*Que pasa*, Johnny? I see you everywhere—have you become my official chaperon in Havana?" Luke asked, his exasperation rising to the surface. He had hoped to relax and maybe catch another glimpse of Eloisa in the open-air bar. Now, he had to deal with this teen again. Recalling the priest's advice, he kept his cool, not wanting to appear rude.

"Just making the rounds. What's up with you, professor?" he asked casually, rubbing his hands on his trousers. Outside, thunderheads were forming and the wind swept briskly off the Straits. A seagull struggled to make headway, bringing to mind Luke's own plight in Cuba.

"I'm trying to order a mojito and just 'chill out' in the bar."

Johnny looked around, waving over a young waiter. "Let me introduce you to my cousin," Johnny said expansively. "Manuel, this is a professor from the States. We'd like two mojitos, please."

The young waiter responded diplomatically, "With pleasure, Johnny. Welcome, professor."

Johnny and Luke sat comfortably in wicker chairs, enjoying the trade winds blowing through. It was a pleasant moment. Luke wondered how the self-acclaimed guide had crossed his path so many times in a city of three million souls.

"So, Johnny, you seem to be everywhere. Do you have clients throughout Havana? If so, is there a favorite place that you take them for salsa and night life?"

"I take people to fun places in the Vedado and Miramar neighborhoods. I favor this swank hotel, where important people come and go. For night life, I enjoy 'The Factory' on this side of the Rio Almendares. It's a maze of rooms full of beautiful people. Everyone goes there to party and to be seen. The manager's well connected, a 'Communist with money.' He invites popular artists to exhibit and dancers to show off their moves. It's a mix of tourists and go-go Cubans, where salsa and disco never stop. Of course, party officials get their cut. Maybe we could go together, later this week?"

"Let me think about it, as I have some tasks to complete. Thanks for the heads up. *La Fabrica* sounds like a lively place."

More people drifted into the spacious bar, seeking seats near the balustrade. They looked out over the restive sea and the gathering clouds.

To shake up this tranquil scene, a group swept in with great fanfare. Surrounded by burly men, the same general, whom Luke had seen two days ago, led the charge. Eloisa followed in his wake without the big policeman. Luke slunk lower in his seat.

"*Que pasa?*" Johnny asked, noting Luke's change in mood. "She's quite a dish, that tall woman—do you like? She's the General's current lover."

"Yes, I understand that she's well connected. I met her briefly. It'd be nice to speak with her again but not in such a public setting."

"No problem, *Americano*. She likes to visit the Factory, too. She may show up tomorrow night at the opening of our famous Cuban sculptor, K-cho. He creates special artifacts out of bricks and is known abroad. He also leaves bricks in poorer neighborhoods to help build their homes. He is popular with the people. He's cut some deal with Google and 'the powers that be.' He's a man on the move. He's also a man of color," he affirmed, envy permeating his eyes.

"Hmm, that sounds like an interesting event, Johnny—do you plan to attend?" Luke imagined how good it'd be to see Eloisa without escorts.

"Yes, I could. I know the outside guards and help them keep the crowd in order," he answered smugly. "There are many rooms in this old Factory, where private encounters can take place."

The mojitos arrived beneath his thirsty stare. Johnny wolfed down half his drink, licking his lips in satisfaction.

Luke couldn't help but smile. "You do like your mojitos and know many people and places in Havana." Luke was amazed how such a young man kept so well connected.

"In the new Cuba, information is my ammunition, professor," he said, flirting with an Afro-Cuban girl holding the arm of a Caucasian tourist. They spoke in halting English.

Luke drank deeply from his mojito while observing Eloisa. He marveled at how she conducted her court of admirers, especially the beaming general by her side. She seemed to stand her ground in discussions with his cohort. Her good looks helped a lot.

Just then, he cringed as the huge major entered the garden bar. Luke ducked beneath the shadow of the palms. He drank the rest of his drink, sensing Johnny's eyes upon him.

"Here are some CUCs, Johnny, for the bill and maybe for a special friend," Luke said, turning away from the General's growing entourage. Johnny looked sideways at him, a question lurking on his lips. Luke anticipated by saying, "I'm leaving as I have an early appointment tomorrow. Maybe we'll see each other at the Factory?"

"As you wish, *Americano.*" He gave Luke a tight hug, his eyes dancing around the bar.

Before leaving, Luke looked quickly at the General's table. In return, he received a pointed look from Ochoa's niece, who held his stare. That moment lasted only a second, but it shook Luke to his core.

CHAPTER 9

Vedado, Havana, Tuesday, 7 a.m.

A LIGHT BREEZE CARESSED HIS SHOULDERS AS he drifted back to consciousness. He opened his eyes and heard a tap-tap sound coming through the door. Opening it, he watched José pounding browned rice with a pestle on a mortar and melding it into liquid form. "Buenos días, professor. This is the poor man's coffee in Cuba. The state store ran out of the Colombian variety. We have to make do. There's no caffeine in it, so it may be better for your health."

He watched his host pour the brown liquid through a homemade filter, adding sugar and cinnamon. The brew had a pleasant aroma but unusual taste. They sipped a small cup and gave each other a light hug. Luke tiptoed past the sleeping family and down the stairs. Outside, he put on his Seattle Mariners cap to shield him from the rising sun. Walking to *"La Rampa"* or 23rd Street, he found passengers jockeying for a share-ride taxi to Old Havana. A battered Chevy stopped in front of him. Luke squeezed into the front seat with two other passengers. A *Colectivo* sign swung wildly from the front mirror as the car veered toward el Malecón.

The driver stopped near the Parque Central and jumped out to pry open the right door, almost pitching Luke onto the street. He gave the driver a one CUC bill and gained another smile. He found out later that residents only paid a few Cuban pesos, or about a dime, for most fares. Luke didn't mind helping this private entrepreneur. He saw the Capitol building gleaming in the sunlight as he tried to get his bearings to Havana Bay.

Pedestrians sought cover from the sun under colonial arcades, but heat rebounded from the mosaic sidewalk. A young man wearing a Yankees cap whooped "*Marinero.*" Luke gave him a thumbs up and continued his trek along cobblestone streets.

He got lost in the maze of Old Havana. He passed the Plaza of the Cathedral, where he'd attended mass and the rectory, where he'd met the priest. At a crossroads, he inadvertently bumped into a middle-aged lady carrying a Gap shopping bag.

"You look lost, *Americano.* Where do you want to go?" she asked, putting down her bag full of clothes.

"Señora, I'm trying to find the headquarters of the National Revolutionary Police in Old Havana."

Bemused, she said, "I hope you're not in trouble, comrade. With your baseball hat, you shouldn't have a problem. Everyone likes baseball here, especially the police. Just follow your nose, straight ahead, and look for an old Spanish fort. It's not in the best of shape. Be safe."

"Muchas gracias," Luke answered, trepidation rising within him. He followed Chacón street until Havana Bay. A commanding structure occupied the corner, surrounded by granite walls and a bolted gateway. At 9 o'clock, two uniformed guards scraped open the wrought-iron barrier, which resisted loudly along the pavement. A fading coat of arms stood vigil above the colonial fortress. Luke walked up to the guards, who rested their hands on their automatic pistols.

"Buenos Dias, señores. The University of Havana said that I'd find the detective on duty here. Where am I supposed to go?" The two guards looked him over and eventually let him pass through the gate.

They pointed upward without words. Luke entered the fortress but sensed the high walls close in. He looked back and saw the guards tracking his climb up the granite stairs.

Reaching the next level, he found a half-opened door and stepped into a dark corridor. He paused to adjust his eyes. Muffled sounds circulated along the stone walls, and a cry rang from deep inside.

He detected movement farther down the hall, where a policeman held a young girl by the arm. Luke followed them into a dimly lit room. A fan sputtered overhead and cigarette smoke drifted over a dozen Cubans of all ages, colors, and dress. Luke hesitated at the door. They turned to check him out.

A wooden counter stood at the end of the rectangular room. Luke drew in his breath and propelled himself through the human sea. He wondered who they all were—perhaps petty thieves, con artists, or even a political dissident?

"Hey, gringo, looking for a program?" asked a slim, androgynous youth, swinging hips in his direction. Another blew smoke in Luke's face.

"Thanks, but no thanks," he responded, pushing himself through the human turnstile.

When he reached the window, two uniformed cops sat in an inner office looking bored. He also saw the back of a large man in a coffee-colored guayabera.

The big man slowly rotated his large body and looked astonished at Luke. He cried out, "You again?"

"Excuse me, señor. The University of Havana asked me to speak with the detective on duty. I've come to ask for a special permit," Luke said, shocked at seeing this colossus again. He took off his Mariners cap as a sign of respect.

"What do you want, *Americano*? You've already found trouble enough in Havana. What is it this time?"

"I need to obtain a permit in order to review trial documents in the National Archives," Luke stammered. Behind him, the morning crowd looked on with interest.

"Stop playing with me! What trial do you want to investigate? As you can see, we have a lot going on. Spit it out."

"I'd like to review the trial records of the former Hero of the Republic, General Arnaldo Ochoa, which took place 30 years ago."

The policeman's face darkened, causing Luke to step back. The detective seemed to smolder like Mt. St. Helena about to erupt. His eyes flashed danger and his voice spewed thunder: "That's impossible. These records are off limits, gringo! As I warned you before, don't poke your nose into other people's affairs. Next time, you'll not just end up on the floor but somewhere worse."

Sweat cascaded down Luke's face. Smoky air grasped his throat. He heard himself plead: "But the University said I could review the transcripts, with the ministry's permission. I came asking for your assistance."

"Not today, not tomorrow, not ever, gringo!" shouted the big man, slamming the grated window shut on Luke. The "Out to Lunch" sign rocked back and forth, as if shaking a finger in his North American face.

Luke shifted slowly from the window but viewed only the backsides of the morning crew. Even the transvestite had glanced away. A path opened slowly to let him pass. He withdrew through a ripple of snickers and stares.

He retraced his steps in the stone labyrinth, touching its walls to keep his balance. He found the half-opened door and shielded his eyes against the blinding light. He put the Mariners cap back on and grasped the handrail to aid his descent. At the guardhouse, the policemen hardly acknowledged him. He was the invisible man without consequence.

They offered no words but pushed the iron gate ajar. It screeched as if begrudging Luke to leave, spewing him into the street.

He stood beneath the seething sun, wondering what to do.

CHAPTER 10

Castle of the National Revolutionary Police, Havana, 9:20 a.m.

"THE NERVE OF THAT GRINGO," ranted Big Man to his fellow officers. The window still reverberated from slamming it shut. "Good riddance," he muttered, hoping that he'd seen the last of that troublesome tourist.

"Major, isn't he the same man who appeared in *Granma's* article today?" said a shorter version of himself. They had served together in Angola and often were called "the twins" by fellow officers.

Big Man looked skeptically at his colleague, who lifted up the newspaper. There on page three was that very gringo, bare-chested and hugging a sleek, black girl. Water dripped from their faces, and the headline read "Tourist saves teen off Malecón." He perused the article and discovered that the tourist was a visiting American professor to the University of Havana. It recounted that the gringo saw the girl fall into the sea and tore off his clothes to rescue her.

He reread the article and noted the reporter's name. As a senior detective, he wanted to know more about this annoying prof and accidental hero of the Malecón.

"Sargent, please get this reporter on the line. I'd like to speak to her. She seems to know a lot about this gringo, yet I know so little.

It's strange that his path and mine have crossed twice this week—*que pasa?*"

"Do we have any real coffee remaining from our precious supply? I could use a pickup after dealing with him and the usual suspects outside," he said, licking his lips in anticipation.

Last night, his wife confessed that she'd been unable to buy coffee with her ration card. She'd only found teabags from Canada and planned to swap them for coffee with the wife of a Brazilian diplomat. After Sunday's meeting at the ministry, he hoped that Cuba would not fall into another "special period." He recalled how tough life became after the Soviets had pulled the plug 30 years ago.

Real coffee put him in a better mood. He savored the café Cubano with his two colleagues, and his pulse rate slowed. Reluctantly, he opened the grated window to the restless prisoners. He asked the sergeant to take the morning head count while his twin worked the phones to locate the *Granma* reporter.

"*Bueno,*" said the Big Man, hearing a pleasant voice on the crackling line. He nodded often and asked about her sources for the story. He took a few notes, thanked her, and asked to keep in touch. Then, he sat down to ponder.

"The reporter got most of the story's details from one of the Inspector's informants. Apparently, the 'thin man' also is tracking this professor on his visit to Havana. He seemed like a 'do-gooder' and not dangerous, but who knows? He's a prof from some American university. Ask around and see what you can discover. I'd like to know what this prof's real agenda is in Cuba and why he's so fixated on the deceased Hero of the Republic."

The Inspector again! He thought back 30 years and how he'd cringed when the "thin man" advised that his former commander was arrested. *MinInt* operatives had sequestered Ochoa at the Reloj Club Boinas Rojas military base. Opportunely, Big Man had distanced himself from General Ochoa on his return to Havana. He'd been able to rejoin the National Revolutionary Police and resume his career. What would have happened if he'd stayed in the Army? Would he have joined other Angola vets and protégés who devised schemes to generate income for Cuba? The country was struggling to survive on the eve of "the special period."

Ochoa's accusers alleged that his inner group assisted the Colombian cartels in running interference against the U.S. Coast Guard. Apparently, they'd secured a number of Miami-based yachts for this purpose to facilitate drug smuggling into South Florida. But how could they have done so without consent from the top?

Big Man couldn't stand drugs, especially cocaine. He had seen the ravaging effects on soldiers in the field. He wouldn't have abided any order to service drug lords. He was thankful that he'd reentered the National Revolutionary Police.

At Ochoa's trial, they'd charged the general of condoning such activity—"free lancing" they called it. The prosecutors implied that Ochoa, his chief of staff, Tony de La Guardia, Major Padrón and Captain Martinez were drug runners on the sly. In Angola, the General was an enterprising commander, but Big Man never knew him to cross the Brothers. They always called the shots. They also called Ochoa *El Moro* or "The Moor" behind his back, because of his darker skin.

His own sources suggested that Ochoa had done their bidding. Such activities would generate dollars during tough times. When these ventures hit the international press, the Brothers needed a scapegoat. Also, they resented Ochoa's growing prestige. They "convinced" the generals of the court martial to find the Hero of the Republic guilty of treason, confirmed by their Council of State. On that infamous morning in July, the four officers were shot by firing squad.

It was strange that this prof wanted to discover what happened years ago to Cuba's hero. The authorities had tried so hard to bury the general's memory. Since the prof seemed determined to research Ochoa in the National Archives, he should learn more about this unusual *Americano.*

* * *

JUST BEFORE NOON, BIG MAN DECIDED to walk to the National Congress building and see a friend who dealt with educational exchanges. Maybe he'd know something about this professor and his university. Big Man usually avoided gringos and hated their superior airs. He also didn't speak English well, which sounded harsh to the ear. However, he enjoyed receiving their Neutrogena soap and Starbucks coffee from "friends of friends."

At the exterior gate, he listened to the policemen's complaints about the lack of food in the stores. He appreciated their sharing concerns with him, even in difficult times. He returned their salute and departed the compound toward shimmering Havana Bay.

Most docks stood empty now, in contrast to winter, when U.S. cruise ships plied the waters. He'd seen herds of foreigners disgorge, buying artifacts, rum and marimba instruments. The tourists always seemed to be in a hurry, which put him off.

Since their arrogant president curtailed these cruises, the sidewalk markets sported few visitors but many crows. He perceived drawn faces on sales attendants and heard Cuban music of lament. One vendor looked nostalgically at the photo of the former U.S. President, shrouded by the words "*Santo Obama.*" For a change of pace, he entered Old Town to enjoy the bustle of fellow Cubans.

He walked by the old seminary building. He'd heard it taught humanities and small-business courses. He peered inside the entranceway and spied a *Cuba Emprende* poster for *auto-propistas* or self-employed entrepreneurs. His wife had talked about opening a beauty salon to feature new styles flaunted by her Brazilian friend. Maybe she'd like to attend.

"My dear countryman, what a wonderful surprise to have you visit our cultural center," he heard from the courtyard. The accent was similar to that of his hometown Santiago, reminding him of childhood days.

He turned to see a willowy man, wearing gray vestments and a Roman collar. "My fellow countryman, it's been too long! Let me give you a hug," Big Man exclaimed, enveloping the slim priest in his powerful arms.

"Jose Antonio, what a pleasure to see you again, here in our Catholic gathering place," the priest replied, a smile growing on his narrow face.

"Father Sebastian, I thought you tended the flock in our hometown? I didn't know that you were visiting Havana."

"I was asked to stand in for a priest on holiday in Spain. I should be here the month of July, and I'm trying to acclimate myself to Havana's frenetic pace. I recognized you at once and wanted to greet you after all these years. Are you free for a cup of tea?" said the priest, his eyes brightening the unlit passageway.

"Maybe another time, padre. It would be fun to catch up. Maybe I could invite my wife, Dolores? She is contemplating opening a beauty salon and could attend the small-business course advertised. May I reach you here?"

"Anytime, José Antonio. If I remember correctly, we both celebrate our birthdays later this month. Perhaps a small fiesta would be in order?" suggested the priest, returning the policeman's hug.

"With much pleasure, padre." His wife always liked the priest. They'd known him during their youth in Santiago. He'd always appreciated his thoughtful tone. He was not surprised that Sebastian had entered the seminary and become a parish priest. They'd shared pleasant times in their serene hometown. The padre had baptized their only son almost 30 years ago. It seemed like only yesterday that holy water had caressed their baby's face at the small church of St. Peter of Santiago. His son gave both parents hope.

As his son's memory sprang to mind, angst eclipsed his mood. It had been more than a year since *Cubana Aviación 972's* disaster flight from Havana to Holguin. They said that the crew was inexperienced and the used Boeing 737 was ill-maintained. The plane crashed just after liftoff that horrible Friday morning in May.

He reminisced how they'd tried to conceive a child, going from clinic to clinic. Fr. Sebastian had said a special prayer. Their spirits soared when the nurse at the *Hospital General de Santiago* announced that Dolores was pregnant. Their baby boy was born at eight pounds and in good health. They felt such joy. Their newborn son had vanquished their worries and despair. Their family had been made whole.

It seemed like only yesterday when they'd moved to Havana. His promotion to senior detective provided opportunity for their young son. They'd navigated the channels of power to qualify Antonio Jr. for the prestigious Escuela Lenin, the top STEM school in Cuba. His son excelled in mathematics and was top of his class. On graduation, the National Revolutionary Police invited his son to work in its forensics department. Junior gained stature and respect as an investigator. He was in high demand. Father and son enjoyed comparing case notes. They often had watched pirated versions of CSI Las Vegas at home together.

In a flash, Antonio Jr. vanished in a fireball with 112 other passengers on board. The plane was heading for Ochoa's home turf in

Holguin. His son was to be lead investigator. In the end, Big Man had been unable to protect him.

He blamed himself for pushing his son to join the forensic service, knowing that the job would require constant travel. Though unsure about God, he thought that he'd led a decent life. He'd always helped his fellow man and woman along the way. If there were a higher power, why had he blessed them with a son and then taken him away? He feared that someone had put a hex on him, calling upon the spirits of Santeria. He raised his fist and shook it at the heavens: Why, why, why, was Antonio Jr. taken from them?

Since Dolores could no longer have children, there would be no one to carry on their family line. Upon their demise, this couple from Santiago would have no one to mark their time on earth. *Nada.*

As he meandered the streets of Old Havana, he reflected on his fleeting youth. How proud his own father had been when Big Man was accepted into the police academy. Later, he was made junior detective and the whole family celebrated. Antonio Jr. was born and they'd moved to Havana. Then his supervisors offered him up to the Cuban Army. They were seeking people of color to fight in Africa. Away he went and rose through the ranks.

His bravery in the field caught the eye of his commanding officer. With the blessing of Ochoa, they'd breveted him to first lieutenant, later captain, then major. At the time, he had reached the top of the world. He'd achieved much for a poor country boy.

Then, his father had died suddenly of a stroke while Big Man was battling rebels in Angola. Big Man's anchor on earth was gone. Again, he was unable to say goodbye.

Why was he able to taste the fruits of power and praise, then, in an instant, be thrown into the depths of hell? Despite soothing words from the priest, he believed that his lot in life was to suffer, along with the rest of the Cuban people.

Not paying attention, he almost ran into a pedicab. He slowed his gait but didn't see a cockroach traverse his path. He usually stepped aside to avoid hurting vulnerable animals, even insects. Not so today. He stumbled and crushed it underfoot. He looked down and concluded that he just might be that cockroach in Cuba—squashed by hidden forces without notice or remorse.

Anger and despair renewed their battle within him. He wasn't sure which force would prevail. Despite his large size, he felt weakened by his son's death. He asked himself whether life was worth living inside his tattered soul.

CHAPTER 11

Old Havana, Tuesday, 10 a.m.

A S THE SUN ROSE HIGHER, sweat streamed down Luke's cheeks and chest. Rebuffed by the police, he decided to walk home to clear his head.

He touched his Mariners cap at a passerby. Despite Seattle's cellar-dwelling team in the American League West, the team cap earned him friendly looks in Havana. Someone offered to trade his cap for one with the Cuban banner, but Luke declined. Maybe he should reexamine his skeptical attitude about his hometown team.

As he wound his way toward Parque Central, ominous clouds rolled in, matching Luke's sullen mood. He felt drops of rain and decided to flag down a collective taxi among those seeking rides to Vedado. The process seemed like a shell game. Crowds surged toward the occasional Chevrolets and Ladas that briefly pulled in. A passenger or two would squeeze inside, becoming filler in its human sandwich. Before the door even closed, the taxi would zoom up the avenue, leaving those on the curb shaking fists.

While savvy locals outmaneuvered Luke, the rain and wind picked up. Several sought shelter under Hotel Inglaterra's covered veranda.

Raindrops mixed with sweat on his Seattle U. polo shirt. Dampened dust pierced his nostrils as the heavens opened up. "One last try," he grumbled, shaking his Mariners cap at a sputtering Oldsmobile. The driver swerved right in front of Luke and pushed the door open. Luke squeezed into a full front seat. Five passengers sat stoically in the back. "So, you're the gringo with the Mariners cap, who pays in CUCs," the young driver affirmed.

Word sure traveled fast among Havana's gypsy cab drivers. The young man hung out with colleagues at the "24/7" convenience store along the Malecón, trading gossip 24/7. He'd learned of Luke's presence while buying a slice of pizza. He was driving his grandfather's Olds and had to pay 10 CUCs in daily rental. The driver knew pidgin English and pestered Luke for baseball news in hopes for CUCs, dollars, or Euros.

Thunder roared and rain pounded on the car roof like bullets from heaven. Instant rivers appeared, carrying refuse to overflowing gutters. The Olds surfed through the waters on Centro streets and made it up La Rampa's steep incline. Pedestrians ran for cover, dodging rain and rooster tails on 23rd Street. As the storm reached a crescendo, sparrows meekly hid under a hostel's eaves. Its sign, "Welcome, European visitors," flapped crazily in the wind.

The driver turned on L Street and stopped at a movie theater across from Copellia in Vedado. Pedestrians dashed for the cinema's lobby, huddling with refugees from the storm. The driver thanked Luke for his two CUCs and held out his card. "I know the ins and outs of Havana, *Americano*. You may need someone to find its out-of-the way places."

"Do you know anything about the Factory? I've heard that a famous artist will exhibit there tonight." Luke thought it prudent to verify Johnny's information and reentered the car.

"You may like that old place, which is full of artifacts and artsy people. Several of your countrymen hang out in this trendy club. *La Fábrica* is a labyrinth of alcoves and foxy women. I think you'd enjoy yourself there."

"If I venture out, I'll let you know. *Gracias*." Luke jumped out and ran to the university's entrance, where he'd visited the dean. Many students were trapped by the rain, standing vigil in the lightless lobby. He noticed the two students he'd chatted with yesterday. They approached him carrying their book bags and greeted, "How are you my friend?"

Both students told Luke they were enrolled as juniors in the university's "Tourism" course. "It's been a hard year without U.S. cruise liners. Hotel vacancies are skyrocketing," complained the taller student, wearing the same "RL" polo shirt of yesterday. "We've seen you here twice. Are you a visiting professor?"

Luke told them that he taught at Seattle University. The students wanted to study in the states but couldn't apply for a visa without a scholarship. "Maybe our well-to-do cousins in Miami will help," said the shorter student. "They threw dollars around when they visited this year. We made extra CUCs by reselling their gifts to buyers here. It helped us get by. The embargo makes life difficult here."

Luke saw a patch of blue sky emerge beyond the gray cumulus, as the rain lessened to a Seattle drizzle. Remembering the priest's advice to confer with "friends of friends," Luke invited the students to share *cerveza* at the California Café, where he'd first met Eloisa. The students agreed enthusiastically and followed Luke toward el Malecón.

The same bartender was sweeping water out of the café's door. He acknowledged Luke and gave the students the once over. Luke sat at the same table he'd occupied Sunday and ordered *Bucaneros* all around.

The students were cousins and self-declared "entrepreneurs." The tall student pitched his aunt's B&B, "She offers competitive rates, and tourists enjoy the informal atmosphere. CUCs off the books help my family survive. Fewer Americans visit now, and even the Europeans are cutting back." He gazed longingly toward the Florida Straits.

Luke asked if they knew anyone at the National Archives. The shorter student said that a classmate worked there in the afternoon and could probably give Luke a tour. He wrote his cell number on the back of the card for their *B&B familiar.*

The stocky student admitted that he loved baseball and used to play catcher. He injured his right foot, ending a budding career. He looked fondly at Luke's Mariners cap. Luke gave it to the wannabe catcher, who beamed ear-to-ear. The *Bucaneros* loosened their tongues and they traded gossip about the University of Havana.

Luke felt a buzz and bid the cousins adiós. He was heartened by a spectacular sunset, exuding a kaleidoscope of vermillion, orange, and yellow. He saw cumulus clouds skitter toward the West and two gulls skim in tandem over the sea. He turned toward Jose's apartment and passed the eternal teens on the corner. They were gaming on their smartphones, their faces reflecting a neon pallor.

Night fell suddenly over Havana.

Luke entered the apartment and thanked Jose's wife for washing his favorite North Face shirt. Their sons were attending another baseball game, and the bathroom was free. Water still dribbled from the showerhead and cooler air refreshed after the afternoon storm. He put on the clean, North Face shirt and splashed on Calvin Klein eau de cologne. The cracked mirror revealed gray hairs gaining more traction in his auburn hair. His Roman nose stood out like a beacon on his sunburned face. Standing up straight, Luke thought he didn't look bad for a middle-aged man.

Feeling upbeat after the beers and shower, Luke left the bathroom in a buoyant mood. He bid "Buenas noches" to the couple, saying that he'd likely arrive late.

Señor José tapped his shoulder and looked him in the eye, "Beware of Greeks bearing gifts tonight, professor."

What a weird thing to say, thought Luke. He fished out the driver's card and called him for pickup at the Hotel Nacional. Despite José's warning, he walked boldly toward the Malecón. He put today's events out of his mind, unleashing expectations for the night ahead.

CHAPTER 12

Hotel Nacional, Havana, Tuesday, 8:30 p.m.

A s Luke strolled along the inner part of the Malecón, a make-shift market sprouted up. On the sidewalk, artisans shared space with vendors pitching roasted maize, fish-on-a-stick, and barbequed meat of uncertain origin. Luke warded off zealous salesmen and set foot on a path, winding up to the hotel's side entrance. Patrons in the garden bar sipped mojitos beneath undulating palms.

Luke stepped inside the lobby and overheard the concierge discuss trendy *paladares* and salsa clubs with French tourists. Ladies in mascara wore tight cocktail dresses and paraded down the corridor with middle-aged men in tow. They spoke in rapid Spanish and cast furtive glances at younger tourists. Luke could understand why Johnny frequented this classic hotel, where Havana's powerful mixed with foreign glitterati.

The doorman limped outside. "Hola, professor. These old legs get tired, though visitors want to use theirs on the dance floor. The clubs are open tonight. Any special plans?"

"I'm thinking of visiting the Factory. I've been told that artists mix with dancers of all types. What do you think?"

"It's a popular place for young Cubans and tourists, but it gets jam-packed in the early morning. K-cho has a show tonight and will draw an artistic clientele. Do you need transportation?"

On cue, the gray Oldsmobile crept slowly up to the entranceway, its muffler growling like an untamed animal. Chauffeurs of shinier automobiles looked down at this upstart gypsy cab. Luke entered the weary Olds and bid the doorman adiós.

The driver wore a sheepish look, muttering, "Buenas noches." He didn't glance at the polished cars but looked straight ahead. After leaving the hotel compound, he exhaled deeply and turned toward the Malecón.

As he shot across the seaside roadway, the young man's face lit up. The Malecón had that effect on people, suggesting romance and laissez-faire. The twinkling stars and rolling waves created an inviting tableau.

"This is the Paseo of the People, professor. Here we're free from daily concerns and from the authorities," philosophized the young driver. He pointed at teenagers hanging out and couples in various stages of embrace. The popcorn man was doing a brisk business, and street vendors plied their trades.

To Luke, the lights along the Malecón resembled a string of pearls. The morning's dismay slowly dissipated into the evening breeze.

At the end of the grand boulevard, the driver turned inward, zig-zagging through a maze of potholed streets. He added, "That's the *Rio Almenderes* and the bridge to chic Miramar. Communists and diplomats with money live there. The neighborhood houses many embassies, including the strange Russian compound. They say that the architect constructed the building to look like a sword. The Russians wanted it to represent power. Here in Havana, we call it the 'syringe.'"

The driver turned once more and stopped at a six-story building with a smokestack on top. The sign read Calle 26. "This used to be a cooking-oil factory but now it's known as *La Fabrica de Arte Cubano*. It's the club that the party swingers prefer, along with international visitors like you. Enjoy your evening, professor. The ride is only five CUCs."

Luke paid him six CUCs, eliciting an enthusiastic response. "These CUCs put me into the black today. *Gracias, Americano.*" The Olds puffed off, leaving Luke behind a serpentine of revelers winding around the block.

The line wasn't moving, so Luke stepped around the corner, heading for the entrance. Its façade cast a subdued blue light, contrasting with the gold-lit entranceway. A tour bus arrived with a guide waving a Canadian flag. He spoke English and French, leading the tourists through the human tide. Security men moved up and down the line, trying to keep order.

Conga beats cascaded from the Factory's roof. Under the marquee, Luke stepped around the tour and aimed for the dimly lit door. He ran into a big bouncer who ordered him, "Get back in line."

"It's OK, comrade, this visitor is known to me," a dark silhouette proclaimed. Luke recognized the voice and saw the bright teeth of Johnny, who appeared from the shadows. The teen wore a sleeveless "I Love New York" T-shirt, a red arm band, and his ever-ready smile. He appeared to have grown a few inches taller.

"Professor, do you have a 20 CUC bill to grease the way?" he asked. Luke forked over a 20 *pesos Convertibles* note, which Johnny passed on to the bouncer. The beefy man took the bill but didn't say thanks. Without losing a beat, Johnny led Luke by the arm through the group of frowning tourists and Cuban escorts. Inside, Luke walked to an open window, where a girl gave him an electronic card. She warned, "Don't lose the card or they'll charge you 30 CUCs when you leave." She acknowledged Johnny with a nod and turned to an entourage of Italians, gesturing boldly with their hands.

Luke followed Johnny to an atelier exhibiting native art under rosé lighting. In the back were two exits, so Johnny asked, "Which way, professor?"

Luke chose the door to the left, leading to a gallery of classic photos of Old Havana. A couple embraced at the end of the hall, so Luke opted for another stairway, awash in reggae sounds. Halfway up, they passed two young men shoulder-to-shoulder. An ash-blonde girl leaned against the wall looking bored. Johnny nodded to one of the guys and began tapping his platform shoes to the music's beat. Luke squeezed past the threesome and climbed to the next level. Disco music poured out the door and pulled Luke in.

Johnny seemed dazzled by the flashing lights bouncing around the spacious room. He absorbed the electronic sound and began grinding his hips. He didn't look back at Luke and whirled off to his own beat. On a raised stage, five young dancers interpreted the music in their individual ways. Luke joined visitors moving to the rap of Kool and the Gang. Bursts from strobe lights bathed the dancers while lyrics ricocheted off the inky walls.

The light beam changed to a rosy hue as Beyoncé's image took over the jumbotron. She sang about an unfaithful lover *en español* while bright colors glanced off the mirrors. Luke looked up to a spinning globe and picked up his pace. Dancers rushed to the floor. Luke searched for Johnny, but he was nowhere to be found.

The music transitioned to another era, taking Luke back in time. Could it have been the '80s when he first danced the "Electric Slide"? Now he formed up with young Cubans who line-danced with gusto and rubbed shoulders with their neighbors. Luke tried his best to remember the steps but went the wrong way, bumping into an attractive couple. Without a word, they took him by the hips and moved him along the floor. Luke liked that.

When the music slowed, the couple smiled and turned to each other, dancing cheek-to-cheek. Luke half-danced toward the exit and climbed to the top floor. Three bars covered the open-air veranda, which overflowed with patrons and waving palms. Bartenders worked nonstop to satisfy a thirsty clientele. Mojitos, Cuba Libres, and *cerveza* flowed freely under the stars. On an adjacent patio, Luke enjoyed a trio of young singers, crooning in the style of Celia Cruz. The clubbers swayed back and forth to the seductive sounds. Jose Marti's poetry flashed across the screen:

"I cultivate a white rose
In July as in January;
I give it to a true friend,
Who offers his sincere hand to me."

Well, it *is* July, thought Luke. He ordered a mojito with extra shots of rum. Following a group of revelers, Luke heard Latino rap bursting from an inside room. On stage, 10 svelte dancers in leotards shifted to the clapping of a slim, older man. Maybe their instructor? They moved in sequence, but a few put more heart into each step. A lively Afro-Cuban woman caught Luke's eye. The ballerina sweated profusely, casting off a steamy mirage.

Luke drank deeply from his mojito as the scene carried him away. He felt anticipation but didn't know why. He enjoyed the sensation of the crowd moving back and forth, brushing bodies with strangers of the night.

Finally, the stand-in instructor clapped once and the performers stopped on the dot. They held their poses and acknowledged cascading applause. After the group sequence, the instructor chose four to remain for a classical piece. The other dancers vanished silently into the throng. The music reset to Debussy's *Clair de Lune*.

A distinctive black man faced off against a willowy Eurasian, while a man with Castilian features stood before the woman in Afro. The four dancers stood erect and motionless as only ballet artists could. When the flute began its plaintive tune, the dancers commenced their pas de quatre. They swayed and swept around the stage. All conversation stopped. Luke traveled to a magical place.

Their steps graced Debussy's notes with dignity and poise. A sliver of moonlight peeked through the door. Paintings of abstract art hung in vigil on the wall. Luke stood mesmerized and closed his eyes to absorb the impressionist's masterpiece.

Someone approached him from behind. He felt two hands cover his eyes and heard a voice whisper, "Lucas, is it time to dance?"

CHAPTER 13

La Fábrica, Havana, Wednesday, 12:30 a.m.

H E ALLOWED HIMSELF TO BE PUSHED toward an adjacent stairwell, where LED lighting intruded from the corner. At the bend of the curving stairs, Luke faced a sphynx in a green dress that matched her gray-green eyes. "Eloisa," he uttered. She stepped forward and stroked his hair. Her touch sent him up the wall. She pressed forward lips-to-lips, nose-to-nose, hip-to-hip. He didn't resist. Musical notes floated down. Suddenly, the classical music changed to a more dramatic piece, ratcheting up their frenzy on the stairs.

Ardor built like a July storm, accompanying Debussy's *Suite Bergamasque*. Under the barrage, his body took on a life of its own. Animal desire pushed through anguish and restraint. He went over the edge.

He heard the door open as another couple entered the stairwell. Luke pressed closer to Eloisa, letting them squeeze by. He heard her say, "You smell good." He closed his eyes, desiring more.

The door reopened and loud voices filled the air. Several couples stumbled down the stairs, chattering like magpies. They stared directly at Luke, dousing his fervor. Though he was charged to go, he should seek a quieter place.

Luke took Eloisa's hand and descended the stairwell into a small gallery. Salsa dancers on canvas adorned the walls, shifting under a rotating light. She seemed to know her way around and nudged him to a dusky corner. He found the zipper to her dress.

Without warning, Eloisa's head rose from his shoulder. She glanced upwards, concern flashing across her face. Another voice penetrated the gallery, one that Luke had heard before. She grasped his hand.

Reluctantly, he followed her down the back stairs. *"Que pasa?"* he asked.

"To be continued, Lucas," is all she said. Above, a door opened and a question bounced off the walls, "Where did she go?" Luke couldn't believe it. How had they stalked Eloisa and him to the Factory? He hastened down the stairs.

He kissed her quickly, his fervor transforming to fear. They hit the ground floor running. Luke's knee cried out. Eloisa turned left without looking back and faded into an obscure portal.

Luke turned right, hopping in front of the exit line. The clubbers didn't seem to mind. They sang *Guantamera* and clinked bottles of *Bucanero*. Luke thrust his plastic card and a 10-CUC note to the cashier. He tried to mask his rising panic.

To Luke's left, a hefty man of color watched him over dark glasses. On his table was a mix of boat paintings and artifacts, some made of small bricks, others of wood. Luke recognized him as the famous artist, K-cho. He would have liked to stop and take a closer look. Instead, he surrendered a harried smile.

The Cuban artist sensed Luke's desperate straits. "Maybe another time, comrade?"

Luke nodded and almost flew out the door, past the burly bouncers and the lengthening line. Johnny wasn't around to rescue him this time.

He turned the corner quickly and began to jog, pain erupting from his bum knee. He ran through dingy streets and tripped on a root sprouting from the sidewalk. He grabbed the cascading branch of a laurel tree to catch himself. A uniformed man on a nearby veranda followed his every step.

Luke resumed his pace, avoiding two scrawny cats chasing a mouse. He stopped under another laurel to rest. Misery bubbled up within him. If he fell into another pothole, would anyone ever know? Would anyone really care?

Despite good intentions, he couldn't catch a break on his mission to Havana. Luke felt an unseen force stalking him. Ever since he'd encountered that airport inspector, his trip had gone downhill. How had he anticipated Luke's every move? Together with that big policeman, they seemed intent on hounding him out of Cuba.

He left the uneven sidewalk for the cobblestone street. Faint light filtered through a huge tree on the corner. In an unlit plaza, dozens of young men and women were hanging out, thumbing their smartphones. Someone began walking toward Luke. Should he hide again?

The young man was examining his phone and nearly bumped into Luke, piquing his curiosity. "Buenos dias. Why are so many of you sitting around the plaza at such a late hour?"

The youth stared at Luke in amazement. Then it dawned on him that Luke was a foreigner. "This is how we get our Wi-Fi. There are fewer blackouts at night. We can access the public Internet after 11 p.m. in the public square. We connect with friends on WhatsApp and watch YouTube videos.

"We also like to know what's happening in the outside world. I'm interested in what the students are doing on the streets of Hong Kong. They are soulmates overseas. I'm also following news about a weird virus and if it's coming to Cuba." He looked down at his phone and said, "Excuse me, *Americano*. I'm late for my rendezvous. *Hasta la vista.*"

He sped off in the direction from which Luke had just fled. The youth probably would join the clubbers in line, excited about his morning encounter. Luke turned and continued past the silent shadows playing their phones like pianos.

Luke squinted at the stone markers on each corner, trying to keep track of the numbered streets. Were they rising or falling? He remembered that Vedado's streets were both numbered and lettered and that Jose's apartment was near Café California on 19th and N Streets. He kept moving in that direction.

Given his misfortune to date, he was anxious about what lurked around the corner. He heard an owl hoot twice. Was that an omen? In this country of inspectors, policemen, and generals, Luke feared that he was in way over his head.

He searched the branches of the Ceiba but perceived only rustling leaves. He caught a glimmer of light on the Eastern horizon.

It now was Wednesday in Havana.

CHAPTER 14

La Fábrica, Havana, Wednesday, 3 a.m.

THE ROOM FOR "*DAMAS*" PROMISED REFUGE from the male voices upstairs. Eloisa went in quickly and eased into an empty stall. She shut the rickety door and sat on the ceramic toilet bowl. She closed her eyes and inhaled deeply to regain some calm.

She heard girls gossiping about unfaithful men and those who couldn't perform. She compared their situation to her own, concluding it was a little of both. What future was there in her so called "relationship of convenience?" When the General decided to cast her aside, as he had past lovers, who would want her then? Given her family ties, she had limited options.

The General, for whatever reason, seemed attracted by her links to Ochoa. He enjoyed flaunting her in public. Her status did provide advantages, including pocket change that dribbled in. Importantly, she gained access to food and fiestas; but the price was high.

She desired more in life. Of the other women who preceded her as the General's "favorite," could anyone remember their names? If she continued on, such would be her fate. She had to break free, but how?

At 39 years, it was time to ask, "What next?" Maybe the middle-aged *Americano* could find a way to get her out. If she went abroad, she'd encounter new people and possibilities. She brightened at the prospect and imagined herself on tour to North or South America. Or even to Spain, where Ochoa's daughter had fled years ago. She heard that her nickname was *La Roja* or the "red woman." She likely was partying at this very hour and then breaking for her churro and chocolate at dawn. Eloisa wanted that kind of life. She was tired of being the kept woman.

However, if the General got wind of her fling tonight, she would be in extreme peril. She shook her head, astonished by her spontaneity. She should better control her bubbly emotions. Sometimes she just couldn't. She saw a gecko on the wall, observing her fretful state. Eloisa began nibbling her nails.

A loud knock interrupted her musings. A high-pitched voice asked, "Are you alright in there, sugar?"

"*Momento,*" Eloisa shouted from the stuffy stall, trying to breathe more evenly. Cautiously, she opened the door into the din of the women's bathroom. Even though she looked down and away, she could feel many eyes on her.

She splashed water on her face and detected budding crow's feet around her eyes. Yet, she still looked pretty good. She caressed her long, sun-streaked hair, wove through the curious onlookers, and tiptoed over the threshold into the gallery outside.

She cocked her head for any untoward sound. She didn't hear the policemen, so she slipped around the corner. At the entrance, clubbers continued rushing in, while others settled their bar accounts with the smiling girl. Some lingered near the door.

She walked unsteadily on her green pumps and joined those in line. She searched her purse for the plastic card, hoping she hadn't lost it during their frenzy. She should have been more careful.

Although Cuba had long been a communist country, the Factory was run by a capitalist crowd. To everyday Cubans, no free rides were allowed. If you were a general or favored by the Party, the club management might let some bar bills slide. Tonight, Eloisa would not pursue this sinecure. She wanted to vanish without a trace.

She fished out the card and paid her last five CUCs for the whiskey consumed. The attendant seemed to recognize her. Luckily, K-cho was busily pitching a Canadian visitor about his boat art, hoping to make a sale. Eloisa slipped by his table without a word.

She joined those heading outside, jostling against others pushing in. She looked away from the security men patrolling the line. She walked in the opposite direction toward the building's shadows.

How had they tracked her here? The General advised that he was going "out on the town," saying she could take a break. She'd taken a *colectivo* and exited two blocks from the club. The General had eyes and ears in all GAESA hotels and clubs. Or maybe it was his arch-rival, that insipid inspector, who had uncovered her destination tonight? That wretched man cast his tentacles everywhere, squeezing Havana's low life. He relished gossip on all his rivals. He and the General despised each other.

Where could she go to escape such men? They always were after her, seeking sex or information. Though no longer a spring chicken, she had more life ahead. If the American didn't help, maybe she'd raft out like younger Cubans. Did she have the courage to evade the onslaught of Cuban patrol boats and Caribbean sharks? She shivered at the thought.

As she ruminated about her future, she turned the corner. Belatedly, she noticed a black car silhouetted by a flickering light. A cigarette flared from behind and a voice asked, "How is Eloisa this fine morning? Dancing up a storm, I hear."

Her heart lurched. Behind her, one of the club bouncers had followed from the entrance. Dead ahead stood the Big Man, and his two henchmen leaned smugly against the Chevrolet. She was trapped.

She shifted her eyes to the foot of an immense Ceiba tree. Inside its twisted roots lay a bleeding rooster, choked by red-and-white ribbons twisting in the wind. She cried out in fright and saw the macho policemen retreat as well. The bouncer spun around and hot-footed it back to the club. Her eyes riveted on this sacrificial rite oozing menace. Who had summoned Santeria's *orishá Changó* to punish her?

She cried out again. The last image was the rooster dripping blood and the dread on Big Man's face.

* * *

A LIGHT WIND BLEW OVER THE TERRACE. and the surf rumbled in the distance. She opened her eyes to a sky with fading stars. She recognized Orion's Belt. Her famous uncle had taught her about the constellations so that she could to find her way at sea or in the field. On her first and last trip to Brazil, the General had pointed out the Southern Cross while they danced on the balcony of the Copacabana Palace. She'd always sensed that these heavenly bodies were her natural allies.

She explored the penthouse veranda and knew that she'd been up here before. It was in the Vedado neighborhood. But how had she arrived? All she remembered was fainting before that horrible sacrifice at the foot of the Ceiba tree.

The Morning Star hung just above the horizon. She murmured, "Have pity on women like me." She yearned that some being, somewhere, might listen to her.

Footsteps echoed up the circular ladder to the veranda. She saw the top of a man's kinky hair and then his broad, brown face. A string of red, white, and blue lights, reflecting Cuba's national colors, shimmered over his salt-and-pepper hair.

"Buenos días, Eloisa," said Big Man softly. "Are you feeling better? How unlucky to come upon that sacrifice behind the Factory. We didn't notice it until you cried out. We'll try to find out who put a hex on that corner. Can I get you something to drink?"

"Buenos días, Big Man. It's good to see a familiar face, despite the circumstances. A glass of water or even a cup of tea would be wonderful.

"Where are we now? Is this a hotel or a private penthouse? I hear the surf from the Malecón."

"I'll find tea for you, Eloisa. We are at one of the Family's apartments in Vedado, which the General uses from time to time. He should be coming soon. He was upset that Santeria had affected you. I'll be right up with your tea," he said, squeezing his large frame down the winding stairs.

She believed that she'd visited this penthouse at a gay rights reception for international journalists. It was hosted by the Family's daughter, who publicly championed LGBTQ rights. The daughter enjoyed the interviews with the press. When the reporters went away, Eloisa had heard her tell disparaging jokes about Havana's gay leaders. She was skeptical of the daughter's conviction but knew that she craved foreign acclaim.

Eloisa pushed herself up from the chaise lounge and glimpsed over the terrace's edge. She saw a shimmering light, heralding a new day. The glow of Venus faded into the sea. A pelican in the distance dove for breakfast, reminding her that she hadn't eaten since midday.

A booming voice blasted up the stairway, with expletives thrown in. She recognized the slurring voice as that of the General, returning from another binge. She cringed at his greeting, "Buenos días, my beautiful one. Have you been waiting long for your lover?"

She turned to face him, noticing his stained guayabera and his hungry look. "Buenos días, *mi General*. Big Man brought me here after we crossed that ritual sacrifice. It was terrifying to me."

"Surely you don't believe in Santeria anymore? I thought you had left that silliness in Holguin. I understand from Big Man that blood was running down the rooster's beak and that you freaked out.

"Let's speak of something more pleasant. Your lover looks forward to your tight embrace." His head was agape, wagging like a puppy dog. He pressed her against the terrace's railing and lunged to hang onto her abundant hips. Being shorter than Eloisa, he had to look up to seek her full lips. He forced his tongue inside.

Eloisa knew the routine by now and doubted that he had much stamina left. She didn't resist his advances, going with the flow. She responded but did not initiate as she had with the *Americano*. She knew that he'd fondle her breasts and then unzip her dress. He always enjoyed ogling her from top to bottom in the nude. He appeared slightly aroused, but she doubted that it would last. He grabbed Eloisa's arm and forced her down on the chaise. He grunted and wailed.

She moved her buttocks to accommodate but felt him quickly go slack. She uttered sounds that he liked to hear but knew that he was done. He pushed her shoulders down and just laid on top of her. He wheezed from his exertions. The Montecristo cigars he preferred did not favor his prowess.

Within five minutes, the General fell asleep. She let her mind pretend that someone else was lying on top of her. When the General's breath tickled her ear, she fancied that the gringo was nuzzling her.

Eloisa wondered if she was to be a lover but never a wife. She was convinced that her fate was to suffer. Nevertheless, she desired something better.

Unfortunately, she had to accommodate the malodorous man on top, whose arms dangled over her. The General could always make her disappear.

Eloisa squinted toward the Malecón and the brightening Eastern sky. Might the *Americano* also be viewing this early sunrise? If so, maybe the heavenly bodies would favor them after all.

She pleaded aloud through the General's snores, "I need a way out."

CHAPTER 15

Vedado, Havana, Wednesday, 10 a.m.

THE KNOCKING GOT LOUDER. WHAT NOW? He'd made it to Jose's apartment by dawn and fell fully dressed onto the bed. He peered at the clock through bleary eyes. It was 10 o'clock, a late morning for him.

Another rap on the door was followed by a familiar voice: "Buenos Dias, professor. You have another call."

Luke wiped his brow. The North Face shirt stuck to him like glue. He opened the door and almost collided with the older man.

"Buenos dias, José. I had a late night. I'm sorry I didn't hear you right away."

"No problem, professor, I'll brew some rice coffee to get the morning started. The phone's in the living room, and the person seems to be an educated man."

Luke found his way through piles of neatly ironed clothes and discovered the phone atop a wicker basket. "*Bueno*," he said, into the reverberating line.

"Buenos dias, professor. Are you well? Regarding the matter that we spoke about over lunch, could you come by my office later this morning? I've received good news from a friend."

Luke realized that it was Father Sebastian, even though he didn't give his name. Perhaps this was how people conducted phone conversations in Havana. He simply replied that he would arrive before noon.

Luke peeled off his sweaty shirt and headed into the bathroom before Jose's kids and wife returned. Standing underneath the showerhead, he recapped his early morning escapade. He was lucky to have broken free from the police. Hopefully, Eloisa made it out without harm. After sharing the home brew with José, Luke said that he'd likely spend a few days in the interior to visit a friend. He promised that he'd telephone to reconfirm.

He packed a change of clothes, an old Nikon camera, and his passport into his backpack. Since consumer goods were scarce throughout Cuba, he included bars of Neutrogena soap as gifts. He discovered another Mariners cap and put it on. He gave José a tight hug and paid him 140 CUCs for the week in advance. He hid the remaining 500 CUCs inside his tennis shoe, along with one Uncle Ben. He left the remaining dollars and clothes inside his Air Force cargo bag in his room.

"Señor José, muchas gracias. Please keep this note with my emergency contact numbers in a safe place. It includes two person's names and phone numbers in Havana. Should I not return after a week, please telephone them, OK?" Jose looked puzzled but inclined his head.

"Please keep me in your prayers." He left the building and passed the California Café, where the grizzled barman was sweeping the floor. Luke flagged down a beat-up Buick *colectivo* coasting toward the Malecón. He shared the front seat with an older lady holding a sack of plantains. Three young men sat in the back, debating their rival baseball teams. Luke enjoyed their heartfelt banter.

A kid sporting an *Industriales* cap spotted Luke's Mariners cap and asked if any Cubans played on Seattle's team.

"Roenis Elias is a relief pitcher. Let's hope they don't trade him away. They've promised to sign a 19-year-old outfielder, Victor Labrada—have you heard of him?"

The baseball aficionados gave him a thumbs up and debated who was the best Cubano playing in the U.S. major leagues. Yasiel Puig, negotiating with the San Francisco Giants, and Yoenis Cespedes of the New York Mets proved to be their favorites.

Luke asked the driver to stop near the rectory and paid him one CUC, earning a look of gratitude. The baseball fans wished him, "*Hasta la vista, Marinero.*"

Luke walked through the baroque building's wooden doors and asked the male receptionist for Padre Sebastian.

"Are you the American professor he's awaiting? The padre would like you to go to *El Centro Cultural Padre Felix Varela,* around the corner. It's the old seminary of Havana. He's at the cultural center with another educator. Let me point it out on your tourist map."

Luke thanked him and found the stately, three-story building that served as the Catholic cultural center. In the inner office, he asked the young nun for Father Sebastian. She telephoned upstairs and asked Luke to wait. The clock showed 11:50. Luke sat on a worn, wooden pew, enjoying the cool relief.

After a few minutes, he stood up to read the posters announcing classes on philosophy and humanities. Another highlighted a new seminar on how to become an "*auto-propista,*" or a self-employed entrepreneur in Cuba.

An attractive woman in a beige pantsuit greeted Luke and led him into the courtyard. They passed by beds of *Mariposa* orchids, Cuba's national flower, where a hummingbird darted in and out of the ivory blossoms. On their way upstairs, Luke noticed rows of plasticized newspaper clippings fluttering in the breeze. "What is this interesting collage, *señorita?*"

"Professor, this is our 'Curtain of Heroes Past'. We've identified brothers and sisters who have acted with kindness toward their neighbors. This is our way to commemorate lesser known heroes of the republic, whose good works go unheeded. This curtain of clippings is our affirmation to them for practicing the Golden Rule. What do you think, professor?"

"What a wonderful testimony. Let me take a photo so I can share it with friends in Seattle and Miami. Gracias, señorita."

They walked up the marble stairs under Roman arches and into a stately corridor. The center felt so serene. Luke followed her into a small library with shelves of books by Catholic scholars. A small window opened toward Havana Bay.

"Please wait here, professor. Father Sebastian should arrive momentarily. You may enjoy thumbing through our books. We have an extensive collection."

Luke was impressed by several editions *en español* by St. Ignatius de Loyola, St. Thomas Aquinas, and St. Agustin. He also perused books from Spain's famous literary generation of 1898, including works by the poet-philosopher, Miguel de Unamuno, and his counterpart, the philosopher-poet, José Ortega y Gasset.

"You've chosen well," said the slim priest, who slipped in quietly from an inner door. His eyes danced in merriment.

"Buenos Dias, padre. I haven't read Unamuno since my Spanish Literature class as an undergrad. I'm heartened that his books are at the cultural center in Havana."

"We try our best, professor, even in difficult circumstances. Would you like some tea? I just received news from my friend in Holguin."

"*Por favor,*" Luke affirmed. The padre added warm water to cups bearing the logo of the San Carlos and San Ambrosio seminary. He put one mate teabag into Luke's cup and stirred it, asking, "Sugar?" Luke declined but saw him reuse the same teabag in his own cup.

"We can find Brazilian tea, professor, but must ration it. As to my friend, Padre Roberto, he plans to be in Holguin this weekend. He'd be happy to receive you and to take you to Ana's gravesite. He could also introduce you to some 'shirttail' relatives of Ochoa. Would you be able to travel soon?"

"Yes, padre. After receiving your cryptic message, I packed some clothes. I'm ready to leave this afternoon." He looked closely at Father Sebastian, who retained an inquisitive look. The priest had the demeanor of an academic and put Luke at ease.

"Excellent. I believe that Padre Roberto knows Ana's son, whom I have not met. It'd be good to speak with him. When we had lunch, I touched upon another Ochoa relative. Eloisa lives in Havana and is close to a powerful General. She may provide information, but you must take care in dealing with her."

Luke gazed down to the floor. In a tremulous voice, he confided, "Father, I met Eloisa by chance at a bar near the Hotel Nacional. I ran into her again last night at the Factory. I felt strongly attracted to her. But then the General's men appeared, searching the club for her. I barely escaped."

The priest gazed at Luke with a look of amazement but not con-demnation. He seemed to be searching for words.

Luke filled the silence, "Father, forgive me. I felt drawn to Eloisa and would have done anything she asked last night. Had her handlers not arrived when they did, I would have consummated the act on the Factory's stairs. I felt consumed by her. Her eyes reminded me of Ana. I should have been in mourning but couldn't resist. I felt like an adolescent again.

"The morning after, I realize that my emotions overwhelmed my common sense. I lost it at the club. What should I do?"

"Are you familiar with Eloisa's history, Lucas? Her mother was Ochoa's occasional lover, and Eloisa is said to have his bloodline.

Her past is not entirely clear. The General, her current lover, is not to be trifled with. You may want to keep your distance, as he is not a forgiving type. Believe it or not, sometimes she comes to the cathedral for confession.

"It's timely that you'll be leaving Havana. The General has many informants in town. Be careful! As a *Norteamericano*, it's easy to 'lose it' in the tropics. You must exercise self-control to survive your visit. Now, please say an Act of Contrition.

Luke stammered through the words but felt lighter afterwards. The priest asked him to seek a quiet place and reflect on Ana. After his reflection, the priest asked him to say a dozen "Our Fathers" and a dozen "Hail Mary's" for penance. The priest wrote a note to Padre Roberto and gave it to Luke. He got up and led Luke downstairs. At a bubbling fountain in the courtyard, Luke observed another man with an Asian mien.

Fr. Sebastian continued, "Let me introduce you to a friend, an independent journalist, who's had a hard time exercising his profession here. When he protested to a university professor about the lack of objectivity in the history class, he was flagged as a troublemaker. His expertise in social media and how to navigate official censorship is extraordinary.

"Thanks to his mother, he has the benefit of a Spanish passport. His father was from China, giving him distinctive features. While he can travel abroad, his Cuban wife and child cannot join him without an exit visa. That's how the authorities maintain control—and keep a dissident's family 'captive'. They also influence Vicente's public reporting; he can't write too critically without personal consequences. He also does work for Spanish maritime firms."

The priest turned toward his friend, "Vicente, how are you? What a lovely surprise. I'm substituting for another padre at the cathedral and should be here until the end of July. Let me introduce you to a new friend from the states. Professor Lucas, here is my friend, Vicente, savvy in how to survive the current state."

"My pleasure, Vicente. I am Professor Lucas Shannon from Seattle University. I understand that Havana is a difficult place to practice your trade. It would be great to speak with you another time and understand how Spanish firms conduct business in Cuba. Could we have a meal together and brainstorm upon my return?"

"Wonderful, professor. Let's exchange cards so that we can get together and compare notes. I'm currently doing some PR work for a Spanish cruise line; it's the only ship in the harbor. I can only work 'off the books'—as I'm a persona non grata with the authorities."

Luke received the journalist's card and gave his own from Seattle U. "I look forward to seeing you when I get back. I'm off to the countryside on a special quest. Fr. Sebastian can fill you in. Stay well, Vicente." Luke gave the journalist and priest tight hugs.

Fr. Sebastian enjoined: "*Vaya con Dios,* professor. Be vigilant during your visit to Holguin. Don't let your guard down. Even though the ambience seems pastoral, police snitches abound. People are motivated by CUCs and food to help them get by. Beware of Santeria and its ceremonies. The people practice it to deflect pain from their daily lives.

"*Atención,*" the priest admonished. His words meant more than "pay attention."

THE SECOND JOURNEY

"*Suffering is the substance of life and the root of personality, for it is only suffering that makes us persons.*"

The Tragic Sense of Life
—Miguel de Unamuno

CHAPTER 16

The Cultural Center, Old Havana, Wednesday, 1 p.m.

BEFORE VENTURING BACK INTO THE HEAT, Luke made two calls from the center's fixed phone line. The first was to José, advising that he was off to the countryside and should return next week. The second was to the young cabbie, asking to rendezvous at an adjacent park where taxis prowled for fares.

At 1:15 p.m., the gray Oldsmobile chugged into the lot full of snazzy cars and hustling chauffeurs. Business must be down, thought Luke. The youth shoved open the door, which cried out in pain. "Buenas tardes, *Americano*."

Luke asked him to head to the train station. Out of the open window, Luke saw the two brothers who'd driven him from the airport. Seated in their yellow convertible looking bored, the cabbies frowned.

"Professor, are you sure you want to take the train? Most of us take the bus, even though it costs more. The *Viazul* is more reliable and doesn't break down as much. Where are you planning to go?"

"I read that the Cuban railway acquired some Russian engines and new Chinese cars. The report said it plans a test run all the way to Holguin province. It seemed like a fun way to visit the countryside, even though it may take longer," said Luke.

"As you wish, but the train may take a day to arrive in Holguin. If the engine suffers a breakdown, all bets are off. They've been remodeling the Central de Havana station for Havana's 500th anniversary. The trains for the country now depart from La Coubre station, farther down the bay.

"By the way, did you enjoy yourself at the Factory? I heard salsa coming from its penthouse and saw many pretty girls."

"Lively it was, with many rooms for dance and diversion. I ran into a new friend, who provided more excitement than I had bargained for. But all's well that ends well," said Luke halfheartedly, recalling how he'd fled the club. And Eloisa—what was she doing now? Despite the priest's counsel, she still made Luke's heart beat faster, as Ana had 30 years earlier.

Looking out the window, Luke saw the Morro Castle across Havana Bay, named after the three biblical Magi. He could use their help today. Along the inner bay sat many empty wharves, with one exception. Looking forlorn on the last pier, a small "MSC" cruise liner was moored, flying the Spanish flag. Luke wondered if that was the line that Vicente consulted for.

A pelican rested on the ship's bowline, searching the murky waters below. From the commuter pier, a ferryboat to Regla was crossing the harbor, seagulls following loudly in its wake. Luke felt hot air rush across his face and hoped that the train had air conditioning.

The young man veered off the roadway and followed official yellow cabs to the pale blue la Coubre's station. It was just around the corner from the more elegant Central de Havana. "Only four CUCs today, professor. Take care of yourself on the train. Let me know how the new cars ride on our old Cuban tracks."

Luke gave him five CUCs, lighting up his youthful face. The official cab drivers in line glowered at them. Luke got out with his backpack and followed a group of students, who were squabbling about money and girlfriends. The people in line were calmer than the clubbers last night. The simply dressed workers and farmers shuffled patiently forward in a lukewarm lobby.

At the ticket window, Luke greeted a heavy-set woman fanning herself and chasing flies. "A roundtrip ticket to Holguin, please," She looked Luke up and down, as if she were assessing his ability to endure. "Very well, señor. Do you know that the trip may take more than 15 hours? I hope you can sleep on board. It makes several stops."

Luke nodded, so she continued, "We have some new Chinese passenger cars, which should make the trip more bearable, if not predictable. Do you want to buy a first- or second-class ticket?

"I've heard that I'll meet more Cuban people in the second-class cars. Permit me to be adventurous on my maiden trip. A second-class ticket will do, señorita."

The attendant stared at Luke, her head quivering slightly. "As you think best, *señor.* You will need patience. That will be 20 CUCs for the second-class, roundtrip ticket to Holguin."

Luke dug out a 20-CUC note, featuring a bearded farmer with rifle in hand. He thanked her and heard her say, "Be safe."

He pulled up short at the same words of caution that the dean had used. He looked around for the entrance gates and got out of the way of patrons pushing forward.

Luke followed others toward the entrance and looked back at the attendant. Her fan beat the air and her head doddered back and forth. He lost eye contact with her among the throngs. In the bustling terminal, a bout of loneliness descended on him. He took a deep breath and searched for the platform.

Luke asked passersby for Holguin's track but received only shrugs. He bumped into a uniformed man and repeated his question, receiving a hand sign of five. He hurried to track #5 and joined the multitude roving back and forth. The temperature was rising, and tempers began to fray. The train to Holguin was late.

A diesel locomotive with fading Cyrillic letters chugged forward and screeched to a halt. Luke saw five newly painted blue cars, all bearing "Made in China" on the sides. The forward car had "1" stamped on it and the following cars the number "2."

Luke followed the hordes of farmers and workers into a second-class car. Luke squeezed into a seat facing backwards, next to a man holding a cage with three young chicks.

The lean man wore cream-colored clothing, checkered with dark splotches. His gnarled hands suggested hard work, and his face was darkly tanned. No doubt a farmer from the country, surmised Luke. The odor of new paint mixed with human sweat in the car's warm interior. The A/C hadn't yet kicked in.

The locomotive blew its whistle twice to hurry laggards along. The train left La Coubre and squealed when it shifted to another narrow-gauge track. Standing passengers had to grab the swinging straps overhead to steady themselves. Following green-light indicators out of the railyard, it slowly picked up speed. The tower of the *Central de Habana,* where laborers scampered up and down the scaffolding like acrobats, whirred by.

As they approached Havana's city limits, Luke's excitement rose. He anticipated serenity in the interior, without hassles from police. Anything would be better than the wild ride so far. He fell asleep with the attendant's face suspended in disjointed dreams.

His body jerked forward, abruptly ending his siesta. He caught his fall on the lap of a middle-aged woman, holding her basket tightly. "*Perdón,*" Luke excused himself.

The farmer next to him remarked, "Only the brave and the poor take the train in Cuba. You must be a daring soul, señor."

Luke nodded and looked outside as mid-rise buildings melded into a hodge-podge of low-rise huts. In more rustic neighborhoods, he noticed older men lounging on makeshift benches, some playing dominoes. They all sought the shade of overhanging mango trees. Luke saw ripening fruit and licked his lips, mentally savoring the plump, orange-colored fruit. He swallowed on a dry throat—he'd forgotten to bring a bottle of water.

The locomotive shrieked around corners, past casitas in yellowing fields. In the fading light, a boy on a donkey pulling a cart plodded across the track, causing the iron horse to halt abruptly.

The farmer next to Luke pointed at the boy. "You see, companion, that lettuce in his cart is likely grown in a family cooperative. Like my chickens here, we've been able to raise more crops and animals without too much party interference. They're always hungry for our food. Still, we must keep a low profile and not show off to neighbors. Though times are hard, we're feeling a ray of hope in the country. I don't sense the same in the big city."

"Interesting," said Luke, heartened by the farmer's spontaneous words.

"I don't like spending time in Havana. I get nervous with all its noise and traffic. I had to visit a specialist at a clinic. I paid for the visit with three chicks. Luckily, the doctor was not greedy, so I was able to keep these three. Afterwards, I always hurry home. The air and life are healthier, which you'll soon discover. Where does your journey take you?"

"My destination is Holguin. This is my first time in Cuba, so any recommendations are welcome," Luke said. The train slowed to an open-air station "Matanzas," and a guard pushed anxious passengers back. A pale-blue tower rose at the end of the tracks, crossed by a Roman arched bridge with crenulated edges.

A few riders disembarked, but more pushed forward into the railcars, carrying baskets of wilted greens and garments. A few shepherded cages with exotic-looking birds. As an amateur ornithologist, Luke perceived the yellow markings of a Cuban warbler. He hoped they were surviving better here than the songbirds of Seattle.

"We just arrived at Matanzas, known for its poets and culture. The Hershey train also stops here, where the American candy company once had its headquarters. Tourists come here and go farther down the coast to Varadero Beach. Its many hotels and clubs attract visitors from abroad. But it's quite pricey, señor.

"As for me, I plan to get off at Santa Clara, a couple hours farther on. It's an attractive provincial capital. Some tourists visit the Che Guevarra Mausoleum and its huge statue. Less well known is Cuba's first Presbyterian Church and its small school for missionaries. I've seen Americans coming and going there. The Cathedral of Santa Clara de Asis is beautiful too. You may like our town and its pace of life."

A frail woman boarded with a basket of cheese *tamales* and carried water bottles on her back. Luke purchased three warm tamales and shared them with the farmer and the woman across from him. He also bought a bottle of water and paid two CUCs, eliciting a smile from her.

"That's very generous. We usually pay with Cuban pesos. We don't often receive CUCs, except from tourists. Muchas gracias.

"You are fortunate to find bottled water. The authorities recently have been hassling private vendors of 'purified water.' The state distributors don't want to compete with them. EcoFinca of Santa Clara is a leading bottler of purified water. My nephew works there." said the farmer, his eyes sparkling in pride.

The train blew its whistle and pulled out of the station. A youngster driving a horse-drawn carriage on a parallel road sped alongside to race. The youth nosed ahead and pumped his fist, before veering off toward the plaza. The train rumbled out of Matanzas and sounded off again. Villagers looked up and waved. Under a large Ceiba tree, they returned to playing cards and chatting with neighbors. Shadows lengthened as the sun began its decline.

Luke was lulled by the swaying back and forth. He slept deeply without dreams.

He awoke with a start. Darkness enshrouded a station with a wide platform, except for an illuminated sign announcing "Santa Clara." The farmer with the chicks and the lady with the basket were nowhere to be seen. New passengers boarded the second-class car.

Luke saw a tall man on the platform, walking briskly up and down. He looked a bit lost. The whistle blew and the Russian locomotive groaned forward. The man cast one last look around the station and began jogging after the train. He grabbed its handrail, boarding like a Hollywood stunt man.

He barged into the aisleway, huffing and puffing from his dramatic leap. The tall, bespectacled man became the center of attention. He surveyed the passengers and meandered toward the rear. The train gained momentum, causing him to wobble back and forth. He pulled himself forward, holding the top of each seat as a handrail.

The man fit his large frame into the seat across from Luke, bumping knees. He looked back at the station once more and exhaled. The A/C continued to blow out lukewarm air.

He turned around and looked squarely at Luke. Luke pressed his seat back and glanced away. He heard the man fidgeting and the clickety-clack outside. Through half-closed eyes, he glimpsed the countryside speed by. He wondered about this man's story but let sleep carry him away.

CHAPTER 17

Santa Clara en route to Camaguey, Thursday, 11:30 p.m.

LUKE OPENED HIS EYES to the panting of a tall, pink-faced man. His grandiose head rested on a large frame, and his jug ears stuck out like radar dishes. The man's brows were knit in worry. He wore a blue-plaid shirt, tan Levi jeans, and a beat-up pair of Nikes. He peered over his dark-framed glasses at Luke.

Only the two of them sat in the four-seat corner section. The Cubans in the car lost interest in the pair of gringos. They began snuggling down under jackets or sarapes for the nocturnal ride. The man asked, "Are you from the states?"

"I'm from Seattle on my first visit to Cuba. And you?"

The man took a few seconds. "I live outside of Atlanta. This is my fourth trip. A colleague should have been at the station but didn't show up. I waited until the last moment to board the train," he exclaimed, extending the last syllable.

"This is my first ride in the new Chinese cars. Let's pray the train arrives at Camaguey without a breakdown. Last time we spent half a day in the middle of nowhere and had to catch a collective taxi to reach our home church." He closed his eyes and moved his lips.

After the man opened his eyes, Luke said, "By the way, I am Professor Luke Shannon, from Seattle University." The man gripped Luke's hand firmly and looked directly at him. At close quarters, his stare unsettled Luke.

"Professor, I am Pastor Beau Barr from Marietta, Georgia. I'm in charge of overseas outreach on behalf of our Presbyterian church," he drawled.

"I was supposed to connect with a Cuban pastor at the station and accompany him to Camaguey. He's assisting a pastor to start a new home church there. Our congregation provides support to him and pastors in the field. We buy land to build them homes with rooms for worship. We also furnish Bibles, training videos, and food. It's our way to help the Cuban people and to share the Holy Gospel.

"This pastor is usually punctual, so I hope nothing happened to him. Occasionally, police checkpoints hold drivers up. They often search for contrabanded fuel or animals, and also gratuities. Sometimes, things happen at home or he may have overslept. It's always a leap of faith to do the Lord's work in Cuba. Two steps forward and one step back. I've learned that persistence pays," he extolled, as if delivering a sermon.

"That's interesting, Pastor Beau. A while back, I read an article in *The Guardian* about home churches. Are there many in Cuba, and do authorities mind if foreigners provide financial support?" asked Luke, his curiosity growing. After all, he was a professor.

"Colleagues at the Santa Clara mission calculate that there are more than 20,000 home churches in all the provinces—mostly evangelical. On a typical weekend, 10-30 people attend lively services in pastors' homes, usually in their backyards. Cubans are more enthusiastic and spontaneous than Americans. They worship for hours on end and enjoy a late lunch.

"The Jehovah Witness activists also knock on doors in the countryside. They 'push the envelope' more than we do but seem to get away with it. The Santería practice is everywhere and is unofficially condoned by the state. In a way, Santeria has become 'the opiate of the people,'" shuddered the pastor.

"As for the greenbacks we bring into Cuba, authorities don't mind as long as we declare our $10,000 at immigration. We usually enter on a religious visa but sometimes are subjected to additional interrogation. Are you a person of faith, Professor Luke?"

"Yes, I am a Catholic, though I don't always go to mass. I went to the cathedral in Havana and hope to meet a padre in Holguin. I read that Raul was quite effusive after Pope Francis's visit but haven't heard much of late. Some Catholics lament Cardenal Ortega's passing. May he rest in peace.

"Are the authorities supportive of your community outreach, as life grows more difficult?"

"There's a delicate balance that people of faith must maintain before the authorities. We try our best to keep a low profile and not get involved in political issues. The regime's snitches are always around, feigning interest in our mission. Some even take notes during our sermons. Someone told me that they report back to some inspector.

"We occasionally receive visits from state auditors, making sure that the land was purchased in the name of the Cuban pastor. Foreign entities, including NGOs, are prohibited from owning real estate. The authorities don't seem to mind if we provide food or medical services. Most doctors, dentists, and specialists reside in Havana. There are few clinics in the field. People in the country get short shrift," pronounced the pastor, his face yielding a frown.

As an afterthought, he added, "The Catholic church has been around for centuries and has found a way to survive the Castros.

Former Archbishop Ortega was a stand-up pastor and helped a lot. The parishes I've visited barely seem to be getting by. They are not growing as fast as evangelical denominations," he opined. His eyes fluttered and began to close.

Luke looked out at the darkness, interrupted occasionally by a sliver of light. Like ghosts, occasional faces appeared at railroad crossings but vanished in a flash. He leaned back and joined fellow travelers in fitful sleep.

* * *

Luke awoke in a start and heard the breaks squeal ahead. Nothing was moving outside. Passengers began waking up, asking, *"Que pasa?"* The pastor pressed his face against the window and scowled.

"God willing, the train didn't hit an animal. On my last trip, the cow's owners got incensed and demanded that the local police get involved. The loss of an animal is a big deal out here—especially if it's owned by a cooperative with political connections. We were stuck for hours without food or water under the hot sun. At least it's night this time. Let's see how long it takes to clear the track."

They sat in the unlit car, peering into the gloom. A few minutes passed, and a man swinging a lantern walked along the track. In reply to a query, Luke heard the man explain that a flambeau tree had fallen across the track. He implored the travelers for patience until the volunteer firemen arrived.

The news was greeted by groans and expletives, a passenger complaining, "So much for their promises of fast rail with a new look." Luke sat back, hugging himself to keep warm. He hadn't thought about bringing a jacket.

He closed his eyes and heard men outside raising their voices while grinding back and forth. The steady rhythm lulled Luke back to sleep. After an hour, the train jerked past a half dozen men holding up two crosscut saws. Several shorn branches with lemon-color flowers reflected faint light.

"The yellow flambeau," grumbled the pastor. "The tree is beautiful by day but loses branches by night. A young pastor recounted how he and his fiancée were romancing one evening but were startled by a huge flambeau branch tumbling on their borrowed car. They weren't injured but had the scare of their lives. We had to repair the car, but it didn't cost much. Cuba is blessed with many mechanics and painters looking for work."

The train inched forward and, within a quarter of an hour, crept into a modest-looking station. A blue-shirted attendant shepherded a few patrons waiting anxiously on a narrow concrete platform. The sign read "Ciego de Aquila" and the clock 2:35.

"Ramón," yelped the pastor through the half-opened window. He jumped up and lumbered down the car's stairs. He walked briskly toward a short, wiry man dressed in a white guayabera and dark trousers. Pastor Beau gave the younger man a bear hug, smiled broadly, and boarded the train.

"Professor Luke, may I present you to my colleague Pastor Ramón. He was detained at a police checkpoint but released. A *colectivo* raced him to this station just in time.

"Thank you for your Divine Providence," exclaimed the tall pastor, raising his hands in praise. Some riders seemed to follow the pastor's broken Spanish and a few shouted "Amen." In the back, a woman dressed in white glared at them.

Pastor Beau continued, beaming at his charge, "With such determination, Pastor Ramón's church should become a community success." His Cuban colleague looked down at his hands.

"My pleasure, Pastor Ramón. I'm glad you made it. Pastor Beau has said good things about you. I wish you well in your mission in Camaguey," said Luke.

"Thank you, professor. As Pastor Beau proclaims, 'persistence pays.' It's good to cross paths with another *Americano,* even at this early hour. Are you on tour, or do you have another reason to visit our countryside?"

"I plan to meet with a Catholic priest in Holguin, who is a friend of a friend. I hope that he'll introduce me to a special family, whose niece I met in the states. I made her a promise years ago. I'm doing everything possible to keep my promise on this trip.

"So far, my first visit to Cuba has been an odyssey of sorts. Please keep me in your prayers, Pastor Ramón."

"Will do, professor. Being a 'promise-keeper' is a noble endeavor in this age of deceit. May you be successful in your mission. In Holguin, you must take care with Santería. This practice has been rooted in Cuba for centuries, brought over by Nigerian slaves. Have you heard of this syncretized Afro-Cuban cult of saints?"

"Yes, Ramón, I spoke with a priest in Havana, who cautioned me too. Apparently, some practitioners even attend mass but pray to African gods in lieu of Catholic saints."

All of a sudden, a woman behind them began shrieking. Her face contorted in fright. She continued crying out until the woman dressed in white stood up and came alongside her. She offered incantations over the seated woman and held her hand. Little by little, the woman stopped trembling and eventually quieted down. The woman in white continued chanting in a low voice, occasionally raising her voice to "*Yemayá.* After several minutes, the seated woman leaned her head back and closed her eyes.

The lady in white stood up and looked around, directing her gaze at the two pastors and Luke. She raised her hands and praised aloud "the spirit of her saint." She tried to engage other passengers, but most turned away, avoiding her stare. Some shook in fear.

Luke looked at the two pastors, wondering what they were up against.

CHAPTER 18

Camaguey, Thursday, 7 a.m.

LUKE AWOKE AS THE TWO PASTORS PUTTERED ABOUT—where were they now? Passengers were exiting the train, including the woman who'd suffered that scary attack of "the spirit."

"Buenos dias, professor. We've finally reached Camaguey, known for its earthenware jars called *tinajones*," said Ramón, who grabbed his small pack from the overhead rack. Pastor Beau was standing in the aisle as the lady in white approached him. Her skirt grazed the pastor as she bobbed her head and mumbled strange words. When she stepped down to the platform, she cast them an eerie grin.

"Buenos dias, Ramón. That woman was pretty intense. I'd be afraid to lock horns with her. She seemed to possess extraordinary powers," confided Luke in a low voice.

"Yes, the woman is a priestess of *Yemayá*, the Yoruba goddess of the sea. In Cuba, that demi-god is interchanged with Our Lady of Regla. Its followers often worship at the Catholic church across Havana Bay. We have our hands full with *Yemayá's* followers all over the island."

Pastor Beau seemed unusually quiet. Pastor Ramón bade Luke adiós and gave him a tight hug. "Here's my card, professor, with my cell number and my fixed phone line in Santa Clara. If I can be of service to you, don't hesitate to call anytime—especially in dealing with Santería. I've served as an exorcist to remove such spirits from people in our congregation. I'm unafraid to do battle with the forces of darkness. However, it demands much personal energy. I always summon the Holy Spirit to guide me. *Vaya con Dios,* my friend."

Pastor Beau shook Luke's hand, stammering, "See you." The American pastor followed his Cuban counterpart down the steps and did not look back. They exited the station and the clock read 7:15.

A few workers wearing homespun clothes came aboard, stifling yawns and carrying bundles. They sat across the aisle and complained about their cooperative's boss. The station master waved his lantern and the train began to move without blowing its whistle. Light appeared on the Eastern horizon, and a cock crowed nearby.

As the train passed the sign "Camaguey, founded 1528," Luke recalled that this town was one of seven original settlements by Spanish colonialists. He looked out the window and saw a horse-driven carriage leaving the station with both pastors. He waved at them through the window but received no sign in return.

Outside of town, Luke spied an unusual pyramid pass by. The worker next to him observed, "That's how we stack tobacco, *Americano,* as it dries in the sun. It's a legacy from our indigenous tribes that once grew '*cohiba*' for themselves. The Spaniards tried it, liked it, and exported it back to Europe.

"Our co-op is a respected grower. Let me offer you one from our unofficial supply," proffering Luke a robust cigar. Luke thanked him and dug out a bar of Neutrogena, "For your wife, *señor.*" The worker's rugged face broached a broad smile

Luke leaned back, closed his eyes, and let his mind wander as to what lay ahead. What would await him a few hours away in Arnaldo

Ochoa Sanchez's hometown? Anxiety slipped inside him, the closer the train approached Holguin and the gravesite of his beloved Ana.

* * *

Luke wandered in and out of sleep, passing pastures and banana trees. He remembered seeing a pile of black beans spread out on a dirt road, drying in the morning sun. He shook himself awake as passengers rustled about. He looked outside at a decrepit water tower and a fading sign for "*Cacocúm*." The train crept into a squat station, where travelers disembarked onto the narrow platform. Luke wondered if he'd overslept the station for Holguin.

A conductor walked down the car, braying, "Last stop! All comrades must leave the train."

Perplexed, Luke asked, "Doesn't this train stop at Holguin? I bought a ticket for there."

"*Señor,* you must depart and wait for the bus. It should come soon and will take you to your destination. Have a pleasant trip," he wished, continuing down the car.

Luke grabbed his backpack and followed the stragglers into the modest station. His hunger was piqued by the scent of fried plantains. He purchased a spiral cup from the young vendor. She clapped her hands when Luke gave her one CUC.

The clock showed 9:40. As the sun beat down, Luke dug out his Mariners cap and put it on. He saw three boys hitting a Styrofoam ball at the end of the station and wandered down. They saw his cap and shouted "*Marinero.*" They peppered him with questions about the major leagues. Luke tossed the first two boys several pitches, resulting in shallow fly balls. The third boy, a little over five feet tall, swung with power, belting the ball over their heads. Luke joined the other boys in cheering the young homerun hitter.

A well-proportioned teen and shorter version of Johnny stood before Luke. He smiled gracefully but looked uncomfortable by the praise of peers. Luke thought he may be looking at the next Cuban star in Major League Baseball. "Muchacho, let me give you a token of recognition for your long ball hit in Cacocúm. Here's a T-shirt from my hometown, Seattle, with its signature Space Needle.

"With your talent, you should think big, even the major leagues. Americans love Cuban players and their zest for baseball. *Mi casa es su casa, muchacho. Como te llamas?*"

"*Señor Americano,* I call myself Hercules the Third. My deceased father named me after my grandfather who died in the war of Angola. He was a strong man and fought under a famous general. He loved baseball like me and my father. I follow in their footsteps.

"My dream is to go to the states and play anywhere I can. *Quien sabe*—who knows—maybe I could play for the Seattle Mariners? It would be wonderful to have an American friend.

"I am Professor Lucas, and here is my card from Seattle University. Maybe a Mariners recruiter could visit you. They scour the Caribbean for talent, even players in their teens. How old are you, Hercules?"

"Outstanding, professor! I will be fourteen this December and hope to grow taller," he exclaimed, standing up on tip toes.

Just then, a grimy yellow bus pulled up at the station. Luke had enjoyed chatting with the boys but didn't want to miss the transport to Holguin. He dug out a three-CUC note and gave it to Hercules, "Celebrate your homerun today with your friends. If you write or email me, I will reply. *Vaya con Dios, muchachos!*" He gave them each a tight hug, surrendering the plantains to the hungry boys.

He ran to catch the bus. Standing in the stairwell, he waved. The bus did a U-turn, and the boys returned to hitting the ball, disappearing into a cloud of dust.

Luke slumped over in the front seat, thrilled yet saddened by the encounter. How would the young ballplayers' lives play out? The MLB's accord with Cuba was unraveling as political rhetoric heated up. But if Hercules contacted him, he would reach out to the Mariners scout.

Caught up in his thoughts, he barely paid attention to the other passengers. All wore looks of curiosity. A tall mulatto, his head shaved bare, looked intently from the rear. Luke wondered if his white clothes meant that he was another follower of *Santería*.

The bus dodged potholes and horse-driven carts. Luke saw casitas appear on the town's edge, followed by colonial homes in improved condition. They must be getting close to the city center. A few Ladas joined several burros with buckboards hauling carrots and lettuce. As traffic grew thicker, Luke asked the driver to drop him near the plaza for the church of San José.

"*Momento,*" the driver exclaimed, "You owe me 10 pesos, *señor.*" Luke gave him a CUC, warranting a thumbs up. "I'll drop you at the next corner. The church is a few blocks away. Ask any villager for directions. '*Preguntando, se llega a Roma',*" he advised, screeching on the brakes to let a donkey pass.

Luke smiled at the driver's words: "*Asking around, you'll arrive in Rome.*" Luke jumped down to the dusty street, hanging on to his pack. He hoisted it onto his back and saw the young mulatto in white reconnoiter Luke's footsteps from the rear window.

He turned into a narrow lane and squeezed the last drop of water from the crumpled plastic bottle. He struggled to find shade to protect him from the relentless sun overhead.

After a 17-hour marathon, he'd finally reached the provincial capital of Holguin. He mopped his brow and breathed in hot air. Expectation and anxiety renewed their struggle within him, as he walked on and on.

CHAPTER 19

Holguin, Thursday, 11 a.m.

THE COLONIAL CITY LAY BAKING IN the sun while humidity smothered pedestrians without quarter. Luke traipsed along alleyways and asked villagers for directions. "It's just ahead," many said. Thankfully, Luke wore his Mariners cap to protect his pate, if not his bone-dry throat.

He saw a vendor grinding sugarcane into *guarapo* juice and ordered a cup. "It's good for your liver, *señor*," said the sinewy man, wiping sweat from a crinkled forehead. Luke even received some pesos in return for the one CUC he paid—the first pesos so far in Cuba.

He turned another corner and faced a red-tiled plaza bordered by many trees. Luke sought the shade of an immense Ceiba. Underneath, older men sat chatting and playing dominoes. Luke greeted, "Buenos días," which they echoed back in chorus. They turned back to their game, slapping the rectangular tiles on a well-used board. So far, so good, thought Luke.

Beyond the Ceiba's branches, a beige colonial church with a bell tower appeared, flanked by smaller columns on either side. Luke thought he saw someone peering out of an upper window. He headed for the church's tall, wooden doors, passing a boy running to lift his kite into the slack air.

Luke sought relief from the heat and opened the arched door. He removed his cap and paused inside, groping blindly with both hands. He went through another wooden door to the church's quiet nave.

Luke stumbled upon a pew and slumped down. He breathed in the cooler air and squinted at a wavering flame, beneath a crucifix on the altar. A votive candle on the right cast plaintive light. He crossed himself and began saying the Lord's Prayer. He remembered he hadn't uttered the dozen "Our Fathers" and dozen "Hail Mary's" prescribed by Fr. Sebastian for his penance. He reflected on Ana, realizing he'd only be able to visit her grave. Disappointment penetrated him again.

Luke presumed that he was alone but heard footfalls approach from an alcove. He sat up and detected a wisp of a woman emerge from its shadows. She walked toward him and ran Rosary beads through her gnarled fingers. She was saying "Hail Mary's" en español, which he had just completed in English.

As she got closer, he stood to greet her, "Buenos días, señora. Is Padre Roberto the pastor of San José parish? I've brought him a note from a friend in Havana."

Her ivory teeth set off nicely against the dark interior. "Buenos dias, señor. Welcome to our humble parish. We don't put the lights on until the evening mass. We use candles to save scarce pesos. Padre Roberto would be glad to greet you, but he's at the farmer's market. Let me take you to this saintly man."

Luke followed her outside, shielding his eyes against the brightness. The air seemed deathly still. The boy with the kite and the men playing dominoes were gone. The limbs from the Ceiba and laurel trees drooped under the blazing sun.

Luke followed her around the church's crumbling corner. They encountered five makeshift stands, displaying tomatoes, bananas, and mangos. A young man was hanging a shank of a butchered animal on a hook. The meat dripped blood, and flies buzzed in frenzy overhead.

A slim man in a Roman collar stood negotiating with a vendor, "My brother, haven't you added a few pesos to last week's price? We're all trying to make ends meet."

"Tomatoes are in high demand with fewer coming from the region. For you padre, as a friend of the people, I'll keep the same price as last week," the swarthy vendor replied. "Have you seen what the butcher is now charging for pork? Its price has doubled since last year. At the rate things are going, my wife will have to serve me Spam for my birthday dinner!"

"Yes, times are difficult, my son, but let me speak with him. I see that the butcher's nephew has brought horse meat today. It is an acquired taste," the padre complained, turning up his nose. "*Hola*, Maria. How are you, and who is your guest?"

"Padre Roberto, I am well, thank you. The visitor comes from Havana, bearing a note from your friend. He seems simpatico."

"Gracias, Maria. Señor, how may I be of service?" the priest inquired, extending his hand with a baffled look. His eyes reflected light on a tanned, wrinkled face.

"Buenos días, Padre. I am Professor Luke Shannon from Seattle. I just met with Fr. Sebastian and bring his note for you. Do you have time to talk?"

"With pleasure, professor. Let's take a walk, and I'll show you about town." Turning to Maria, "Many thanks, my sister. *Vaya con Dios.*"

Luke picked up his pack and retrieved two bars of Neutrogena soap. "Please accept these in appreciation, Maria and Padre Roberto."

Their faces beamed more brightly than the tropical sun. The padre took Luke's arm and asked, "Did you know that Holguin is acclaimed for its parks? The plazas are popular with the people, especially in the afternoon." He pointed out young girls practicing salsa steps and boys riding fast on shaky bikes. They passed an open-air café, exhaling scents of fried garlic, onions, and plantains.

Luke's stomach growled. "Padre, may I invite you for a coffee or a bite to eat?" The priest bobbed his head enthusiastically. They bent under a tattered tarp but were thankful for the shade. They sat around a metal table, and Luke slid off his pack onto a wobbly chair. A waitress appeared and offered them the "plate of the day," *ropa vieja,* which Luke translated as "old clothes." He ordered bottles of *Bucanero* to beat back the heat.

Over *cerveza,* Luke recounted how he had met Fr. Sebastian and confessed his secret mission about Ochoa. He admitted his unkept promise made to Ana 30 years ago and how he'd come to see her in Cuba. The padre touched Luke's shoulder in consolation. Luke handed him the note and saw more furrows crease the priest's forehead.

"Ana's passing was tragic, and the accident report hasn't been released. Her son took her death badly and became unmoored. He recently turned to Santeria, seeking retribution against the driver. He's a troubled soul," the priest sighed, adding: "Professor, did you know that Ana named her son Lucas and baptized him in our church?"

Luke sat up abruptly, spilling his beer. He felt his pulse speed up and his throat constrict. He managed to say, "What, her son's name is Lucas? Are you in contact with him, padre?"

"I've served as priest in Holguin province for more than 40 years. I've known her family and was aware of Ana's aspirations. Her son was the apple of her eye, her purpose in living. She doted on him. Throughout Lucas' school years, she tutored and encouraged him. As her son had no father figure in life, she assumed all of his burdens. She even taught him basic English.

"When she couldn't secure a place for him at the University of Holguin, she was devasted. She became even angrier with the authorities. They already had banned her and all Ochoa family members from state employment.

"Her son absorbed her anger and rebellious spirit. Lucas turned to art. He paints water colors of humble Cubans from the countryside in tones of red and brown. If you study their faces, they seem distressed and vulnerable. He often sells paintings to foreign tourists. Meanwhile, the authorities keep him and all Ochoa's kin under scrutiny."

Luke tried to absorb this news. He wondered what his namesake might look like. "How old is Lucas, padre, and does he live close by?"

The padre tilted back his head, "He should have celebrated 29 years earlier this year. Since he turned to Santería, I haven't seen much of him. I should do more to reach out to him. After all, I christened him and promised to help him in good times and bad."

The padre looked down. "I believe that he lives in Cacocúm in a cottage belonging to his former great uncle. An aunt of sorts lives in Holguin's outskirts. She is the living memory of the Ochoa family. If you'd like, we could visit her and ask for news. We also could visit Ana's grave on return."

The waitress brought their food, and the padre offered a blessing. He picked at the "plate of the day" and opined, "Professor, I'm sorry that the taste may be a little strong. I doubt that the chef used beef flank steak to prepare this traditional dish. He probably mixed it with 'exotic meat'. The spices make it more edible, as do the *Moros*, the rice mixed with black beans. The chef does the best he can with limited resources."

"The *Moros* are tasty, padre. I always love the sweet banana *maduros* too," Luke said, washing them down with more *cerveza*. Neither he or the padre finished the main course but savored a splendid coconut flan for dessert.

Luke paid the waitress five CUCs and followed the priest outside. They passed men riding old bicycles and tired horses, while empty Chevrolets prowled the streets. Luke saw no tourists but many simply dressed peasants. Luke kept up with the priest's brisk pace through back alleys. The cobblestones eventually petered out into a dusty lane. They were heading out of town.

At the trail's end stood a mud brick home, overshadowed by a huge Ceiba tree. The padre turned and asked Luke, "Have you encountered Santería before? This woman is a priestess in the Cuban cult. Occasionally, she comes to pray before the statue of St. Barbara, *Changó*'s syncretic counterpart in the Catholic church. *Changó* is one of the most powerful spirits or *orishás* of the Yoruba nation. He is renowned for anger."

"Padre, I have witnessed Santería up close in the train, where a priestess summoned another spirit, *Yemayá*. Scary stuff for me," said Luke, shaking off the memory.

The padre slowed his pace and sighed again. He knocked three times on a thick wooden door, shrouded by red-and-white pennants drooping above. After a minute, the door opened. Darkness and incense engulfed them as they crossed the threshold.

A voice commanded, "Buenas tardes, padre. How befitting that you have brought a visitor to see me. I had a vision that someone would arrive from afar. Enter."

Luke swallowed and followed the padre into the gloom. He heard the padre say, "*Saludos,* Severina. The visitor has come from *el Norte* on a mission. As you are a respected relation of the Ochoa family, I suggested that he come to speak with you. Our visitor hopes to learn about Ana as well as our deceased Hero of the Republic. May their souls rest in peace.

"He also would like to meet Ana's son, who bears the same baptismal name. Might you have time to speak with us?"

"Eternity is my timeframe, padre. How does the visitor call himself? And what does he want to know about Ana and Arnaldo, whose spirits roam this land?"

Luke's eyes adjusted slowly but focused on a dark woman dressed in white. Her large body was in sharp contrast to the slender residents in town, where food proved elusive and dear. The robust priestess's face was lit intermittently by the Kerosene lantern's flame. He heard water boiling and a teapot whistling toward the back.

"Señora Severina, I am Professor Lucas Shannon at your service. I spent time with Ana 30 years ago in Washington, D.C. I promised to tell her uncle's story to the world, including why the Castros shot him against the infamous wall. I'd like to discover why both Ochoa family members met an early and untimely death. I want to keep my promise to her."

"Ah," she said, her voice fading. "Before speaking about the Ochoa's, please share this herbal infusion with me. It helps release our human concerns and invites visitors from other realms. Please sit on my couch-bed while I prepare our special tea. Then, I will tell you why Arnaldo's and Ana's spirits are not resting in peace."

Luke shivered at the thought of spirits loose in this den. He heard something rustle in the inky corner. His hair stood on end.

CHAPTER 20

Outside Holguin, Thursday, 3 p.m.

LUKE BALANCED HIMSELF on the rickety bed against the damp wall. The padre slid in beside him, touching elbows. Luke struggled to breathe through the incense-filled air. Light shone weakly from the lantern and gas burner. He squinted to see what was lurking in the corner.

Luke almost fell off the narrow couch. Two yellow eyes were staring at him. A dark animal sat as still as a statue. Luke steeled his nerves to ask, "Severina, is that a cat over there?"

"Don't take fright, professor. It's just my companion, Ibo, who has adopted me and my home. He protects me from unfriendly beings both near and far. I see him eyeing you. Do you have any feline friends?"

"A neighbor has a tabby cat—more social than Ibo. Your cat seems to be *en garde,*" said Luke. The cat didn't move, though its eyes seemed to glow brighter.

Severina scooped herbs into a cracked porcelain pot and placed it on a small wooden table. The tea had a hint of lemon grass and chamomile. "He's assessing you, professor. He knows Padre Roberto and feels no threat. Let's have some tea," she said, pushing the table closer to them. "Let us see if she comes to you," said Severina, pouring the steamy liquid into three small glasses.

She lumbered to the oversized chair next to the bed. She grazed Luke's leg, causing him to jump. His heart beat accelerated. He cautiously sipped Severina's special brew. The cat remained in the corner, keeping an eye on him. Severina began her family story.

"Arnaldo was a curious but competitive child. He always liked to win. He also asked many questions like young boys do. As an adolescent, he asked me how to tell a liar from a truthful man. I told him to always look into the person's eyes. Did he sense any flicker or twitch on the person's face? Maybe a movement of arm or leg? Even if the person were able to hold Arnaldo's stare, body language would render the truth or the lie.

"He followed my advice and young men followed him. He brooked no cowards or liars. They followed him all the way to the Sierra Maestra mountains. He joined the commander there and led his group of wannabe soldiers to fight for the Revolution. He impressed Fidel with his courage. Arnaldo always led from the front. Against Batista, the Angolans, or the Ethiopians—he didn't care. He was a leader of men.

"Sure, he liked women and fast cars. He got himself into trouble for bedding someone's wife in Africa. But when he led men into battle, he was in his element. That was his world, and he was unafraid. He was very good at fighting. He exercised savvy judgement on the battlefield. When he came back to Cuba, he missed the smell of war. He was used to blood, sweat, and tears. He never did well with tricksters or spies. Unfortunately, they abound in our homeland.

"As to playing the political game with the Castros, he didn't fare well. When he returned from Africa, Arnaldo was full of himself. In restaurants and public places, people stood up and applauded him. It went a little to his head. He forgot that the brothers did not condone competition from any man, including Cuba's beloved Hero of the Republic."

She took a break and sipped more tea. The cat left its space and came unbidden, rubbing Severina's leg. Luke heard purring and felt the cat's tail swishing back and forth. He forced down his tea, hoping that its chamomile would calm his nerves.

"Ibo seems to like your manner, professor. That's a good sign. As to Ana, she had a hard life on her return from the states. With a Master's Degree in History, she tried to teach at the university but was refused. And she tried teaching at grade or high schools without success. The hidden bureaucrats in the Education Ministry rejected her at every turn.

"She was forced to live by her wits to support her son. She served as guide to foreign visitors and did translations to survive. She was returning with tourists from Cayo Coco, the beautiful key in north Cuba. They said a truck crashed into the car she was driving. She lingered between life and death but passed three weeks ago. The two Canadians barely survived. The accident remains a mystery."

She fell quiet again but gazed intently at Luke.

How long could he stay in this room, full of incense and weird beings? To break the silence, Luke asked, "Ana's son, Severina, what has become of him? Padre Roberto said that he was close to his mother and distraught by her death."

She continued regarding him, inclining her head. She finally said, "Come to the large Ceiba tree on the outskirts of Cacocúm tonight, just before midnight. There you can ask him yourself, professor.

"Gentlemen, Ibo is growing restless. The spirits are moving about. We must take leave of you now. Adiós."

The cat continued observing Luke, coaxing his retreat from the den. Padre Roberto followed him outside to a sagging sun.

They retraced their steps back to the city. The padre opened a squeaky gate to an overgrown cemetery. He led Luke to a narrow headstone, "Ana Maria Sanchez, 1966-2019." Luke knelt down. Thirty years of regret and sadness caught up with him. He shook uncontrollably. "Ana, please forgive me," he cried out. The padre took a step back.

Minutes passed and Luke finally arose. From an overhanging branch of the *almendro*, almond tree, a Cuban Emerald released its high-pitched trill. Maybe the bird missed its companion, as Luke did Ana now. Padre Roberto kept his silence. Luke reluctantly left her burial site and wavered at the gate.

The sun withdrew its light from the horizon, leaving melancholy in its wake.

CHAPTER 21

Holguin to Cacocúm, Thursday, 6:40 p.m.

THE SAME DINGY BUS TOOK LUKE back over the same bumpy road. He arrived at the station after dark and bought more fried plantains. The girl remembered him and thanked him for another CUC. Luke heard someone approach from behind.

"*Buenas noches, Americano.*" Luke turned to see the young home-run hitter jump down from the train station.

"Hola, Hercules—you spend a lot of time around here. Where are your friends who were hitting the ball with you?"

"They went home, professor. My grandmother is ill at the hospital in Holguin. I'm out and about tonight," said the boy, whose eyes scoured the plantains.

"Help yourself, Hercules. Do you know where we could grab something to eat? I also need a place to overnight and may need your help."

"There's a cantina a few blocks away. The owner is a friend of my grandma and rents a room upstairs. It's not ritzy, but her food tastes good. Does that sound OK?"

"Lead the way, my young guide. I'm flexible about places to eat or to sleep, as long as they're clean." Luke followed Hercules and saw a darkened sign for "Los Pinos." They continued walking to the next block and entered the swinging door of "Cantina Familiar." The small room was illuminated by a lantern and furnished with two metal tables and six metal chairs. Luke's nose sniffed tangy odors coming from the kitchen. A hunch-backed woman emerged slowly and greeted the teen, "How is our baseball star today?"

"Very well, auntie. How are you? Let me introduce you to Professor Lucas from the U.S.A. I met him at the station today. He played ball with us. He's an *Americano simpatico* and needs a place to stay. Is that possible?"

"Of course, Hercules. A friend of yours is a friend of mine. The Canadian tourists just left the upper room with the double bed. Professor Lucas, be welcome as our guest. We still have our Cuban version of Osso Bucco, leftover from the tourists' lunch, but it tastes fine. May I serve you some?"

"Señora, that's most kind of you. It's been a long day. I believe both us would love to taste your home cooking," Luke affirmed. He followed Hercules to the corner table and dropped his backpack with a thud. Had the fragrant bouquet not perked him up, Luke probably would have fallen asleep on the spot. The overnight train trip had finally caught up with him.

The steaming broth and oxtail arrived under their hungry stare. They devoured dinner without words. Afterwards, Luke told Hercules his purpose in returning to Cacocúm. He wanted to get to know this person also named Lucas. Would he be able to recognize his namesake? Luke wavered about a midnight session of Santeria but felt compelled to attend.

Hercules's aunt was clearing the dishes but stopped on hearing Santeria. "Professor, be very careful there. Its spirits even affect visiting tourists. I've had to minister to some Canadians with herbal tea. They were slow to recover. Do you really have to go? If so, you shouldn't go alone. Hercules should join you.

"Hercules, his grandmother, and I are baptized Catholics. As a person of faith, he could watch your back. You never know what might happen at these sessions. Drums beat nonstop and followers chant mumbo-jumbo. *Atención,* professor!"

"If Hercules is willing, *señora,* I'd be grateful for his presence. I've witnessed the effects of Santeria on the train. Amigo, what do you think?"

Hercules squirmed in his seat but nodded his head. "Professor, I'm willing to be your companion tonight. I hate Santeria, but I'll stick close to you." His auntie tilted hear head in approval.

"Gracias, Hercules. By the way, I know padres in Holguin and in Havana. I'll write down their points of contact for both of you. As you are Catholic, they may be able to help sometime. If you have a fixed phone line, we could stay in touch with you."

The woman wrote her number and admonished Hercules, "You take good care of our guest. If you become afraid, summon the Holy Spirit."

"Gracias, señora. I'll include Fr. Sebastian's fixed line at the Havana Rectory. He is a thoughtful priest and could counsel Hercules in his pursuit of playing professional ball. He has given me wise advice. I plan to see him on return."

Hercules' eyes began to droop as he mumbled, *"Americano,* shall I show you to the room? We have time for a siesta before the midnight session. We'll need all the energy we can muster before those crazy spirits."

"Good idea, Hercules. If we wake up by 11:30, that should give us time."

* * *

LUKE AWOKE SLOWLY AND ASCERTAINED someone breathing nearby. He turned to see Hercules peering down.

"Don't take offense, professor. I just wanted to feel your presence, even your breath on me. I've never shared a room with an *Americano*. This moment means much to me.

"The alarm just rang. We should get going to arrive in time. I will do all that I can to protect you tonight."

"No problem, muchacho," Luke said, scratching his head. He got out of bed and splashed water on his tired face. His nose reflected a brilliant red. He put on tan trousers and dug out has crimson Seattle University shirt. He wore sandals but left his Mariners cap in the room. He followed Hercules down the stairs into the silent street.

They walked past the railway station. Its clock showed 11:50. Human voices drifted over from the other side of the tracks.

Luke saw a bonfire in the distance and heard steady drumbeats. He approached cautiously and saw people dressed in white circling a huge Ceiba tree. Their incantations rose to the stars above. A crescent moon shone meekly through cumulus clouds, which grew thicker by the moment. The air seemed unsettled.

Luke and Hercules slowed, trying to take in what was going on. Neither had witnessed a Santeria session nor its alien sounds. They both stood outside the circle of followers and heard a cry come from within: "*Changó*, come visit your loyal followers circling this sacred tree. Be present! Send your spirit, wherever it roams. In the Yoruba nation, you were a royal prince of the Oyo kingdom. You traveled with your tribesmen across the sea. You shared thunderous power with us in the New World. Your breath hovers o'er this island. Come to us tonight."

Luke stood transfixed. It was Severina's voice rising from the middle of the throng. Two other women were puffing cigars and raising their arms in the air. A breeze began to blow, and clouds covered the slender moon.

A willowy man slipped from under the tree's shadow. He began twirling a necklace of red-and-white beads. To Luke, it appeared like a coral snake writhing in anger around his neck. The man uttered unworldly sounds and raised his eyes above. Luke heard a crow caw.

Young men pounded harder on the Conga drums. The men and women accelerated their pace around the tree. They shouted in unison, "*Oh, lei-lei oh, oh, Changó.*" The constant refrain and beat seemed to transport the followers to another place.

The tree rustled before the wind. A flash of lighting pierced the sky; a thunderclap rumbled in reply. Luke felt Hercules grab his arm.

"*Momento,*" is all Luke said, engrossed in the moment. A booming voice escaped the thin man twirling beads, "He has arrived!" Suddenly, one of the women inside the circle began to swoon. Severina came alongside to break her fall.

Two young men stepped outside the churning circle and removed a white chicken from a cage. They crossed back over and held the hen at the foot of the tree. The thin man approached holding a large, shiny knife. He raised his hands above his head and plunged it down. "For you, *Changooooooo,*" he bellowed. He cut off the chicken's head. Uncanny screams and ululation erupted from the circle.

One of the young men with a shaved head turned back to look at Luke. He was the same mulatto Luke had seen on the bus to Holguin. He broached a sly smile. Luke took a step backward. Hercules clung to his arm.

Another young man joined the tall mulatto and stared over his Roman nose. His dark, curly hair waved in the wind and his eyes glowed in expectation. He took one step forward and then another. He approached Luke in cadence. They came face-to-face, their eyes reflecting the fire's dying flames. Hercules released his grip on Luke's arm.

Luke regarded the young man before him. For a second, he viewed himself in earlier years. He was Luke's height with a square and determined chin. His face was tanned and he was long-legged. His body was lithe like a swimmer's.

When Luke regarded his gray-green eyes, another person came to mind. For a second, Luke was observing his beloved Ana, transfigured before his very eyes. Luke held his breath.

The young man didn't waver in his gaze. Electricity filled the air. It was not from the lightning from the heavens or from *Changó's* spell. It came from a different sphere. Two humans unbound years of heartache and despair. They released their hopes and emotions into the morning air.

Luke felt their gene pools mix and match. Such energy had but one source. It came from a son meeting his father for the very first time. And from a father overjoyed by seeing his son, whom he'd never known.

"You've come, at last," escaped the young man's lips. He dropped to his knees before Luke. Rain began to fall.

The storm picked up in tempo, and rivulets flowed down Luke's cheek. He knelt and put his arms around the young man's shoulders. Their bodies heaved under the pounding rain. Luke didn't care. He'd exceeded beyond his dreams. He had finally found his son, of the Ochoa clan, bred by passion 30 years ago with Ana. Luke had so much to say. He could only utter, "My son." He didn't want this moment to end. It had been so long in coming.

Under the downpour, the fire flickered and embers sparked. Sheets of water cascaded down. The circle broke up, and people dashed for cover. Their vestments lost all whiteness and quivered in collective shadow. The only person Luke could discern was the tall mulatto. His teeth shone like a lamp in the darkness. Then lightning struck the holy tree of Cuba. Current surged through the air.

Not everyone was left standing.

CHAPTER 22

Cacocúm, Friday, 11 a.m.

H E AWOKE ON THE DOUBLE BED, damp from sweat and rain. Feeling woozy, he tried to piece together how he'd arrived back at the B&B. He remembered the flash of lightning that had thrust him to the ground. Then Luke's memory faltered.

He recalled the Santeria session under the tree and the bizarre actions of those dressed in white. Beside him slept his new-found son, his once-glowing vestments coated in earthly tones. It was he who approached Luke from the circle, as the rains began to fall. It was he who said, "You've come, at last." Now, they both shared this room, safe from the storm, safe from spirits, safe for the moment.

Luke regarded the curly haired youth. His chest was rising and falling in soothing rhythm. His son's clothes were steaming in the late-morning warmth. The rising mist spawned a halo around his body.

Someone sighed on the other side of the room. There sat Hercules, contemplating the two of them. The teen attempted to smile, though his eyes suggested sorrow.

"Buenos días, amigo. How did we get back here?" asked Luke, trying to clear his head.

"I didn't want to go last night, professor. Santeria is scary to me. I will never attend another session, ever. Do you remember the lightning strike? You seemed dazed, along with the rest of us. We helped you home.

"I am glad that you met your son. I have known him as 'Lucas, the painter of Cacocúm.' I am happy for him. He finally knows that he has a father. When he lost his mother, he became angry and turned to the worship of the saints. But now he's found you. I wish I were him. Will you take him home with you?"

"Wouldn't that be wonderful!" Luke replied. He nurtured hope that the priest would have an idea of how to get Lucas out. As the local U.S. Embassy had curtailed its staff, there'd be no help there. But maybe Fr. Sebastian's journalist friend, an entrepreneurial sort, would conjure a plan? He would definitely want to brainstorm with him.

Luke slid off the bed and stood up. He was thrilled to witness his son waking for the first time. His son's eyes opened wider, and a smile graced his handsome face.

"Buenos días, my son. It makes me so happy to say 'my son.' After so many years without knowing you existed, I never want to lose you."

"Father, you are the answer to my prayers. Yes, even if I made them to the saints of Santeria. I'm so glad that you found me. After the death of my mother, I lost all hope. Now, my heart is burning to know you. I want to hear about your time with her. Let's find a quiet place where we can speak without haste. We have so much to catch up on."

His son's words were interrupted by knocking on the cantina door. Hercules darted to the window and blurted, "It's our local policeman. Why is he here? It's unusual for him to visit us. What should I do, professor?"

Luke couldn't believe this was happening again. Why were the police pursuing him, even to the countryside? Without giving a second thought, he threw his clothes on and shoved the rest into his pack. "Lucas, it's time to go. I've already had a run-in with Havana's police. I want to avoid trouble, and I especially don't want to involve you. Is there a safe place to go?"

"Father, we could head for my great uncle's casita just outside of Cacocúm."

"Hercules, is there another way out besides the front door?" Luke finished packing as Hercules peered outside.

"This way," Hercules said, pointing to the back. "Hurry!" The policeman's knock became more insistent. A deep voice demanded, "Open up, police."

Hercules unlocked the window. The roof slanted toward a dusty alley. "Go quickly. I'll send you word." He turned and raced down the stairs to the front door. Luke tossed his pack to the ground and slid awkwardly on the asphalt shingles. His right knee buckled when he hit the ground. His son followed and landed neatly on his feet. They dusted themselves off and walked quickly through the alleyway.

"So much for our tete-a-tete. We're off and running again. I am in your hands, Lucas. By the way, do you mind if I call you Junior?"

His son gave Luke a quick thumbs up and picked up his pace. Entering a narrow passageway, they began jogging.

Luke's knee shouted in pain. He kept pace as best he could. He followed Junior into a copse of banana and flambeau trees. When Luke tripped on a root. Junior stopped to help his father up. He lifted Luke's backpack onto his back and said, "I'm sorry, father. We must put distance between us and the village policeman. He knows me. He was unkind to my mother. It'd be best if he didn't see us together. We don't want him to connect the dots. My studio is not far. We can find refuge there."

Luke put on a brave face and followed in his son's footsteps, watching the dirt path beneath his feet. He ducked in time to avoid a cluster of bananas hanging above. His right knee ached, but Luke kept moving toward a clearing ahead.

"Father, it's the casita surrounded by bougainvillea." Junior took a narrow path winding up the hill. He ducked under low-hanging branches and pushed open a wooden gate. He opened the door to a beige-stucco blockhouse, overshadowed by a Ceiba tree. The small room exuded scents of must and paint. Canvasses greeted Luke from the walls and from the easels in various stages of completion. Light filtered through a small window, facing East. A painting of Ana hung directly above a door.

Luke limped into the room, startled by Ana's gaze. He stood there spellbound. His son turned and joined his father. Luke knelt on the blanket covering the packed-dirt floor. His son followed suit. "Ana, forgive me for my unkept promise. Let me make amends. Our Father, please show my son and me the way."

* * *

Over aguardiente and stale bread, father and son delved into their pasts. Memories rushed in and out, and angst and regret overflowed. Their eyes were not often dry.

Lucas Junior confessed his fear of attending grade school. He remembered how other boys boasted about their fathers. On Father's Day, he'd lowered his head, hoping the instructor would not call on him. Sometimes, he stayed home pretending that he was sick. When the teacher finally asked him what his father did, Lucas didn't know what to say. When someone dubbed him a "bastard," he didn't let that comment pass. He fought three of them after class and took his hits. Even though he didn't know who his father was, he'd brook no disrespect toward his mother.

Ana tried hard to get him into the university. "You would make me and your father proud," she often said. She pleaded to many "friends" but they turned their backs on her. The Ochoa family name was taboo. Word came down from the university rector that her son was "unqualified." Its doors remained closed to both of them. Ana's son would have to seek a different path.

Despite his mother's love, Junior felt incomplete. Without a notion of who his father was, how was he to act? Every time he asked his mother, she'd reply that his father was an *Americano,* who had made her a promise. Despite his constant questions, Ana never gave a full answer. His father remained a mystery.

Often, when Junior regarded himself in a mirror, he'd ask what resemblance he bore to the *Americano.* Was it his muscle tone, his long legs, or even his solid chin and nose? Would he recognize him if their paths ever crossed? Not knowing his father haunted him as a boy, as an adolescent, and as a young man.

He'd often speculate about the promise his father had made to his mother. Was it to marry her someday? Now, she was gone and had taken her secret to the grave.

When Luke heard his son's lament, he put his arm around his broad shoulders. It was Luke's turn to confess.

"Son, I didn't honor my promise to your mother. I was supposed to inform the world what really happened to her uncle, General Arnaldo Ochoa. I came to Cuba to find Ana and to discover why the Castros had him shot 30 years ago. I want to honor my promise to her, one way or another.

"But now, I've found you, the son of my very blood. How can I honor my promise to your mother and keep you out of harm's way?"

"Father, thank you for telling me. I know that you want to keep your promise. Let me help—take me with you. Together, we could proclaim Ochoa's story to the world!

"We are sitting on the Angolan blanket, which my great uncle gave my mother upon his return from Africa. He particularly liked its diamond-shaped design and earthy colors. I've adopted some of them into my own artwork. Let's take the blanket and some of my art abroad. We'll give witness to the truth, as father and son.

"I will follow you wherever you go. Please don't abandon me in Cuba." This time, it was his son whose eyes turned moist.

The moment was shattered by pounding on the door. Junior wiped his face, exclaiming, "Father, go into the back room and lock the door. Let me see who arrives without warning."

Junior spied through a peephole. "Hercules, you gave us a fright. If you'd texted or rang my cell, that would have alerted us. Come in. Do you have any news? Father, it's our homerun hitter. You can come out now."

"Buenas tardes, Hercules. What did that policeman want? I hope he didn't rough you up."

"Professor, the policeman sought an *Americano*. Someone has denounced you. You are not safe in Holguin province. He said nothing about Lucas the painter. But if anyone from the Santeria session opens their mouth, they'll come here too." He looked directly at Luke, "I told him that you'd left my auntie's home and maybe returned to Holguin. He seemed to buy my story. I stood up to him."

Luke gave him a high five. "Hercules, you did very well. I will not forget you. You know how to reach me in the States or through Fr. Sebastian in Havana. Now, we must flee. But how or where?"

"Father, I know a truck driver who leaves Cacocúm every Tuesday and Friday afternoon. He works in the black market, buying and selling merchandise. He's often given me a lift to cities along the *Carretera Central* to exhibit my art. Let me call him and see if we can hitch a ride. He will have to pass police roadblocks and will need CUCs to facilitate passage. He makes several stops but ends up in Santa Clara. What do you say?"

Luke replied wholeheartedly, "Let's go!"

Lucas texted the truck driver and then telephoned on his beat-up smartphone: "Samuel, all is well? Yes, this is your local artist: are you going north this afternoon? *Excelente!* I'd like to catch a ride with you and bring a family friend. Would that be OK? Yes, I'll bring artwork. Also, my companion is shy and wouldn't want to be seen. Is there a place he could travel inside the trailer? He'd pay handsomely in CUCs."

Junior waited and then said, "150 CUCs? That's a princely sum. Let me confirm with my friend." Luke gave a thumbs up. His son concluded the arrangements to rendezvous.

"Father, we are to meet at an unused shack just beyond the banana grove. He asks us to arrive in 30 minutes. He must arrive in Camaguey tonight. He's had problems finding diesel fuel, which is costly on the black market. I agreed that you'd finance his fuel costs and give him a bonus. I hope I didn't over promise. It's likely our only way out. If an alert is sounded, the police will be inspecting documents of all passengers on buses and trains."

"You've done well, my son. Let's pack up your artwork and the Angolan blanket. Hercules, please keep an eye outside. Let's go— *Vámonos, amigos.*"

They packed up quickly. Junior carefully removed his mother's portrait from the wall and added four small paintings to his home-made backpack. He followed his father outside and turned to touch the top of the door frame. Junior led them down the trail and glanced back once at his hideaway, disappearing into the bougainvillea.

Luke took note of the oblique angle of the sun and followed Junior into the woods. He stopped abruptly. Someone was coming through the banana grove.

He prepared himself to fight.

CHAPTER 23

Ministry of Interior, Havana, Friday, 5 p.m.

THIS TIME HE RETURNED to the nine-story building, following in the steps of his superior officer. He was asked to be his escort, one of his many roles. He'd always said, "Yes sir." It was the way to keep his little family afloat. Ever since he'd tackled the angry peasant with a machete on Varadero beach, the General wanted him by his side. Being favored by the General had its perks. Things he'd do for food and gasoline. Sometimes he loathed himself—especially when the General went wild during his early morning bacchanalia.

Today's summons to the Interior Ministry was unusual. Friday's often were avoided, as attendees, including the General, readied themselves for outings not involving wives. Sundays were preferred. Few around the table admitted to attending church. What was today's crisis—lack of gas, lack of money, lack of food?

Big Man saw the General waver. He wondered if he'd already tossed back a few. Che Guevarra's image towered over the plaza, where some kids were kicking around an old soccer ball. His thoughts abruptly returned to his missing son. He felt being pulled down to that darker place.

The General peered at him. "Big Man, you seem quiet of late. Are things right with you and the Revolutionary Police? Are home fires burning brightly? Or has a lover gone astray?"

"No, General. A bout of nostalgia hit me on seeing the kids play. No lover or unusual activity to report. Today, I only have Dolores at home."

The General frowned and asked no more questions. He ploughed straight ahead and through the heavy front doors. The soldiers at the Ministry stood at present arms. Big Man returned their salute, casting a shadow over the shorter man ahead.

They went up to the same conference room and were the last to arrive. A somber atmosphere hung over the "who's who" of the intelligence apparatus of the Republic of Cuba. With the arrival of the General and Big Man, they totaled nine, compared with 22 last Sunday.

"Gentlemen, thank you for coming on short notice. However, too much is going on to stand pat. I believe that you know Mr. Dong from Vietnam's Embassy. Let me introduce Mr. Zhao of the People's Republic of China."

Both Asians inclined their heads. Big Man had met Dong at a previous forum but had never laid eyes on Zhao. The Chinese visitor's face stayed immobile while his jet-black eyes swept the room. His gaze hung on Big Man an extra second. As the only mulatto in the room, he felt self-conscious. The Army's chief medical officer moved one seat away from Zhao.

"You're aware of the grave situation in regard to petrol. The Venezuelans have shut the tap, and the Mexicans are afraid to cross you-know-who up North. Gas shortages are rampant. Pirates are siphoning off thousands of liters of diesel and gasoline every day. Often, it's taken from our official stations!

"Our transport system is breaking down. This theft shall stop. No one—including family and friends—will be shown mercy. In one of

Raul's tirades last night, he threw a crystal glass in anger, barely missing my head. 'This will not stand,' he ordered. 'I will personally shoot the first thief caught stealing petrol from the government stations. I will line the thieves up against *El Paredón*. We will return to the days of Che. The wall will run red again!'

"Gentleman, I take him at his word. We must lower the boom—even on our subordinates. Check with each of your drivers, and find out who's stealing the petrol. We are supposed to be the cream of Cuban intelligence. Let's demonstrate that with results.

"Ferret out the kingpins behind this massive leak of oil. Who are the 'go to' guys in the black market? The situation is dire in the countryside. We have demonstrations in Cuba's second city for insufficient water. Santiago's pumps don't have the juice to lift H_2O to high-rise buildings that host several ministers and generals. *Que pasa?*"

When the Vice Admiral glanced his way, Big Man felt himself grow smaller. He was the only one from Santiago in the room. Others around the table examined their notes. The Inspector gazed at the ceiling. The two Asians remained taciturn, taking in the scene.

The Vice Admiral exhaled, glancing at the Chinese spy for moral support. "Mr. Zhao, I understand that you have news that may help us on the I.T. front. Your software program, I understand, is called *Dragon's Teeth?*"

Big Man saw the Army doctor frown. He'd heard the doctor warn about a new virus emanating from China's interior. The Chinese operative didn't look the doctor's way but began mumbling incomprehensible Spanish in a half-closed mouth. Big Man picked out the words that the People Republic's spyware would "chew into firewalls like dragon's teeth."

The Inspector piped up: "So, secure firewalls could be penetrated—including those of foreign NGOs and church organizations?

Your hackers have helped us infiltrate Google's encryption in Cuba. You referred to that as 'kid's stuff.' We need your help now. I hear rumblings of discontent everywhere on social media."

The Chinese muttered under his breath about special algorithms to seek out targets. Big Man didn't understand much about the World Wide Web. What he did know was that youth around the country were glued to their Chinese smartphones. In hometown Santiago, students had organized "pop up" marches via WhatsApp. Hundreds had marched in the street to protest the lack of food, water, and gasoline.

More and more people were using Wi-fi, installed this year by Huawei in public squares. These very Chinese had opened Pandora's box.

He glanced at the Vice Admiral, whose eyes began glassing over. Most older hands around the table stifled yawns. Only the Inspector tuned in, trying to read the Asian tea leaves. The thin man was tech-savvy and rumored to cruise the Dark Web for live videos of kinky sex, especially of Asian women with African men.

"Thank you, Mr. Zhao. Now, let's hear from the Inspector. Any chirping from your canaries about town?"

"We've locked up more journalists and artists. They're writing more anti-government propaganda for the international press. Let's see how they feel after a few nights in the Eastern Compound outside Havana. Thousands of inmates are licking their chops. They're always hunting for new bait.

"The group from that Miami foundation has brought in new Apps to spread amongst the young and the restless. They're providing free downloads to facilitate access to international sites. They've teamed up with Spain's *El País* for a special feed about Cubans living abroad—especially in Madrid. Students are downloading these Apps and seem engaged. Maybe *Dragon's Teeth* can help us block access abroad? We've already warned this group to stop transmitting this

App. I'll probably throw a few Miami agitators in jail just to remind them where they are.

"There's also been grumbling among veterans of the African wars. Even though they're dying off, they complain of long lines at clinics and lack of medical help. My canaries have heard Ochoa's name bandied about. I'm sniffing around for any vets planning to commemorate the anniversary of that traitor's death. There are relatives around with a public profile who may tacitly support that effort. We must combat Ochoa's ghost."

The Inspector glanced at the General, who tensed in his seat. The General stared daggers at his rival. Tension lit the air between these intel heavyweights. The older hands avoided looking at either man.

After a pause, the Inspector continued: "There's also an annoying professor from the States asking questions about this traitor. He's from Seattle and has visited the University of Havana. We have canaries there who keep tabs on him. Our 'lone wolf' at Hotel Nacional has also ingratiated himself with this 'do-gooder.' Another source confirmed that the prof visited Ochoa's hometown near Holguin. He was seen last night at a Santeria session in Cacocúm. The local police are searching for him as we speak. I've dispatched an all-points bulletin to law enforcement along the main highway, *la Carretera Central*. I want to interrogate him again. If I squeeze him just a little, I'm sure that he will sing.

"Other than that, it's business as usual—small fries trying to make noise."

Big Man listened carefully. It dawned on him that he knew this professor. He'd confronted him twice. He asked himself why the gringo wanted so badly to learn about his former commanding general? The prof seemed out of his element. Big Man doubted that he'd foreseen the consequences of his foolhardy actions. He'd also heard that the prof was at the Factory the same night as Eloisa. Did they cross paths? He should find out.

When the American prof was mentioned, the Vietnamese diplomat leaned forward in his seat. It appeared to Big Man that he had something to say. The Admiral's assistant intervened and rang the bell, adjourning for a late afternoon break. *Añejo* rum and Montecristo cigars awaited them in the elegant *Sala de Recepción*. Big Man decided that he'd speak with Dong over some shots of *Havana Club*.

Big Man observed his superior officer, whose eyes blazed in fury at the Inspector. His nemesis feigned nonchalance. The General shoved back his chair, causing it to teeter back and forth. The most senior officer rose up and bulled his way toward the parlor. He'd likely want to drown his sorrow in Whiskey Sour. Big Man wondered which one of the two would gain Raul's ear. Who would ultimately prevail?

The Inspector winked at him. Big Man's face darkened as he stood up. He flexed his muscles but bit his tongue, tamping down his volcanic temper. He turned his back on the snide thin man. He joined the Vietnamese diplomat exiting the room. He breathed deeply for a few seconds in order to regain some calm. Later, he made small talk with Dong.

Big Man felt comfortable in the diplomat's presence. He'd like to spend time with him outside these formal gatherings. Maybe they could forge a dialogue beyond the official façade? Together, they might gain an edge to fend off threats from intelligence rivals.

Perhaps, they'd also compare notes on this peripatetic American prof, who had drawn so much of the Inspector's ire.

THE THIRD JOURNEY

"Yea, though I walk through the valley of the shadow of death, I will fear no evil: for thou art with me. Thy rod and thy staff, they comfort me."

The Twenty-third Psalm
—King David

CHAPTER 24

Cacocúm, Friday, 5 p.m.

L UKE CAUTIOUSLY ENTERED THE BANANA GROVE. He heard rustling and a human grunt.

A man with a machete was moving through the copse but stopped when he saw Luke's party of three. Maybe he didn't like the odds. Keeping his eyes on them, the man hoisted a large bunch of bananas onto his back. His machete in hand, he backed out of the thicket. Everyone had to eat, thought Luke.

Luke raised a finger to his mouth and stealthily trekked out of the woods. Under an almond tree sat a farmer stoically holding the reins of a white, Brahman cow. He scanned the threesome then looked away. Luke inclined his head and skirted the hillock on a well-trodden path. He made out an abandoned shed under a Flambeau tree ablaze in red.

In the shade loomed a late-fifties International Harvester, with the contours of a garbage truck. If they could only export this classic van, it'd pay for their trip back to the States. Luke wondered how this contraption would make it all the way to Santa Clara. Importantly, where would he fit in?

The driver's door was ajar. A middle-aged man in cutoff sleeves and shorts leaned back against the headrest. On his lap, the official paper, *Granma,* fluttered under a current of air. The three of them rested briefly at the open door. The sun was setting, but heat waves swelled beneath Luke's feet. Riding the air currents, a vulture circled overhead, looking for prey.

Junior raised his voice, "Samuel, all is well?" When the driver opened his eyes, Luke did a double take. He saw a darker version of actor Sam Elliott, flaunting a handle-bar mustache and strong arms. His brown eyes said, "Don't mess with me." They matched the color of his weathered skin. The driver swung down to the ground and gave Junior a bear hug.

"Ready to go, Lucas? I'm running late. Which one is your 'family friend'?" asked the driver, peering at Hercules then back to Luke.

"This is my friend, Esteban. He also knows Padre Roberto. He needs a lift but prefers riding in the back. Is that acceptable to you?"

The driver squinted at Luke and then back at Junior, caressing his mustache with care. "Sure, Lucas. My pleasure, Esteban—be my guest. I've carved out a little nook that used to house the garbage compactor. It won't be too comfy, but it will keep you beyond curious eyes.

"There's a blanket back there, but you'll have to shift around. Just don't do so when we're at a police checkpoint. We'll pound twice on the trailer when we come into contact with the highway patrol. Three knocks mean 'coast clear'. Understood, *señor?*"

"Very well, Samuel. Let me advance you 50 CUCs to help with the police. How do I get in, and will I share the space with any merchandise?"

"You'll enter into the curved bin in the back. I'll bolt it closed during the trip. If you're getting ill or have an emergency, just beat on the bin. But don't do so when we're at a check point or if the truck is stopped. Remember, Esteban, two knocks bad and keep quiet. Three knocks good. Thanks for the CUCs, but I'll need more during the trip for petrol. You won't be riding in the bin with other goods. As for other creatures, you'll have to play it by ear," the driver grinned, twirling his mustache with gusto.

"Our first stop is Las Tunas an hour-and-a-half away. Use the Flambeau tree now to do your business. Here's a bottle of filtered water, Esteban. We have to go."

Luke and his son gave Hercules a tight hug. Luke slipped a 10-CUC note into the ballplayer's front pocket. "I'll give your auntie a call when we arrive in Havana. In the meantime, keep hitting the long ball, amigo." The boy nodded reluctantly when Luke touched his shoulder.

After hugging Junior, Luke slipped into the back of the old garbage truck. The Cuban Sam Elliot gave a thumbs up and slid the bin upward, locking Luke in place. In the dark, Luke reconnoitered with his fingers, trying to decipher the cramped space.

The truck jerked forward on the dirt road, jostling Luke back and forth. He covered his head with his arms and shoved his pack behind him to protect his back. He wondered how he was going to survive the 350-mile trip.

Reverting to an old habit in times of distress, Luke began reciting the 23rd Psalm. Dust flicked into his nostrils as he felt the truck stop and go. He sensed that they'd arrived on the smoother streets of Holguin. After 10 minutes, the truck accelerated, likely reaching the *Carretera Central.* He returned to the Psalm and curled himself into a fetal ball. He managed to fall into an uneven sleep. He awoke with a start and heard knocking. Was the village policeman after him? He was locked down and couldn't budge.

Two knocks reminded him that he was in the back of the garbage truck. He couldn't remember if two knocks were good or bad. He was sweating, awaiting word.

After a few minutes, the truck started up and cruised at a steady speed. Luke tried to drift back to sleep, but his right knee hurt. He needed to move, and his leg was cramping. As the truck was moving, he decided to bang for help. He hit the bin over and over again. The truck decelerated and eventually stopped. He heard the locks being undone and saw the apparition of Sam Elliott.

"Buenas noches, Esteban. We just passed Las Tunas' checkpoint. The police asked if we'd seen a gringo hitchhiking. Come out to stretch your legs quickly. It must be a little cramped back here."

Luke wavered as he climbed out of his garbage cell. His legs felt like rubber, and his head throbbed. His son rushed to lend him a hand. Luke limped off the road and breathed in the humid air. After a couple minutes, Samuel cautioned.

"Stopping along the roadside arouses suspicion, especially at night. The cops are on the lookout for black marketeers. Let me fit another blanket into the back, Esteban. Let's go before a police car arrives." He helped Luke back into his space and locked him inside.

Luke shifted around his cubby hole. He fingered the water bottle and took a long swig. The second blanket provided more cushion from the swaying truck. He managed to drift off to sleep, until he heard banging again. The truck slowed down and voices seeped inside the bin. They seemed to be arguing about money. "Why that's highway robbery," he heard. Then all went quiet.

CHAPTER 25

On the Carretera Central, Friday 9 p.m.

H E WAITED AND WAITED. The voices diminished and Luke recited the psalm again. He faded off to tumultuous dreams.

He was bouncing around the Caribbean though no one was in sight. The swells grew larger, making him tumble. He hit something sharp and cried out. He opened his eyes to blackness. He heard a high-pitched sound, which did not hail from the sea. It came from a screaming engine in proximity. He bumped his head as the vessel swung hard to starboard. Then all engines stopped.

All was quiet, until it wasn't. A metallic knock resounded three times and a shaft of light touched Luke's face.

"That was close," complained Samuel, pulling nervously on his stash. "A dark sedan began following and tried to push us off the road. I had to zig and zag to keep him at bay. He was another corsair trying to hijack my scarce goods. It's getting dangerous to drive on the highway at night. People are getting desperate.

"When they passed me, I swerved into this narrow lane and doused my lights. I've hidden here before. Let's keep mum for a few minutes and hope they don't double back. Camaguey is just 20 miles up the road. Someone is waiting there for most of my cargo."

Luke heard footfalls in the underbrush and saw a glint of metal. "Samuel, someone is coming up behind us."

Suddenly, footsteps crumpled branches and voices rose close by. Samuel dashed for the truck's cab. Luke saw the glint again, this time off machetes in the hands of two hooded men. Luke and his son backed into a Ceiba tree seeking protection against the blades. Luke grabbed a fallen branch and his son another. Together, they tried to fend off the *desesperados*.

Luke pushed the branch into the first attacker's hooded face. With one swoop, the man cut off a third of the branch. On his backward slash, he chopped the remaining branch in half. Luke tried to fend with the stub, but a glancing machete blow drew blood on his right shoulder.

Junior roared like a panther and leaped at the attacker, hitting him in the solar plexus. An NFL tackler could not have done better. Junior began pummeling the man. He hit the man's hooded face again and again.

Samuel jumped from the cab, swinging a three-foot machete at the second man. Luke witnessed a dramatic battle of Cuban martial arts. Steel blades clanged back and forth and sparks lit the night. Samuel was relentless in his thrusts, sporting the bigger blade.

The second man appeared winded and bellowed to his cohort, "*Vámonos*—let's go." The corsair backed out the way he came. Samuel pulled Junior off the other man, ordering, "Let him go. We have bigger fish to fry. You've done well."

Luke heard an ignition start up and a vehicle drive away. He looked at his crimson Seattle U. polo shirt, which matched the color running down his arm. He let Samuel splash rum over the cut and wipe it down. Blood was flowing, so Samuel tied it off with a towel. "Let's get moving, Esteban. We will tend to your wound later. I'll ring my associate for help. You'll be riding up front with us until we reach his warehouse. Let's hope there's no checkpoint before Camaguey. We'll turn off before the city center."

"*Muchas gracias*," Luke said, leaning on his son. They squeezed into the front seat, with Luke on the right. Luke applied pressure on the impromptu patch covering his cut. Samuel backed the garbage truck out and eased it onto *la Carretera Central*. Luke drank some water and leaned back, feeling lightheaded. He saw dark fields of sugar cane fly by. Cumulus clouds blanketed the wavering moon.

A vehicle drove up behind them, following their every move. Samuel touched his machete on the floor. The black sedan pulled alongside the truck. Two men stared at Samuel, who glanced casually at them. He turned his attention back to the road and saw another vehicle's lights rise over the hill. It came rushing down the left lane. The sedan accelerated and missed the oncoming truck with few feet to spare. Samuel's garbage truck maintained a constant speed. The red tail lights ahead pulled away.

Luke and his son took deep breaths. Luke now viewed Samuel as a marketeer with nerves of steel. He had underestimated him. Sam Elliott's darker twin could teach him a thing or two, especially how to navigate the treacherous roads in Cuba. He was glad that Samuel was on their side, at least for now.

Lights reflected off the overhead clouds. A suggestion of rain was in the air. Samuel down-shifted and turned off *la Carretera Central*. He nosed the truck into General Gomez Street, easing past horse-drawn carriages and empty taxis. A few pedestrians gaped at the truck, maybe wondering why it was picking up garbage at this late hour?

"We've arrived in this industrial district, where my associate's warehouse is. I'll text him and ask for a doctor 'off the books' to stitch up Esteban's gash. I'll need another 50 CUCs and no prying eyes at our next locale." Samuel made his call and maneuvered the truck through narrow streets.

A few people were hanging out, and salsa floated through the air. A light rain began falling. Samuel turned into an alleyway without music or light, stopping at a two-story, stucco building. A garage door opened, and a flashlight beckoned the truck inside. Lightning outlined a heavyset man in guayabera. He slid the door shut and shambled up to Samuel, offering a loose hug.

"Comrades, this is my associate of many years. We will not exchange names or pleasantries tonight. We'll offload the electronic goods and the crates of eggs as silently as we can. Colleague, has your medical friend arrived?"

"He's waiting upstairs. Stack the Huawei crates in the back of the garage, but bring the eggs to the first floor. I'll leave you the lantern to find your way."

Luke followed the man trudging up the stairs. The man opened a door into the kitchen and turned back without a word. A masked, young Eurasian in a white coat awaited Luke, backlit by a kerosene lantern. He had a stethoscope around his neck and wore plastic gloves. A gas burner heated two small pots of water in the corner.

"Señor, let me see your cut. You've lost a lot of blood." The doctor rolled up Luke's sleeve and dipped a wash cloth into a pan of hot water. He washed Luke's shoulder with homemade-looking soap, causing him to wince. The doc dipped another cloth into the water and did his best to wipe the cut clean. Blood still dribbled out.

Luke wondered why the doc wore such protection to mend his shoulder. "Why the mask, doctor?"

"You may not have heard, but there's a strange virus stalking the world. It's just arrived in Cuba. I plan to leave tomorrow for Havana to be part of a research team. We'll be experimenting with interferon as a possible treatment. We must begin taking precautions, *señor.*"

He gave Luke a double shot of rum, "Drink up. I'll have to sew you up. It won't be without pain." Luke gulped another drink and bit down hard on the towel. The doctor dunked a large needle into a pan of boiling water and began stitching up the wound. Luke bit through the cloth but didn't cry out. He gasped and the doctor stopped momentarily, wiping Luke's brow. "Let me pour some *añejo* on the wound again. We've run out of antiseptic at the hospital. Here's another shot for you. We're almost done. Hang on, my friend."

Luke closed his eyes and chomped harder on the towel, hoping that his teeth would withstand the pressure. When pain was about to breach his threshold, the doctor patted him on the back. "Done! I've inserted a sterile rubber band beneath the suture, leaving part of it outside. It'll help drain the shoulder. You never know what bacteria may be hiding inside. We have to be creative in Cuba," he concluded.

He wiped Luke's brow again and gave him a thumbs up. He also gave Luke a couple of aspirins—it was all the medicine he had left.

They both looked out the window as the rain came thundering down.

CHAPTER 26

Café Boné Ma, Vedado, Havana, Saturday, 8 a.m.

"Buenos días, Major. I trust this *paladar* with a Turkish twist is agreeable to you. One of my sources, who works at Reuters across the street, gave it glowing reviews. The breakfasts are tasty and reasonably priced. It's calmer here than the whirlwind inside the Hotel Nacional. What do you think? Please don't take offense if it lacks prestige."

"Buenos días, Señor Dong. I am always on the hunt for a café *'bueno y barato'*—good and cheap! Hidden inflation is eating up our wages. I thank you for the invitation to exchange ideas more informally. Even though we run in similar circles, I'm never quite sure who's confiding in whom at our official briefings.

"Let me also congratulate you on speaking Spanish. Many foreigners have problems. You speak our language correctly, without much accent. Have you been here long?"

"I've just completed my second year in Cuba. The Ministry plans to retain me another year. It would mean much to me to have an open dialogue with a thoughtful person like yourself.

"By the way, *Café Boné Ma* usually has a supply of fresh eggs and bacon, thanks to special relationships with farmers in Santa Clara.

They also get fresh bread from an in-house baker. Shall we order breakfast, or would you prefer its shish kebab?"

Big Man followed Dong's lead and ordered breakfast with bacon and eggs from the countryside, accompanied by a plate of delicious papaya, mangos, and pineapple. With fresh bread and real butter, Big Man ate with relish. When Dong suggested they top it off with a cappuccino, Big Man felt amply satisfied. If only he could eat this well every day. He was tempted to slip some bacon into his napkin to bring home to Dolores. He cleaned his plate instead. He almost burped in exultation. He kept it down, not wanting to appear uncouth to this smooth diplomat from Southeast Asia.

"Now that we've breakfasted, Major, please permit me to raise a professional question. Do I understand correctly that you've encountered this American prof a couple of times? He sat next to me on the plane trip from Miami to Havana. We had a lively conversation. What was your opinion of him?"

Big Man took a few seconds to respond. "I believe that the *Americano* should take care in asking questions about the fallen Hero of the Republic. As you're aware, It's a very delicate subject here. He seems to have a personal interest in discovering more about Ochoa. I can't figure out why that is."

"Yes, he spoke briefly with me about his personal mission. Apparently, he met a niece of the General many years ago. He made a promise to her. It may be that he went to Ochoa's hometown to discover her whereabouts. I learned that he's also a Catholic. It was strange to hear that he attended a Santeria session in the interior."

Big Man paused at the sound of Cuba's syncretic religion. The nocturnal image of the *Chango's* sacrifice flashed across his mind. "Yes, even Catholics are affected by Santeria in Cuba. For centuries, both religions grew up as brothers, like Cain and Abel. When the first slaves from Africa arrived, they brought their Yoruba gods. It's sometimes difficult to separate the two—especially in the countryside.

"Though I don't often attend mass, I try to avoid *Santería*. It appeals to the darker side of human nature. There's already too much of that in the world for me."

"Well said, Major. I also keep my distance from any syncretic practice, even in Vietnam. My wife and I like to attend mass at the Cathedral, usually at its 10:30 service. Do you ever go?"

"Not often, Señor Dong. However, a padre I know from my hometown of Santiago will likely officiate there this month. He is substituting for a travelling priest. You may enjoy meeting Fr. Sebastian, as he's a bit of a scholar. I'd be happy to make introductions."

"That's kind of you, Major. A friend of the cloth is always welcome."

Just then, two boys passed in front of the café, bouncing a soccer ball back and forth on their knees and heels. They seemed to be having fun, showing off to girls on the sidewalk. Big Man nodded approvingly.

Dong followed Big Man's gaze and watched the kids control the ball with deft moves. When they disappeared down the street, he said, "Those boys remind me of my youthful attempts at soccer. Not as able, mind you, as these Cuban boys. Do you have any children, Major?"

Big Man's eyes turned down. "I'm sorry to say, Señor Dong, that our only son was killed last year in a plane crash. He was going to Holguin. His memory returns whenever I see other kids play. Jose Antonio also loved soccer and baseball."

The Vietnamese diplomat leaned forward and touched his arm. Big Man appreciated his gesture and noticed that the diplomat's eyes were full. Then Dong looked away and removed his hand.

"I'm sorry for your loss, Major. Our children are our legacy on earth. Their early death must be devasting to any parent. When my father was killed 30 years ago in a border incident with China, our whole family lost its anchor. Imagine, losing your only son. Please let me know how I can be present for you, either day or night."

Big Man's emotions bubbled over. He placed his arm around the short Vietnamese diplomat and squeezed him tight. He hoped that he'd finally found a friend. He needed one so badly.

CHAPTER 27

Carretera Central 20 miles east of Santa Clara, Saturday, 8 a.m.

L UKE WOKE UP TO A RISING SUN. How long had they been driving since slipping out of Camaguey in the wee hours? Junior leaned on his left shoulder. Thanks to Ana and his only begotten son, his heart had been pried open again. He couldn't believe that they were riding together to Santa Clara and, hopefully, out of Cuba.

Luke observed Samuel driving on the *Carretera Central* in light traffic. He seemed transfixed on a salsa beat blasting from Samsung earbuds. Could he hear anything outside his audio world? The trucker moved his head up and down.

The truck passed a horse-drawn cart piled high with sugar cane. Luke craned his neck out the window to smell its earthy aroma. Two farmers riding up front waved back as the garbage truck zoomed by.

"Esteban, it's best to keep your head inside the cab. Someone could report a gringo on the highway. My associate listened to the police radio last night. They're searching for an *Americano,* though their description was vague. We should arrive within an hour.

"With your shoulder wound, I thought it best to let you ride up front. You wouldn't survive long in the back. We're risking a lot, so let's not take chances. It'd be best to roll up the window. We don't want anyone to grab a view and report you to the Revolutionary Police. They'd get a small reward. Everyone is seeking an advantage here."

"I'm sorry, Samuel. I forgot where I was for a moment. I'm grateful for your help," said Luke, sweating more without the breeze. He felt his son stirring, which made him happy. He had to catch himself from saying, "son." He asked himself if Samuel had figured out their blood relationship.

"Buenos días, Lucas. How did you sleep? We're getting close to Santa Clara and will have to figure out where we go next."

"Buenos días, *papá*. I slept well and you? Let me take a look at your shoulder," he said, lifting up Luke's right sleeve, where a little blood still seeped out. He wiped it dry with a paper towel.

Luke looked quickly at Samuel. Did he note how his son had addressed him? If so, the driver didn't let on.

"I'm going to pull off of the highway before the main entrance to Santa Clara. You're going to have to ride in the back until I reach my associate's garage in town. You should be OK for a few miles, resting on your left shoulder. It's better this way. It would be hard to explain your presence, or your wound, to the Revolutionary Police.

"Have you thought where you'd like to go next after Santa Clara? The *Americano* should not travel on the main highway. The closer you get to Havana, the more police check points you'll encounter. A slower but safer route would be along the coast. The northern beaches are popular destinations for tourists. You could fit in without drawing much attention. I won't be able to help you beyond this town."

"An excellent idea, Samuel. I met a pastor from Santa Cruz, who may be able to help. He's involved with several congregations in the region. Maybe he has a home church near Varadero. When we get into town, I'll try to reach him."

"Very well. You can borrow my cell now. I have the rest of Huawei smartphones to deliver to my other associate. Afterward, I plan to pick up cases of filtered water at a secret location. I could drop you off downtown."

Luke found Pastor Ramon's card and telephoned his cell, leaving a message on his voicemail. He texted too, hoping that he'd remember him. A half hour passed but no return call. Maybe the pastor was conducting a worship service in one of the many home churches.

"OK, Esteban. I'm going to pull off the road up ahead. You'll have to ride in the back again. It won't last long."

The truck slowed down and stopped at a turnabout with overhanging Flambeau trees. Luke got out of the cab and returned to the back bin. He faced inward, leaning on his left shoulder. "We're almost there," said his son, lightly touching his arm. Luke was enclosed in darkness again.

* * *

Luke stayed in the bin until the trucker offloaded the rest of the smartphones. On a side street, the driver released him, offering the middle seat in the cab. Samuel decided to drop them off before his pick up of filtered water. "I'll leave you at the historical center, favored by tourists. You'll be able to find a *colectivo* or a ride to Varadero beach."

Luke viewed a bronze Che Guevara brandishing a rifle, before his mausoleum and straggling tourists. Samuel skirted by the plaza and proceeded downtown Santa Clara. Just then, his cell rang. He handed it to Luke; Pastor Ramón was on the line. Luke agreed to join him at the Café Europa in an hour's time. So far, so good.

Samuel seemed to be in a hurry and asked for another 50 CUCs. Luke paid and thanked him again. Samuel pulled over and let them both out, his manner gruff. Luke wondered if something had transpired between him and Junior while he was ensconced in the bin.

Luke and Junior each gave Samuel a light hug and waved as the gray garbage truck chugged off. Wearing their backpacks, they wound their way to a pedestrian walkway.

At a kiosk, Junior negotiated the purchase of a blue bucket hat, sporting a Cuban flag, and planted it on his father's head. Luke hoped it made him appear like a typical tourist rather than a prof on the run. They walked past youth hostels, cafés, and art galleries. They stepped away from gray-clad policemen swinging billy clubs and eyeing passersby. Luke saw the sign for Café Europa and selected a back table on the terrace. A boyish waiter took his order of fried plantains and mojitos. It had been a long 24 hours, and Luke and his son were ravenously hungry. They wolfed down the plantains, and Luke ordered more.

An hour passed and the temperature rose. Luke spied Ramón walking slowly toward the restaurant with a young boy in hand. The pastor saw Luke and smiled.

He gave Luke a tight hug and introduced his son, *Juanito*. Little Juan was attending second grade and loved baseball. "Pastor, let me introduce you to someone very special, my only son. Lucas, this is Pastor Ramón, about whom I've spoken. We met riding a train to the interior. He's active in Cuba's home-church movement and is a thoughtful man."

Pastor Ramón blinked twice and gave Junior a tight hug, exclaiming "Wonderful" several times. He nodded enthusiastically. "Indeed, professor, so this was the important mission—hallelujah!

"I'm happy we are able to meet again, especially with your son. I just returned from Camaguey. Our new church is growing fast, but its finances are strained. The pastor there conducts services in the garden. Pastor Beau plans to return with farmers from Georgia to plant peanuts and maize to feed our community. I hope to go back then."

The waiter came to take the pastor's order of *Ciego Montero* orangeades. When the sodas arrived, he asked, "How may I be of service? Wisely, you didn't say much over the phone. As you know, big brother is always listening."

Luke retold his story of coming to Cuba, intending to honor his promise to Ana. He mentioned the Inspector's interrogation at the airport and the huge loss he felt upon learning of Ana's death. But then such joy, when he met his son at yesterday's Santeria session. "But the Cacocúm police were knocking on our door and we had to escape. Thanks to Lucas' friend, we arrived here this afternoon. Now we must find a way back to Havana, while avoiding the police."

The pastor squinted at Luke and Junior, a new wrinkle crossing his brow. He observed his son and saw other boys tossing a baseball back and forth in the plaza.

"Hmm, professor. I'm glad you were able to survive Santeria without lingering effects. Since Pastor Beau encountered that priestess on the train, he's not been 100 percent. Lucas, how are you feeling?"

Junior twirled his straw inside his mojito. "Pastor, if Santeria brought me and my father together, then I'm OK with that. It was a scary experience under the Ceiba tree, but maybe an invisible force intervened in our behalf. Who knows? I won't pursue that anymore. I just don't want to lose my father. Can you help us get out of Santa Clara, maybe to the coast?"

Pastor Ramon looked again at his son and then up at the sky. He seemed to be having a silent conversation with himself. "So be it. Let us put our heads together and find a way out of here." He frowned toward the plaza and exclaimed, "Professor, trouble is coming our way. Please go inside right now."

Luke turned away and saw two patrolmen's reflection off the window panes. They were checking a hand flyer and then the restaurant's clientele. Luke walked briskly inside to the WC.

He went in and locked the flimsy door. He sat on the toilet basin, surrounded by newsprint on the floor. Luke counted off five minutes and lifted his feet away from the roaches skittering underneath. He heard three knocks on the door and wiped his sweaty palms. He examined the narrow window; it'd be tight a squeeze. He tried to balance himself on the toilet bowl and almost slipped in. He tried to push himself through the narrow frame.

He heard another knock. His shoulders got stuck. He couldn't move either way. The pounding became more insistent. Luke wondered if this was how his trip would end—in tragi-comedy.

CHAPTER 28

The Rectory, Old Havana, Saturday, noon

SHE PEEKED AROUND THE CORNER OF the neoclassical building. Was the entrance being monitored by those street cleaners or the couple sitting on the outdoor bench? She passed by the wrought-iron fence and walked around the block. Fifteen minutes later she came back and the sweepers had moved on. A different woman was resting on the bench under the laurels.

She entered the Rectory and asked for Fr. Sebastian. The receptionist told her to await his return from morning mass. She walked around restlessly but enjoyed the Rectory's cool air.

Suddenly, she heard a familiar voice coming from the passageway, "Eloisa, what are you doing here? I didn't know you were a Catholic. I thought you favored the worship of the saints."

She almost threw up her modest breakfast. Taking extra seconds, she tried to compose herself.

"Why, Major, it's nice to see you again. I was reading the posters advertising a small-business course. My mother always wanted me to become a hairdresser. I might speak with the priest about it. How about you, do you come to mass here?"

"Every now and then are the operative words," Big Man said, dragging a comb through his salt-and-pepper hair. Like Eloisa, he turned his attention to the Rectory's floor, grappling for words.

Their silence was broken by another voice, "Jose Antonio and Eloisa—to what do I owe the pleasure? Be welcome here," said the priest, lighting up the anteroom with his bright smile.

"Umm," Big Man murmured, "It seems that we have a mutual interest in that *Cuba Emprende* small-business course you mentioned earlier. I came to enroll Dolores and encountered Eloisa here with similar thoughts."

"May I invite you both for tea? We have a little Brazilian *yerba mate* and brown sugar as well."

Eloisa and Big Man nodded and followed Fr. Sebastian up the marble stairs. They passed the open-mouthed assistant and into a library full of scholarly books. The priest used one teabag to make three individual cups: "This brown sugar was just delivered by a country priest. Please help yourselves."

Eloisa sat on one end of the scuffed-leather sofa and Big Man on the other. She crossed her legs and wondered what to say next. She really came to have a one-on-one conversation with Fr. Sebastian. She needed his advice about how to escape the General, Big Man, and her miserable life in Cuba. But now, she had to sit and play nice. She was tired of playing nice.

* * *

ELOISA DECIDED TO ATTEND THE 5 P.M. MASS, slipping in a few minutes late. The procession was halfway down the long aisle in the cathedral's nave. She sat in the back pew and bowed her head. She asked herself if God would listen to her. As she'd dabbled in Santeria and prayed to Venus, wouldn't He judge ever so harshly because of her lifestyle? Eloisa remembered the story her mother told about the Samaritan woman at the well. She also had many "husbands," but Jesus had shown her mercy. Maybe God would listen to her after all.

The church's lights were subdued. She closed her eyes and tried to clear her head. The General's image, unfortunately, reappeared. She wondered if Big Man would be sent to find her at that Centro apartment. The General expected her to be at his disposal 24/7. He'd likely be angry if she wasn't awaiting him. She'd left her cellphone there so he couldn't track her here.

The mass began and she muddled through words learned as a child. She followed what the others did—standing up, kneeling down. Catholic mass was confusing to her. Her favorite part of worship was giving the "sign of peace." She loved greeting and hugging other parishioners while saying, "Peace be with you." When communion was offered to the faithful, Eloisa did not go forward. Given the life she led, she felt unworthy. She remained on her knees.

After the blessing was given on the congregation, Fr. Sebastian walked down the aisle and caught her eye. A smile fluttered on his lips. She waited until other parishioners had had their chance to speak with him.

"Eloisa, another pleasant surprise. This must be my lucky day." She felt more upbeat with his words.

"Fr. Sebastian, I'm sorry about my hasty departure. I was hoping to speak with you privately. Would you have a moment?"

"Let's walk back to the Rectory and have more tea." The padre smiled at passersby who ogled Eloisa with interest. She followed him upstairs to the salon for more *yerba mate*.

Eloisa unburdened herself about her affair with the General, pushing her over the edge. She wanted desperately to escape Cuba. She told the padre about meeting the *Americano*, but getting a U.S. visa at the embassy was nearly impossible. She retained her passport, arranged by the General for their trip to Brazil. She confessed that she'd considered rafting out on a flimsy boat. She wanted out any way she could.

"Eloisa, did you know that the *Americano* knew your distant cousin, Ana, 30 years ago? He came to Cuba to find her. Unfortunately, I had to share the sad news that she'd passed away last month. As we speak, he may be in Holguin visiting her gravesite.

Eloisa erupted into tears. After the authorities had "black listed" Ana and her son, she'd barely maintained contact. Now Ana was gone, her last link to that side of the family. She felt her body shake as many regrets gushed out. Her family in Cuba was no more. She was alone again.

The padre touched her shoulder, provoking Eloisa to hug the priest. He held her until her tears had run their course. With calm restored, she listened to the priest describe his friend with ties to a Spanish cruise liner. He said that he'd be willing to speak with him about a passage out. In the meantime, he counseled Eloisa to keep up external appearances and not share her plan with anyone—including the *Americano*.

Eloisa wiped her eyes and sipped the tea. A plan was forming in her mind.

CHAPTER 29

Café Europa, Santa Clara, Saturday, noon

LUKE FELT SOMEONE TUG HIM from the narrow ledge. He was relieved to hear laughter. Junior had jumped ahead of the restroom queue and pushed through its flimsy door. He pulled Luke from his precarious perch. Together they excused themselves and walked quickly past the restless patrons.

"Let's go, *papá*. Pastor Ramón has arranged a ride to the coast. The police still are looking for you, but they've left the restaurant. Your airport photo is on the flyer. Keep your hat on and let's get sunglasses too."

Luke followed Junior out of Café Europa and turned onto a quieter street. His son bought a pair of cheap Chinese shades. Luke fit them on his pink nose.

He waved down a pedicab to take them to Santa Clara's First Presbyterian church. Luke inclined his head and looked away. The pedicab driver talked non-stop, swerving to avoid carts and pedestrians on bumpy roads. After 10 minutes, he dropped them at the church for a CUC.

Luke gazed up at four concrete pillars with a cross on top. Its symmetrical array of raw concrete would make Le Corbusier proud. "Brutalism" was how the famous French architect described this style.

It also seemed an appropriate description of the current state of Cuba. Luke found an opening through the church's wrought-iron fence and aimed for two sloping concrete blocks. He found the gate ajar.

Luke climbed the sandstone steps, his son following behind. They sat in the back pew, awaiting Ramón. In 10 minutes, the pastor arrived with a man of similar age and build. "Let me introduce you to Pastor Raul, who has a home church near Varadero. He plans to depart early Sunday morning and invites you to overnight at his home. How does that sound?"

Luke saw a nut-brown man of medium height, with hooded black eyes. He seemed lithe as a panther. "Thank you, Pastor Raul, that is very gracious. I am Lucas, and may I present my son, Lucas Junior. We're traveling together but keeping our relationship quiet." He exchanged a light hug with the shorter pastor, as did his son.

"Understood, Lucas, father and son. I've seen the flyer circulating on the streets about the American prof. It would be prudent to depart before people arrive for the afternoon service. We never know who might be listening. I'm aware of your situation."

Luke gave Ramón a tight hug, holding him an extra second. He'd gained confidence in this stand-up pastor. In a country of shifting alliances, he was trying to get a better sense of Pastor Raul. A friend of Ramón should be O.K., right? Luke and his son followed the pastor through the church and out the back door. They squeezed into the front seat of a chartreuse Lada, the back seat covered with New Testaments, CDs, and saltine crackers.

Raul's brows were furrowed, and his words were few. His was a different personality than the ebullient Ramón. As the sun drifted toward the western horizon, Luke hoped he could trust another "friend of a friend."

* * *

HE HEARD THE RUMBLE OF THUNDER and flashed back to the Santeria session. Sweating profusely, he had to think twice about where he was now.

He looked around the tiny room and saw his son on the straw mattress. A glimmer of light shone through a small window. Outside, someone was moving about. The door creaked open and a gas lantern flickered.

Luke sat up and sputtered "Buenos días" to the shadow. His son turned over in his sleep, inhaling the humid morning air.

"Buenos días, professor. It's 6 a.m. and we should depart. We'll have to take the back way to Varadero. It's a taxing drive," Raul's voice informed.

Luke got up first and left to wash his face in an outdoor basin perched on stilts. As he entered the outhouse, he heard pigs grunting on the other side. He smelled fried plantains coming from the neighbor's hut. His stomach reeled. He stepped over an anthill, brushing fire ants off his feet. He dodged a pile of tiles and went inside. A cock crowed twice.

He touched Junior's shoulder. "Buenos días, son. Pastor Raul is ready to leave for the coast. Are you ready for another adventure?"

"Of course, papá. As long as we face it together." Thunder sounded again and brought them to their feet. They joined Raul at a wooden table under a mango tree and breakfasted on tea, mangoes, and crackers. Parakeets chattered in the branches, and a gecko reconnoitered from above.

They put their packs into the trunk, taking special care with Junior's art. Luke sat in front with Raul, who wove through quiet streets to the edge of town. They soon were surrounded by cane fields and flowering trees. Clouds lumbered in from the coast.

"I'm avoiding the main East-West highway and its checkpoints. I'll follow the windy route to the north. You'll see more peasants and potholes, but fewer police," Raul said. He maneuvered the frail Lada to avoid a burro laden with coconuts. On these rural roads, the young pastor impressed Luke with his driving skills.

Luke drifted off, subconsciously following the car's tortuous moves. At Sagua la Grande, he awoke as Raul screeched on the breaks. Two oxen had broken free from their yoke, wallowing about the road.

They passed a neoclassical parish near la Libertad Park. Luke spied a woman frying plantains and asked to stop. He gave his son some CUCs to buy three plantain cups, wrapped in newsprint. Raul nodded thanks and crossed the Sagua River, turning west along Cuba's northern coast. He continued driving expertly through cane fields, stray animals, and pueblos.

"It's too bad we don't have time to visit, *papá*. Mogote de Jumagua's limestone caves are spectacular and close by. Maybe another time," Junior remarked wistfully.

Luke took a closer look at his son. He believed that he was doing right by bringing him out of Cuba. Yet how prepared was Junior to abandon the pastoral ways he'd known all of his life? If and when they made it out of Cuba, how would he adapt to the faster pace in America? Luke would assume all responsibility for his son's well-being but fretted about the path ahead.

CHAPTER 30

On the Bay of Cardenas, 20 miles south of Varadero, Sunday, 9 a.m.

THINGS WERE GOING SO WELL. Raul had driven through several dusty towns without hitting a burro, ox, or farmer. Slowly but surely, the pastor arrived without incident at the crossroads of the Northern Circuit and Route 101. Varadero was not far off.

Raul's cell tone broke the tranquil morning. He answered while maneuvering the Lada around a horse-driven cart. He listened intently, grunted twice, and rang off. After a minute, he said, "Professor, I have to make a stop in Cárdenas. A friend at church is having problems with local authorities and requires my presence. It would be unwise for you to come. The police will likely be there. I'll drop you on this road to Varadero but can't take you farther. Sorry, amigos."

And just like that, father and son found themselves standing at the intersection with their backpacks and paintings. Raul turned the Lada toward the Bay and gave a quick wave.

"What a guy," Luke grumbled, wondering how Raul and Ramon got along, given their different personalities. Luke took a deep breath and put on a confident face for his son.

"*Papá*, there should be a spot farther down where buses and *colectivos* stop for Varadero. It'd be best to keep your cap and sunglasses on just in case."

Luke walked along the paved road, the heat hammering him from above. His throat was dry again. He reverted back to counting his steps to break the monotony and stress. He turned off his mind and plodded on.

The earlier thunder clouds had dissipated toward the west. Without rain this morning to tamp down the temperature, the sun inhaled liquids from the earth, including Luke's sweat. As his water bottle was empty, Luke gleaned the remaining saliva in his mouth. A bus passed without slowing, even though Junior tried to wave it down.

Father and son walked for another 15 minutes and 420 steps. Junior stopped and pulled out a red bandana and lent it to Luke. Luke wiped his brow, returning it to his son, who put it over his head. "Maybe the red will attract a patriotic driver, *papá*." Luke was reminded of the red stripes of the Cuban flag, displayed on his cap.

They continued toward Varadero, their backs to the traffic. Junior walked with his left thumb raised to any vehicle approaching from behind. A truck rumbled by. Minutes passed and Luke wondered if they'd have to walk the whole 20 miles to the famous beach.

He heard a car decelerate. Junior turned around, shock on his face.

A dirty, white Lada crept by, driven by a man in a gray uniform. The car pulled ahead and stopped on the gravel. *"Policía"* showed through the dust on the car's side. Luke murmured to his son "I'm a Canadian tourist, and you're my guide to Varadero."

Junior greeted the policeman through the car's open right window. "Buenos días, officer. The summer sun is intense. Can you spare us any water? My Canadian tourist is not used to our Cuban heat."

"Buenos dias, young man. I'll get you some filtered water for you and the tourist." The mulatto officer appeared a little older than Junior but was shorter and thicker around the waist. He wore the questioning look of a policeman. He passed a water bottle to Junior. "Where are you heading?"

"Muchas gracias, officer. We missed the bus to Varadero and are trying to hitch a ride. Is it very far from here?"

The policeman looked them over. "It's several kilometers away. If you'd like, I could give you a lift to the beach's turnoff. Later, I'll be heading West along *la Via Blanca*, the coastal road to Havana."

"How gracious of you, officer," effused Junior. Luke chimed in accented Spanish, "*Muchas gracias, señor. Merci beaucoup.*"

The officer opened the front door to Junior and said, "Señor, you may sit in the back." Luke took a deep breath and wrestled the backpacks onto the seat. He drank from the water bottle but continued to sweat—out of thirst or fear, he knew not which.

He avoided the policeman's eyes reflecting off the rearview mirror. He wiped his brow again but kept on his cap and sunglasses. He was grateful that his son kept the conversation going with the officer about the heat, baseball, and a tropical storm heading their way. Luke rested his eyes to avoid the policeman's stare.

"Señor," said a familiar voice, wooing Luke awake. He opened his eyes and felt his son's light touch on his healing shoulder. He winced but tried to smile.

"We're almost at the crossroads to Varadero. The officer would like to know where you'd like to go. Is it that Spanish hotel chain?"

"Umm, yes," Luke replied in broken Spanish, "I think its name is Meliá."

The policeman acknowledged Luke's answer by downshifting, causing the Lada to shudder. He pulled over before the crossroad but seemed reluctant to let them out. Junior came to the rescue, offering lavish praise, "Señor, would you mind if I commended you to your supervisor? You are an example of a true comrade." Luke thought his son deserved an "A" in creative dramatics.

"Very well, be on your way. There are many hotels along the beach, some run by Spanish and other international chains. Beware of the occasional pickpockets and riptides."

Father and son thanked him again and hoisted their packs. They turned right toward Varadero, as cars whizzed by. Luke looked over his shoulder at the policeman's Lada still parked at the junction.

They sauntered up the *Autopista Sur* to a covered stand, where uniformed cooks and doormen shifted under its shifting shade. When Luke turned around again, the Lada was gone. An off-beige coach rumbled up and screeched on its brakes.

Luke followed the workers into an open-windowed bus, similar to the one he'd taken in Cacacúm. His son paid in Cuban pesos, not CUCs, like the rest of the passengers. The bus pitched forward with a herky-jerky motion, passing hotel billboards along Varadero's expansive beach. The turquoise waters captured Luke's imagination. He yearned to dive in.

Luke saw cheap-looking motels and hotels, including one for "Adults only." The farther they proceeded along the beach, the more elegant the hotels appeared. In the distance, Luke saw a high-rise and pointed to the *Meliá Internacional Varadero* sign. His son shouted, "Driver, please stop at this hotel." Each grabbed their packs and exited the vibrating coach.

Luke led them to a roadside bar and ordered seltzer waters with fresh limes to quench their thirst. Under its thatched roof, Luke found a spot of shade and two wicker chairs.

"Junior, let's discuss our next move. As you recall, my reservation at the Hotel Nacional was canceled after the airport inspector held me up. The desk clerk found me a room at his friend's apartment. He invited me to join this tour to the Meliá resort today. An older couple from Miami and some American coeds may also be present. There also will be the *Cubatur* guide.

"It's 11 o'clock, so they should have arrived. Let's get our 'stories' straight. The tour agent may be on the inspector's payroll. Let's not present ourselves as father and son. That would put you at risk. It'd be best for you to continue as my guide from Santa Clara.

"OK, *papá*. I'll just be Junior, the tour guide. Let's say that we met at one of the galleries there."

"*Excelente,* Junior. Thanks again for engaging the policeman. You saved me from answering his questions. This morning, please represent yourself as a local artist, trying to make a few CUCs as a guide."

"With pleasure, *papá*. I forgot to mention that I used to act with Holguin's theatre guild. I played Romeo in that classic play. Today, I look forward to serve in another role. For *mamá*, I helped several tour groups to Cuba's northern keys—especially Canadians. I loved working with her." Junior's voice faded, as he gazed out to sea.

Luke touched his son's arm, causing each to recollect how Ana had touched their lives. They finished their drinks in silence.

"Son, let me give you Fr. Sebastian's phone number at Havana's Rectory, close to the Cathedral in Old Havana. I'm also going to write him a note. Don't take offense, but we may have to split up, especially if the *Cubatur* agent asks many questions. Remember that I am a 'wanted man' according to the police flyer. Here are my last 100 CUCs and 100 dollars, should you need to grab a bus or collective cab back to Havana.

"This is our alternative plan, if things get squirrely. I will signal you with my fingers in a 'V.' If I do, please excuse yourself immediately. You should be able to find a bus to Havana. Seek out Fr. Sebastian in the Rectory in Old Havana. Understood?"

Junior frowned, batted his eyes, and murmured, "I understand, *papá.*"

Luke continued, "When you reach the priest, have him telephone Señor Jose to say, 'The package has arrived.' The line may have another listener, so we must take precautions. Understood, my son?"

"Yes, *papá*, but let's hope that we don't have to split up. I feel safer with you."

The hotel's tree-lined driveway and bright-green golf course had the look of a deluxe resort. The five-star hotel sprouted wings, like spokes in a wheel, which emanated from a chic lobby.

Luke led them up the long driveway, where Mercedes and Impalas rested near the grand portico. Feeling self-conscious with his shifting pack and dripping shirt, Luke made his way to the hotel's sliding door. He passed through a potpourri of bellhops, security guards, and tourists speaking English, French, and German. The middle-aged doorman frowned. "How may I help you, señores?"

"We've come to join the *Cubatur* group from the Hotel Nacional. Have you seen them, señor?" Luke looked the doorman straight in the eye.

"It may be the tour that just arrived. Check inside the main lobby or by the pool." The sliding doors opened, and Luke and his son entered an immense circular concourse of tourists in guayabera and Aloha shirts. The lobby seemed more like an upscale train station in the tropics. People milled around in every direction. The A/C felt great.

He recognized Arturo in the far corner, chatting with other tourists. As he approached the hotel clerk, he heard from behind, "Our long-lost visitor, where have you been hiding out? I've heard interesting stories about you, professor."

Luke turned and came face-to-face with the agent, dressed in tight jeans and a tighter blue shirt. A '*Cubatur*' lanyard swung recklessly around his neck. The guide's eyes jumped between the attractive coeds and the burly security guards making the rounds. He had a Cuba Libre in his hand.

The young guide forced a smile on his tanned face. His eyes, however, told Luke a different story. They switched between suspicion and aggression, a toxic combination.

Luke took a step backwards and glanced quickly at Junior. Pivoting toward his son, he raised his right hand, showing two fingers, alternating between the sign of peace and the sign of victory.

Junior acknowledged with a thumbs up. He now had to play the lead role of his life—for both of them.

CHAPTER 31

Ministry of Interior's conference room, Havana, Sunday, noon

THE CLOCK STRUCK 12 TIMES.

Twelve men and one woman gathered around the mahogany table, looking expectantly at the heavyset man at its head. His leathery skin contrasted with his Navy whites. He emitted a troubled air.

No one was joking around. All he heard was the relentless ticking of the nautical clock. Big Man thought the Vice Admiral's silence melodramatic. After Friday's impromptu meeting about black-market gasoline, he fretted that another crisis was afoot. Had Raul fallen ill again?

"Gentlemen and Maria, thanks for coming. I thought you should hear the news first before President Diaz-Canel makes an announcement later on." He gazed fondly toward the bank assistant, dressed today in a pink pantsuit. "Maria, please share the latest news from the *Banco Central de Cuba.*"

She pushed back her abundant bangs and forced a smile. "Thank you, Admiral. As mentioned last week, our external accounts have not fared well. The chief culprits continue to be U.S. sanctions, declining tourist revenues, and less-subsidized Venezuelan oil. This month, 'black market' activity is surging among the *doleros* or dollar marketeers. On the QT, private tourist agencies have accelerated their exchange activities, buying dollars and selling CUCs. The rate has been one-to-one for years, but now the dollar has appreciated 10 percent.

"The Central Bank soon will announce that the Cuban Convertible peso or CUC will transition next year into the Cuban peso. One CUC today is exchanged at 24 CUPs or Cuban pesos. The Central Bank will return to the policy of 2004, permitting all retail establishments to accept U.S. dollar transactions.

"The Central Bank concludes that such measures will entice more foreign currency into official coffers. We have monitored Venezuela's experiment to use dollars to settle transactions and have seen its hard-currency balances rise. We plan to pull the rug from under the feet of the dollar marketeers. Our dual-currency system of decades has given middlemen room to wheel and deal. It will soon disappear. *Atención*—be prepared.

"We recognize that this is a major change. After the announcement, the government plans to assist the transition by increasing subsidies to some workers. After an adjustment period, things should settle down. Cuba finally will have a more tenable currency. Any questions, gentlemen?"

Big Man sat in stunned silence. What would happen to his and Dolores's savings in CUCs, painstakingly gathered over many years? What would these CUCs be worth after the official communique? Though nominally one-to-one with the U.S. dollar, people like him likely would dump the short-lived Cuban Unit of Currency in favor of the gringo's Ben Franklins.

Others around the table mulled over the assistant's words with long faces. Only the Inspector appeared taciturn. Big Man thought he knew why. He'd heard from several sources that the thin man kept dollar accounts in Panama for "intelligence activities."

"So, what steps does the Central Bank propose to stem speculation in the dollar?" inquired the Inspector through tight lips. His thin fingers pointed upward as if in prayer. Big Man had never seen him inside a church or synagogue but noticed him going into and out of many brothels.

The assistant continued to caress her chestnut hair through slender fingers. Big Man speculated that she was trying to hypnotize the men in the room. If so, she almost succeeded with him.

After a few seconds, she admitted, "Stores and tourist agencies will be able to accept CUCs through 2020 but likely will opt for dollars or Euros. Hopefully, our foreign currency levels will rise. As you know, a dual-currency system is difficult to sustain."

She looked down at the other end of the table toward the Vietnamese diplomat, who sat motionless and untroubled. He'd told Big Man over breakfast that he received his salary in U.S. dollars and not in CUCs.

No one else braved a question. The old hands probably were evaluating how this change would impact their personal lives. They retained perks as military officials but not the largesse of the Family or their favored ones. Big Man observed a sea of frowns around the table.

The Vice Admiral pondered a minute and offered: "On the good-news front, we've broken up a gang of gas smugglers in Santa Clara and Camaguey. We're planning to have the culprits face a public trial. However, some official drivers have been implicated, and Raul is demanding retribution.

"Does anyone have more news to report?"

The question reverberated inside the conference room. Big Man said nothing and remained in shock. Only the sound of the ticking clock filled the spacious room.

The Vice Admiral sighed again. "As to the dissidents, Jose Daniel Ferrer got interviews published again in the international press.

The Inspector is planning a surprise for him next week in Santiago's compound. Get ready for more outcry from the likes of Amnesty International, *The New York Times,* and *El Pais.*

"Inspector, anything else?"

"We have been able to penetrate Ferrer's Google email traffic and intercepted his hand-written notes. We've also secured a witness who will testify that Ferrer struck him. We will charge this troublemaker with assault and let him feel the full force of Cuban justice. As the newspaper worms always seem to find a way to snitch information, I've asked the prison commandant to rotate outside soldiers into the prison and move the regulars out. That should keep a tighter lid on the dissidents' favorite spokesman.

"As to the blogger Yoani and her husband in Havana, we've slowed down *14ymedio's* Internet connection. They're now booting up in public Wi-Fi plazas, using stringers to do their legwork. We're tracking her husband and daughter's movements around town and have learned more about their sources. As you're aware, this website is blocked inside Cuba but finds its way abroad. The international press and Amnesty monitor *14ymedio's* status closely. But they are on borrowed time."

The Inspector paused. The Vice Admiral prompted, "Is that all, Inspector? I plan to speak with the president shortly." The admiral looked at his Rolex and at the pert bank assistant.

"One of the worms from that Miami foundation has been in touch with Ferrer, so we'll pull him in for questioning. We'll do so when we arrest Ferrer next week in Santiago. Get ready for an uproar. If he's not careful, we may use him as a guinea pig like we have other prisoners.

"As you may have heard, a joint Cuban-Chinese medical team is testing Interferon Alpha 2B treatment with prisoner volunteers. They are hoping that it will prove antidote to this novo coronavirus. It has probably already come to Cuba, so beware*!*"

Big Man wondered what this was about as he didn't follow foreign press reports. Should he be concerned about the Inspector's warning? One more thing to worry about. He saw Dong raise his eyebrow and decided to ask him afterwards.

"As to the American prof, he was last spotted in Varadero by a highway patrolman. He was traveling with some Cuban artist. We'll find out what he's up to and surprise him when he returns to Havana."

"Thank you, comrades. Please help yourself to espresso and Havana Club next door. Enjoy the rest of your Sunday afternoon," the Vice Admiral intoned. He lifted himself out of the large chair and offered his arm to the chic bank assistant. They didn't stop for coffee.

Big Man glanced at Dong in bewilderment but said nothing. The Chinese representative did not attend today's session, despite the P.R.C.'s many loans to Cuba. Should he be concerned by the spy's absence?

He joined the other silent men on their ride down the elevator and exited onto the Plaza of the Revolution. Big Man looked at Che's angry gaze down from the concrete obelisk. The revolutionary hero must be turning in his grave. The government was about to abandon the Cuban Unit of Currency and embrace the U.S. dollar.

Neither he nor his fellow Cubans would escape its consequences. It was time to batten down the hatches. Another type of storm was brewing. He had no clue how it would end.

CHAPTER 32

Varadero Beach, Sunday, 1 p.m.

LUKE WATCHED THE HOTEL CLERK with pride, reminding him of
students experiencing their "ah, ha" moment in class. Arturo
looked so pleased, afloat on the rolling waves. This was Luke's tried-
and-true way to teach beginners how to swim. First to float, then
to kick, next hand strokes, and finally to breathe in and out. In the
buoyant sea, Arturo showed off his elementary backstroke to the
cheering American tourists.

Only the *Cubatur* agent glowered from the shore. He sat solo on
the beach towel of Hotel Meliá, his Cuba Libre having spilled. The
American coeds and Miami couple left to encourage the hotel clerk
splashing in the surf. Afterwards, the girls invited Arturo to build
castles in Varadero's pearly sand.

Luke left the group and dove under the breaking waves. He did the
butterfly and then plunged underwater. Ocean waters cleansed him,
washing worldly woes away. He dove down, touching the sandy bottom, and saw a Goliath grouper beneath a coral reef. Luke swam closer
but spotted a moray eel. It was time to say adiós to Varadero's depths.

He rose to the surface and turned onto his back. He closed his
eyes, the swells lulling him to reflect. Luke marveled at his son's moxie

in excusing himself from the tour without raising alarm. He was a born actor and an accomplished painter. Though his son proceeded well in the countryside, Luke hoped that he'd arrive to urban Havana without incident.

A rogue wave hit Luke, upsetting his reverie. He opened his eyes and saw that he had floated 100 yards from shore. Belatedly, he recalled the policeman's warning about Varadero's riptides. He looked back at the beach and saw stick-figures waving at him. A different hotel drifted into view.

Luke tried not to panic. He began swimming parallel to the shore. On every incoming wave, he bodysurfed a few yards before the current reversed. Luke tried to preserve his energy until the next breaker in. Sometimes, waves would rise up, making him adjust on the fly.

He was making headway to the beach but was sliding toward the end of Varadero. He had to make it ashore before the peninsula came to an end. If not, the current would pull him out to the open sea.

He swam with all his might as the point was coming up fast. The swells lost regularity, spinning whirlpools in odd directions. In desperation, Luke flung himself onto a huge roller and flew over its breaking crest. The wave pummeled him, tossing him around like a ragdoll. He didn't have a clue which way was up or down.

The riptide returned with ferocity, though Luke did all he could to resist. He bumped into a submerged rock and grabbed onto a crevice. He held on for dear life. Saltwater pushed its way into his mouth. How much longer could he hold out?

The tide changed and a monster wave hurled Luke off the rock, making him somersault underwater. More seawater gushed down his throat, making Luke fear that he was drowning. With all he had left, he swam for his son, he swam for Ana, he swam for his life.

Another comber crashed, throwing him onto the sand. Luke spewed seawater and gasped for air. He dragged himself ashore and crawled on all fours. He was a human animal trying to survive. He threw up more water, lost his balance, and flopped about like a fish.

He collapsed at the end of Varadero's shore, the waves lapping at his feet. A seagull pecked seaweed from his hair. Luke drifted off to an unknown place.

* * *

He felt a heavy force pressing down on him. Pain surged inside his chest, though it came and went like the tide. Had his overconfidence as a swimmer pushed him down to the first circle of Purgatory? There, human pride was expunged in never-ending flames. The burning pressure persevered. Then someone's hand touched him.

His eyes popped open, and a geyser shot out of his mouth. The wiry, bronzed man on top of him, threw back his head and laughed. Luke did not think his predicament funny but was heartened by smiling faces. Maybe he'd escaped Purgatory after all. He heard a human chorus cry, "*Viva!*"

"Professor, what a swimming lesson you gave us, as well as a bout of fright. You must have swum over a mile to reach this spit of sand. The fisherman saw you wash up on the beach and helped bring you back to life. What an extraordinary feat by both of you. Someone upstairs wants you around," exclaimed Arturo, raising his arms high.

Luke focused on the people above, including the coeds and the middle-aged couple from Miami. A few locals and tourists rounded out the group. Luke grabbed the fisherman's strong hand and rose to his feet, giving him a tight hug. "Muchas gracias, señor. May I thank you by your name?"

"I call myself Pedro. I'm glad I could lend you a hand. It's marvelous to see you up and regaining color. You were so pale when I pulled you from the surf."

"I am indebted to you, Pedro. My name is Lucas. I've met several fishermen during my stay in Cuba. How may I repay your kindness?"

The brown man looked down and simply said, "Maybe you'd like to buy some fish, Señor Lucas? If you like red snapper or even this *centolla* crab, you could enjoy a tasty lunch."

Luke saw the huge orange crustacean with extended claws held by the fisherman's veined hands. "Arturo, can you lend me some CUCs? I'd like to buy some seafood from Pedro. We could grill them for lunch over the fire pit on the beach. What do you think?"

"With pleasure, professor," the clerk replied and gave the fisherman a 10-CUC bill and a handful of Cuban pesos. The fisherman signaled to a hearty black woman wearing a red bandana, who observed them from a beachside hut. She carried down a wicker basket, followed by a boy, lugging a bunch of yellow-green plantains.

She plopped a large towel around Luke's shoulder, wiped away the water and gave him a big hug. He flinched when she touched his right shoulder but didn't care. Her face radiated kindness. She reminded him of the other fisherman's wife in Havana.

Luke examined his right shoulder and saw that the stitches held fast. The doctor in Camaguey had done well, despite the painful ordeal. So far, so good.

He helped the woman gather driftwood and built a bonfire in an open pit. His Boy Scout training kicked in again. Luke luxuriated in its warmth. The woman lathered the snapper and *centolla* with canola oil, fresh lime juice, and a sprinkle of salt. Luke's stomach sounded off.

He helped her to remove the plantain skins and cut them in half lengthwise. He placed them on the grill and wiped saliva from his lips. He drizzled the woman's special concoction over the sizzling plantains, turned them over, and removed them from the fire after five minutes.

The fisherman brought out a bottle of homemade rum and passed it around the impromptu crowd. Maybe it was the savory seafood or camaraderie under the afternoon sun, but to Luke, it was the best meal he'd ever had.

As he was sucking the last morsels from the *centolla* crab, a shadow blocked the western sky. The *Cubatur* agent strode toward them, forcing a smile. "You're at it again, professor, but this time at your peril. Beware of Cuba's cross currents, very different from your Puget Sound.

"Travelers, it's time to go back to Havana. It's time to face the music."

CHAPTER 33

Traveling west on la Via Blanca to Havana, Sunday, 6 p.m.

THE *CUBATUR* BUS WOUND THROUGH CHECKPOINTS along the coastal road toward the setting sun. Often a few CUCs passed hands. When the highway patrolmen boarded to inspect inside, Luke lowered his eyes. Hopefully, the cheap shades would hide his anxious look.

Luke heard the guide extol the "*Playas del Este*" and saw signs for the beaches of *Santa Maria, Tarará,* and *Bucaranao.* He thought how pleasant it'd be to return someday and relax with his son—as unlikely as it seemed. He wondered if Junior had made it to Havana and found refuge with the priest. He felt isolated without his son or any cell. He saw the sign of San Carlos and San Ambrosio Seminary peek through the date palms at kilometer 13.

Lulled by the bus's motion, Luke was about to close his eyes. He felt the bus slow down and heard one of the American coeds inquire, "What's that hidden behind the trees? I see guards holding guns at the gate." The blue bus passed a nondescript entrance, surrounded by trees. A couple guards glanced their way, wielding AK-47s.

The guide frowned. "That's the Eastern Compound, where we lock up the bad guys. The guards have a hard time keeping these criminals in check. There are some mean hombres inside."

The balding attorney, Mitch from Miami, piped up: "Yes, the Eastern Compound, or *El Combinado del Este,* holds thousands of inmates, including 'criminals' like journalists and political dissidents. Sometimes there are riots inside. The prison is overcrowded and is said to be the largest in our hemisphere. I've heard reports that they conduct medical experiments on the prisoners too." His half-moon glasses jangled around his neck, as the bus rolled on.

The Cubatur agent glowered. "That's a gross exaggeration. Remember that our legal system is different here than in Miami. Let's not forget that. It's best to stay on tour and not to freelance about." He caught Luke's eye and drew his hand slowly across his throat.

Luke turned away and placed the hat over his face. The adrenalin rush that had saved him from the surf abandoned him to deeper slumber. He had weird dreams of moray eels morphing into snarky guides, holding him underwater. A mermaid with emerald eyes rescued him, guiding him to the surface.

"Professor, we've arrived at last," said the desk clerk. "You're back at the Hotel Nacional. I hope you enjoyed your siesta. I heard you murmuring about someone, maybe an old flame?

"Thanks for teaching me how to swim. I'm going to pass on your lessons to my stepbrother and sister. I am so glad you survived your swimming ordeal. This was the most exciting trip I ever had to Varadero beach. I'm so happy you were able to join us."

Luke gave Arturo, the coeds, and the Miami couple tight hugs. "Please get in touch if you ever land in Miami, professor," offered the upbeat attorney, Mitch. Luke avoided the *Cubatur* agent, who murmured something to a heavyset man in guayabera. He grabbed his pack and walked briskly down the hotel driveway.

Someone followed him behind. Luke almost jumped when a hand touched his right shoulder. There appeared Johnny, like Houdini, with his constant smile. What was he doing here? The red-and-white beads of *Changó* swirled around the young man's neck.

* * *

It was all Luke could do to keep his cool. He regarded Johnny's smile but wondered what lay behind his shiny teeth. He begged off a drink and conversation, though Johnny followed him to the apartment building's door. There, Luke drew the line. He did not invite the pushy teen up or accept his offer to "see more sights." He was exhausted and simply desired rest. "Adiós," he bade, hoping that would be the last of him. Luke climbed three flights of stairs and heard a creak from below.

Out of courtesy, he knocked on Jose's door. The older man opened it slightly, then wider, to let Luke in. He was alone in his apartment. While Jose's eyes remained kind, they flickered with concern.

"*Que pasa, Señor José?*" Luke asked. The pink spread and sheets smelled like they'd been recently laundered. A warm breeze blew in from the Malecón.

"More or less, professor. While you were traveling, you had an unusual visitor. She is the head of our neighborhood Committee for the Defense of the Revolution. This busybody questioned me about where you had gone. I told her that you were seeing a friend in the countryside but thought her coming a bit odd. Did I speak correctly on your behalf?"

Luke tried to hide his shock but inclined his head. He didn't know how to respond. To fill the silence, he took out the remaining coffee his son had brought from Cacocúm. "*Señor José*, thank you for the heads up. Please excuse me if I've caused your family any trouble.

"Here's some coffee from Holguin province for you and your kind wife."

"No problem, professor," Jose responded gravely. His eyes lit up at the coffee. He gave Luke a long hug. Luke liked this man and his family and hoped he hadn't put them at risk.

As dusk settled over Havana, Luke released a yawn. "*Señor José*, it's been a long day. Do you mind if I turn in early?"

"Of course, professor, but let me warm up some *ropa vieja*, which my wife prepared today. It is my favorite dish. We celebrated our 40th wedding anniversary in style. Please sit down with me."

"Congratulations, José." Luke obliged and sat around the worn Formica table. His host heated up the shredded-beef casserole, which cast off enticing aromas. Luke inhaled the savory scents of garlic, onions, and olive oil. José served the typical Cuban dish with *Moros*. Luke loved the mix of rice with black beans and the sweet banana *maduros* too. The homemade *ropa vieja* tasted so much better than its "exotic" variety in Holguin.

Though Luke's body cried for rest, he engaged in small talk with his amiable host. He also shared his tale about his ordeal on Varadero's beach. José listened intently and shook his head. "Professor, you must take better care of yourself.

"I forgot to tell you that I received a cryptic message from someone who's telephoned here before. I recognized his steady voice. He said to tell you that 'The package was received'—does that mean anything to you?"

Luke couldn't suppress his relief and touched Jose's arm, "Thank you for sharing that message."

José went to the cupboard and withdrew a bottle of what looked like rustic aguardiente. He poured double shots of "white lightening" into two glasses, raising his arm in a toast.

"To your health, professor," to which Luke replied, "To many more anniversaries for you and your wife. *Salud!*"

With his stomach warm and good news from his son, Luke got ready for bed. He wished José, "Buenas noches" and gave him another hug.

He pushed the more ominous news away and let sleep overtake him. The clock showed 8:05 p.m. and darkness invaded his room.

CHAPTER 34

Vedado, Havana, Monday, 3:35 a.m.

They came for him at night. He was tossing and turning on the narrow bed when he awakened to the banging door.

He heard José's voice call out, "How may I help you?" No response came back, but heavy steps pounded on the squeaky floors. A man demanded, "Where is the gringo?"

Luke had heard that voice before.

The door slammed open to Luke's stuffy room and rebounded off the wall. "So, you've decided to conduct research in the field, without our permission? I warned you, professor. You can't hide from me. My canaries are everywhere. You won't escape the Cuban state. You'll now have a chance to check out the interior of a different kind of place. Get up!"

Luke rubbed his eyes. In front of him towered that thin man with his snarky smile. It was the same inspector from the airport who had interrogated him a week ago. Though the room was dark, he wore the same guayabera and Ray-Ban glasses. He inclined his head as if to say, "I told you so."

The Inspector turned on the overhead light. Two hefty cohorts, a man and a woman, grabbed Luke's arms, yanking him from bed.

"Put on your pants to cover your pallid legs. Let's not shock the keeper of your new abode. Say adiós to Jose's hospitality in Vedado."

They released him to slip on his Levi's and Patagonia shirt. Then they cuffed his wrists behind his back and pushed him through the kitchen and living room. Jose's family stood cowering in the corner. When the police turned their backs, Luke saw the older man cross himself.

Luke stumbled down the stairs, pushed by calloused hands on each shoulder. The Inspector led the way to a black SUV outside. The woman shoved Luke into the back, where he bumped his head against a steel grate. Luke saw lights though the night was overcast.

This was beyond a bad dream.

The SUV revved its engines and spun its wheels. Maybe this was the Inspector's reminder to people peeking out their windows. Do not to mess with the powers-that-be. The SUV surged toward the Malecón and turned away from Old Havana. It sped west, retracing the route taken by the cabbie and his brother a mere week ago. Their warning about the fortress, where nights were days and days were nights, haunted Luke's mind.

As Luke bounced around in the SUV's back cage, he recollected another ride taken years ago. After college, he'd joined the Navy to qualify for an elite force but washed out. He'd failed the P.O.W. escape training in an undisclosed location. His task was to survive "off the land" for 24 hours. If caught, the prisoner would be submitted to intense interrogation. Luke was apprehended within 12 hours.

The ride back to the naval compound was as rough as the one in the back of this Chinese SUV. Then as now, twin devils reared their ugly heads

The first devil, *Shame*, first visited Luke years ago for not making the grade. Luke tried to bury that feeling deep inside. Now, *Shame* escaped its boundaries and hounded him again. With his hands cuffed and his body ricocheting off the grate, Luke's image reflected off the blackened windows. He had no professorial airs now. What would the university dean and colleagues say when they discovered his sorry state? He could almost hear someone ridicule him as a "bridge builder."

The closer the SUV approached the prison, the more Luke's confidence slipped away. He sensed the second devil close in, pushing *Shame* away. *Self-doubt* clawed its way back, making Luke distrust his ability to survive. After all, he'd washed out once before. How would he hold up against a harsher interrogator? This time he would be in the hands of a foreign power and not someone from the U.S. Navy. The devil whispered into his ear, "It'd be easier to give up."

His intention to take his son abroad began to fade. Luke was way in over his head. How could he honor his promise to Ana, let alone his son? One university skeptic had christened him "quixotic." Maybe he was right.

Now, a third and more powerful devil thrust the other two aside. It called itself *Fear* and squeezed Luke's right shoulder at will. Egged on by the other devils, *Fear* opened the floodgates to a widening black hole into Luke's soul. It called itself *Abyss*.

The SUV turned abruptly off the highway onto *Avenida Independencia* and entered a dead-end street. To Luke's right rose the citadel, surrounded by a steel enclosure. A simple sign read "*Ministerio del Interior.*" When Luke viewed *la Villa Marista* prison in daylight, he had felt unease. This early morning, its malevolence grabbed him by the throat. As they approached the barrier, Luke tried to resist darker spirits pulling him down.

Two uniformed soldiers with AK-47s let the SUV pass through. Someone must have forewarned them, as they didn't bat an eye. They closed the gate, locking the chain link-fence behind them. As they drove by, Luke heard an owl mock him from a ceiba tree.

They approached the penumbra of a two-story building, a faint light escaping its side. The SUV headed for the entranceway and jerked to a stop. The Inspector's cohorts removed Luke from the cage and impelled him inside the compound. The guards marched him down the ochre corridor, passing many steel-plated doors. One door opened and a guard pulled a prisoner out. The guardsman whistled. The policewoman holding Luke commanded, "Face the wall." The other prisoner groaned and brushed Luke's elbow passing down the narrow hall.

Luke counted 162 steps until they detained him before an open, steel door. "You are now prisoner 217," she said. The guard removed the cuffs and propelled him into the cell. "Welcome to the penthouse, *Americano*. Your fellow countryman stayed here a few years back. Maybe you can beat his record of survival in Cuba." They slammed the door, which reverberated on its bolted frame.

Luke recollected how Alan Gross, an American USAID worker, was arrested in 2009. Cuba's presiding Minister Raul Castro orchestrated his trial. He'd been accused of "crimes against the state" for bringing Wi-Fi equipment to Havana's Jewish community. Gross had languished inside the *Villa Marista* and other prisons until 2014. Obama's diplomatic rapprochement encouraged Castro to release him in a "goodwill" gesture. The prisoner's health suffered serious decline. Would Luke follow his course? If so, for how long?

He looked around "the penthouse," measuring 10-by-12 feet. It was about the size of Jose's guestroom but had no window, only wall vents spewing musty air. There was no breeze from the Malecón. The overhanging lamp, enclosed inside a wire mesh, beat steadily on Luke's bruised head. There was no water or chair inside, but cockroaches knocked about its corners.

After minutes of walking back and forth, Luke's tired body slid down onto the black-and-white checkerboard floor. Despite being detained in a soundproofed space, the three devils screamed loudly into the ear of Prisoner 217.

CHAPTER 35

Villa Marista, Havana, Monday, 5 a.m.

"**G**ET UP, PRISONER 217! You're not on holiday in Vedado or Varadero. This is not a place for rest and relaxation. Stand up. It's time for you to perform."

The Inspector grimaced at the gringo's arrogance. Never did he permit detainees to loll about when they first arrived. It was he who established the ground rules, not the other way around. He fancied observing what a detainee would do when overwhelmed by physical and mental fatigue. Would the gringo cry, whimper, grovel, or just pass out? At first, each prisoner reacted differently, but each one would eventually submit. The Inspector stood up straight and reminded himself that he was the alpha male inside the *Villa*.

He observed the gringo struggle to his feet, tottering as he walked around the narrow space. The Inspector liked to keep his quarry in suspense. It was his decision when he'd open the door and haul him into the interrogation room. He was curious to see what the gringo would do and how long he'd stay standing.

Looking through the portal, the Inspector saw a man of similar age. The thin man stood a few inches taller. The gringo's eyes were blue, like his American jeans, and his manner was subdued. Let him amble more and see how long he'll keep his cool. The *Americano* wavered but steadied himself against the wall.

He speculated what this man's life was like in the States. He wore no wedding band but what did that mean anymore? Did he earn enough as a professor to support a family, children, or lovers on the side?

He recalled cross-examining exiles returning to Havana about their lives in Miami. They touted their material comforts, homes, and lifestyle. When pressed, each one confessed how hard it was to hustle a small piece of turf in Hialeah, Houston, or some nondescript suburb. He wondered how he'd do in a capitalist country, where his livelihood was not guaranteed. Havana had less "stuff" than Miami, but here he knew the rules.

He felt proud that he had excelled inside the revolutionary state. Wasn't he an example of Cuban "success"? It was he who had become chief Inspector of Havana, securing favor, perks, and power for himself. Dissidents like Ferrer or troublesome gringos soon would bend to his will.

His memory drifted back five years when his last wife divorced him. He didn't give a damn when she rafted out with their impudent son and other "worms." Good riddance! She and 10 others had drowned in the Florida Straits. Thanks to the U.S. Coast Guard, his son had managed to survive. An informant recently saw him promenading down Ocean Drive in South Beach with a motley group of *amiguitos*. There, he'd embraced a gay lifestyle. What did the Inspector care?

His memory flashed back to his son's last words, "You only care about yourself. You don't give a damn for me, my mother, or anyone else. I'm ashamed to be your son."

The Inspector slammed shut that door of reminiscence. He turned his attention back to the detainee and checked his watch. It'd been a while since the gringo had been inside the cell. He was barely holding out. The prisoner tried grabbing the wall but slowly slid to the checkerboard floor. By the Inspector's watch, it'd been 57 minutes since prisoner 217 set foot inside. He set a new record for someone under his watch. He wondered if the gringo was former military. He'd try to find out.

The *Americano* then did something unexpected. He fell to his knees and bowed his head. Was he trying to pray? The Inspector couldn't remember the last time he'd entered any church, though he'd attended a Santeria session or two. Did this wishful thinker really believe that anyone would intervene in his behalf? That this prison used to be a Marist school years ago was irrelevant. Today, it only hosted "enemies of the state." It was he who'd decide the prisoner's fate and no one else.

The Inspector's English was passable, though he couldn't quite catch what detainee 217 was babbling. He saw sweat rolling down the prisoner's face and his arms keeping him from falling over. He heard the gringo cry out for some shepherd to save him from the valley of death. What was that about?

Just then, a guard rang him from outside. Two intelligence officials had arrived and asked to see the Inspector with urgency. He looked at his Rolex, whose hands pointed straight up and down. For a few prisoners, it'd be reveille at *Villa Marista*. Who on earth would arrive at this hour?

* * *

THE INSPECTOR LEFT HIS POST and headed to the entranceway to check out the untimely visitors. His face must have broadcast surprise when he spied two known agents. Quickly he retrieved his official smile.

"*Que pasa*, Big Man and Señor Dong? To what do I owe the pleasure? If I remember correctly, we just met a few hours ago."

"Buenos días, Inspector," said Big Man more courteously than usual. "I believe that you, like I, was curious as to why the gringo was so fixated on Ochoa's hometown. Señor Dong shared some information that I thought would interest you."

"Good morning, Inspector," said the Vietnamese diplomat, bowing slightly. "I discovered from a source that the professor had a love affair with Ochoa's niece many years ago. Her name was Ana, and she returned to her hometown. The prof came to Cuba to find her. His meeting at the University of Havana was sanctioned but not his visit to Holguin. Inopportunely, his former lover died last month from injuries suffered in a traffic accident. He was only able to put flowers on her grave."

The Inspector drew back and looked skeptically at both intel pros. How had Dong discovered this link when he had not? When had these two become confidants and how had they found out about this gringo's detention? "What's your interest, Señor Dong, in coming here in the prisoner's behalf?"

"Good question, Inspector. At 3:55 this morning, I received a call from a José, who hosted the professor in Vedado. I'd given Shannon my card to telephone if anything untoward happened during his first visit to Cuba. He seemed a bit naïve but had occasionally provided small services to our government. When I was informed of his lockup, I thought I should advise you about his trip to Holguin and his past love affair with Ochoa's niece."

"That may explain one thing, Señor Dong, but why did he attend a Santeria session? He's been rambling inside about some shepherd in the valley of death. I've asked myself if he was affected in some way."

"Inspector, would you mind if I listened in for a moment? Maybe I could provide insight into the prisoner's utterings."

"As you wish. Follow me. He's in a special cell at the end of the corridor." They passed an orderly whose prisoner faced the wall. The Inspector arrived at the last cell and opened the portal for Dong. The gringo was repeating his mantra about death and was struggling to stay on all fours.

After a minute, Dong replied, "I believe Professor Shannon is trying to recite the 23rd Psalm, which is considered the soldiers' psalm. It was written by King David centuries ago and is recited by soldiers when they face battle or death."

The Inspector was non-plussed. He had never heard that one before. How was he to know anything about a psalm?

Dong looked at him intently, "If you would do me this small favor, Inspector. Please consider releasing the prisoner into my custody. I would be grateful and would keep you informed about his whereabouts and any news surrounding Ochoa's deceased niece. It may help your inquiry. A less threatening environment could encourage him to speak more freely."

The Inspector looked Dong straight in the eye. The Vietnamese intelligence chief held his stare. He heard himself say, "I'll consider your request Señor Dong as your government is a friend of the Cuban state."

"Guard, please take these men to the entranceway and await my orders." He turned back to prisoner 217's cell and heard him mumbling on.

CHAPTER 36

The Rectory, Old Havana, Monday, 7:50 a.m.

THE PRIEST WASN'T SURE if he could digest all that had occurred in the last 12 hours. He prayed that the next 12 would not prove as dramatic.

First, Ana's son showed up at the Rectory at dusk with a wild tale about meeting his father, Professor Luke Shannon, at a Santeria session. They'd escaped the police in Ochoa's hometown, fought black marketers yielding machetes, and hidden Luke inside a garbage truck. They'd somehow found their way to Varadero beach, where Luke encountered his original tour group at the Hotel Meliá. As the *Cubatur* guide acted suspiciously, his father asked Junior to seek out Fr. Sebastian. His account was so unusual that it might even be true.

Luke's son had taken a *Viazul* bus to Havana's national terminal on *Avenida Independencia,* where he grabbed a *colectivo* to Old Havana. This was his first time in "the big city" and he shook like a leaf when he arrived at the Rectory. He got lost in the old city's maze and dodged honking cars and pimps pitching sex of all varieties. He ran into a friar leaving the Cathedral by chance, who graciously guided him here. Together they banged on the front door until a friar opened up.

Fr. Sebastian had found him, lugging a pack with artwork, looking harried and unglued.

After hearing his incredible story over mate tea, the priest asked a friend to find Junior a room in a private B&B. He took Junior's cell number and gave his extension at the Rectory switchboard. He cautioned Junior not to speak openly by phone. The priest promised to ring him when his father arrived and asked the friar to take him to the *B&B familiar*.

Fr. Sebastian read the professor's note again. It requested him to telephone a Señor José to say that "the package was received." He did so and heard José question the message, which he repeated and then hung up. As he'd received no word from the professor by 11 p.m., he went to bed, wondering what had become of him.

At 4 a.m., José rang, stuttering that the professor had just been dragged away by the police. Luke had left him an envelope with two persons to telephone in case of an emergency: the priest and a Vietnamese diplomat.

At 6:30 a.m., a Mr. Dong rang, advising that he and Major Sanchez had just freed Luke from the *Villa Marista*. He was currently at the diplomat's residence. "Father, I spoke with the professor, who's cleaning up after his incarceration. He asked to meet up at the place where you had coffee last week. If so, I could stop by before I go to work. Would that be possible?"

Fr. Sebastian looked at the wall clock and remembered that he had to officiate mass later this morning. "Thank you, Señor Dong. I could be there at 9 a.m. It would be a pleasure to meet you."

He hung up the phone, aghast. He said aloud, "Lord, you sure work in mysterious ways." He prepared himself to leave but took off his Roman collar.

After walking around Old Havana, he perceived no surveillance. He strolled by the old Bank of Boston building, housing the administrative offices of *el Banco Central de Cuba*. Two ladies sat at the corner, selling *tomales*. He continued around the corner and slipped inside the European hostel. He greeted the hostess at the desk, who did a double take at his civilian attire. "I'm receiving special visitors that desire to keep a low profile, señorita. Is the private room available by the fountain? They'll probably arrive around 9 a.m."

She led him through the French doors, across the courtyard to a room with a wooden table and four chairs. Pink roses in a vase emitted a delightful fragrance. "Would anyone need to stay the night, padre? We have one room remaining."

"How thoughtful to ask. Yes, please make a reservation for him under my name." He sat down and listened to the fountain's bubbly water. He closed his eyes and breathed in the rose's bouquet. Slowly, tension slipped away.

A ruckus outside shattered his glimpse of serenity. He heard raised voices and someone say, "Grab him before he gets away."

What on earth was happening now?

CHAPTER 37

Vietnamese diplomatic residence, Miramar, Havana, Monday, 8 a.m.

LUKE FACED THE TORRENTS from the shower for minutes on end, hoping all his woes would flow down the drain. He scrubbed his body up and down, despite the pain. He avoided touching his abdomen and thighs, where they'd beat him with a rubber hose. It was the Inspector's way to say *adiós*. Mercifully, his shoulder suture had persevered.

He remembered the guards leaving the cell door ajar and hearing the Inspector's words: "You are no longer welcome here. If I ever catch you inquiring about Ochoa again, I will personally haul you into the Eastern Compound for the surprise of your life. This *Villa* is kid's stuff by comparison. Get out of here and stop wasting my time."

Luke almost broke down but restrained himself. He didn't want to exhibit any weakness to his captors. They'd get no more satisfaction than what they already had gleaned. Two orderlies lifted Luke under his armpits and dragged him down the corridor. Only the fading shadow of the thin man followed his retreat. The devils' voices finally were quieting down.

He breathed in the humid, morning air. The orderlies opened the back door of the dark Chevrolet and thrust him in. He glimpsed the first light of dawn and heard cock-a-doodle-do. His night had finally become day at *Villa Marista*—one little victory.

As the Chevy slipped out of the compound, he tried to raise his head. Up front, Luke was shocked to see Big Man driving and the Vietnamese diplomat raising a finger to his lips. Their presence at this moment pushed his emotions over the edge.

The guards opened the barrier without a word. Departing the *Villa*, Luke let out a prolonged sigh. The more distance the Chevy put to the prison, the more hope Luke gained that he was truly free. He was finally leaving this living nightmare. He tried reciting Psalm 23 but shuddered uncontrollably.

The Chevy turned left onto the Malecón, away from Vedado. Luke saw the familiar scene of fishermen casting lines and joggers along the seaside promenade. He looked down at his bruised arm, reminding himself of another reality, beyond tourists' eyes. Unintentionally, he'd become a new soulmate of the thousands locked up in Cuba's Gulag Archipelago.

They drove past *la Fábrica*, making Luke recall his careless fling. It seemed so long ago. Where was Eloisa now? The Chevy crossed the bridge over the *Rio Almendares* into the posh neighborhood of Miramar. Well-kept residences with red-tiled roofs alternated with august embassies and armed guards. Luke saw drivers polishing black Mercedes and BMWs. Big Man took a sharp left and approached a small but elegant home of Spanish-colonial design. Its wrought-iron gate opened automatically into a sandstone driveway. Dong thanked Big Man profusely, touching his shoulder and offering a slight bow.

Big Man opened the back door to help Luke out. He gave him a light hug. Luke saw him turn away with moist eyes. As his father had counseled, "Don't judge a book by its cover." The Chevy departed and Dong led him inside. No one was at home except a Vietnamese servant.

* * *

Now Dong was driving him back along the Malecón toward the rising sun. They passed the Hotel Nacional, making Luke wonder if Johnny, Arturo, and the older doorman were working the crowds. They passed the cracked wall where Luke had saved the young girl and the train station where he'd left a few days ago. It seemed to Luke that he'd been in Cuba forever. It was time for him and Junior to go.

Dong advised, "You're safe for the while, professor. However, it'd be wise to depart soon. I'm unsure if the Inspector will honor his word to leave you in my custody much longer. He's a man who likes ultimate control."

Luke examined the Vietnamese diplomat, who seemed to be having a conversation with himself. Luke looked out the window toward Havana Bay and saw the Spanish cruise liner. He was supposed to chat with the Spaniard on his return. He should do so today. Maybe the priest's friend could find a way out by sea.

"Mr. Dong, thank you very much. You have shown friendship to me as a brother. You should not put yourself at further risk. I hear your counsel and accept it. I will make plans to leave Cuba. Fr. Sebastian may have some ideas."

Dong seemed lost in reflection. "As Ana has passed on, is there anyone else involved besides you, professor?"

How could Luke escape this man's clairvoyance? Luke admitted, "Mr. Dong, I went to the Santeria session in Cacocúm and discovered that Ana had had a son. It was her legacy to both of us. I would die to get my son out of Cuba."

Dong continued nodding but offered no reply. He turned into Old Havana and followed Luke's directions through the narrow streets. The hostel was sandwiched between two fading, colonial façades.

Outside, a policeman held a teenager with a purse in his hands. An older woman was yelling, "You sneaky thief."

Dong parked on a narrow sidewalk and said, "Professor, it'd be wise to put on your sunglasses. Let's wait a few minutes for the police to leave.

They waited until 9:10 and saw the curiosity seekers go their separate ways. They entered the hostel and the amiable receptionist led them through the courtyard to the private room. Fr. Sebastian stood to greet them. He gave both Luke and Dong a light hug and a pensive look. "Professor, I am so happy to welcome you back to the land of the living," he said. "It must have been a horrible trial, but let's not rehash the unpleasant past.

"Instead, let me offer you each a cup of green tea, which our receptionist found especially for you. Señor Dong, thank you for all the good you've done for your neighbor in need." His eyes glowed and his lips formed a crescent smile. "Haven't I seen you at our 10:30 Sunday mass?"

"Yes, father. My wife and I attend on occasion. We are from South Vietnam and practice the Catholic faith. At the embassy, most colleagues are agnostic or nominally Buddhist. I do not share my beliefs with them. Please count me as a friend."

Luke was glad that their words and body language came across as cordial. Each leaned forward as they spoke, Fr. Sebastian occasionally touching Dong's arm.

"Father, I told Mr. Dong that I discovered Lucas Junior in Holguin. I would like to leave Cuba with him. Thanks for your message last night. I was so tired I forgot to call back. Where is my son today?"

"Professor, your son is in a safe place but not in this hostel. I have reserved a room for you here under my name. Last week, you asked to speak with my Spanish friend. He could come and brainstorm with you. Let's shoot for 3 p.m. As to Señor Dong, it is impolitic to involve him further. His position and family could suffer repercussions."

Luke nodded. "Mr. Dong has done so much already. It'd be best for me and the Spaniard to speak one-on-one. However, I will have to retrieve my luggage and pay Jose his due."

"Professor, let me retrieve your luggage later today and settle your accounts. Please write Jose a note. Promise me that you will not venture outside this hostel. Remember that I am personally responsible for your whereabouts with the Inspector. Since Friday, your face has been on the website of the Revolutionary Police. It has not been removed. Please stay put. Agreed?"

"Agreed, Mr. Dong. I will never forget that you rescued me."

The diplomat nodded somberly. "Thank you for your hospitality, padre. I will telephone you after 5 p.m. today, advising the hour of my arrival. Please note that I'll have to leave by 7 p.m. to attend a diplomatic reception."

The priest nodded and clasped the diplomat's hand and arm. Despite Luke's bruised and battered body, he gave Dong a long hug in gratitude. He felt a ray of hope.

Now, he had to prepare himself to run the gauntlet one more time.

CHAPTER 38

The Rectory, Old Havana, Monday, noon

H E LEFT MASS QUICKLY. Usually, he spent time with parishioners, hearing their concerns or providing advice whenever he could. Now, he had to ring Vicente, his Eurasian friend, during the lunch break at the Spanish ship. At 1 p.m., Big Man was stopping by with someone requiring "special treatment." In the last 24 hours, he had played an unbidden part in a James Bond thriller. Just a few weeks ago, he arrived in Havana believing that he'd merely serve as substitute priest.

In retrospect, he should have stayed in Santiago. Nevertheless, with fewer clergy in Cuba, he had to do his part. After all, he was God's servant and was charged to help his neighbor. Fr. Sebastian hoped that his Spanish colleague was enjoying his stay on la Costa del Sol. "Please, St. Peter, help me persevere," he said, hoping someone was listening.

"Vicente, do you recollect our conversation with the foreigner before he traveled? Yes. He'd like to see you today at 3 p.m.—can you manage that? Please stop by beforehand. Ciao."

The phone was a dangerous medium in Cuba. He'd learned to carefully choose his words. He asked the receptionist to hold all calls until the policeman arrived. He closed his eyes, his energy fading fast.

He needed to restore himself for whatever lay ahead. He leaned back on the recliner.

The phone rang insistently and his assistant answered outside. She knocked gently on the door, and Fr. Sebastian shook himself awake. The wall clock read 1:15 and the open window channeled in the bay's sultry air.

"Buenos días, padre. Your police friend has arrived with Eloisa. She has suffered a setback. May I bring them upstairs?" Her eyes were downcast, alerting the priest that something bad had happened.

"Gracias, Monica. Please do so in a couple minutes. Permit me to freshen up. Today has proven to be a very long day."

He inhaled deeply and splashed water on his drawn face. In the mirror, he thought that he'd aged a couple years during his two weeks as substitute priest. His olive skin reflected a ghostly pallor. He felt his ribcage and feared he'd lost weight, though he didn't have much to spare. Havana was an acquired taste with its hustle, bustle and intrigue. He yearned for the slower pace of Santiago and its less complicated people. He heard the tap on the door and tried to appear serene.

"Buenas tardes, Antonio and Eloisa. May I prepare you both a cup of tea?"

"Please, father," responded Big Man. Eloisa didn't reply, her eyes hidden behind dark glasses.

The priest caught sight of bruise marks along her cheeks and a swollen right eye. He prepared himself for the worst. He had one *mate* teabag remaining and apportioned the warm water equitably into three cups. He served them, forcing a smile, despite the frown on Big Man's face. He thought it'd be best to keep his silence.

"Fr. Sebastian," began Big Man after a minute, "We have a tough situation on our hands. The General blew up about Eloisa's carousing at *La Fábrica* last week. He roughed her up pretty bad and cast her out of the Centro apartment. She has nowhere to go."

Eloisa's mouth quivered and tears were brimming in her eyes. The priest's compassion overtook him. He left his seat and placed his arm around her shoulder. The dam burst over her rouged, discolored face. Her body shook like a palm tree before a storm. Big Man came alongside, offering quiet consolation.

Minutes passed. Eloisa said, "Father, I have sinned so many times. I don't deserve to be in your presence, nor in the land of the living. I just want this to end." Her tears flowed again. Big Man and the priest looked at each other, wondering what to say.

"Eloisa, even though things look hopeless now, there will be a morrow. I love you, Eloisa, and Big Man too. Yes, it's good to seek forgiveness. But it's also time to sit up and be counted. It's time to make a plan."

Maybe it was his lack of sleep, but the priest shed his mellow self. Who did they think they were to beat down fellow Cubans whenever they saw fit? Yes, Jesus had said to "love your enemy." However, he also acknowledged the widow's plea for "justice" against the corrupt judge. Wasn't it the priest's turn to act and stand up for the innocent? But first, he had to talk to Big Man, one-on-one.

"Eloisa, please take a minute and ask the Lord's forgiveness. Permit Antonio and me to have a short walk outside."

She inclined her head. When the priest took the Big Man's strong arm, he heard Eloisa quietly recite the Lord's Prayer. They walked under the colonnade on the second floor, lost in thought.

"Antonio, Eloisa looks so desolate, does she have anywhere to go? Her second cousin, Ana, passed away last month, so she can't go to Holguin. I'm unsure what to recommend."

Big Man matched the priest's slow pace. He looked upon his childhood friend and detected deepening lines on his placid face. Everyone living in Havana had a price to pay. Big Man confided, "She is talking about rafting out, padre. She's desperate to escape Cuba. She'd like to join Ochoa's daughter in Spain but doesn't know how."

"Let me reflect on this, Antonio. A friend from a Spanish cruise line should arrive this afternoon. I will ask him for advice. In the meantime, do you have a place Eloisa could stay overnight? Our local hostel is full.

"Regarding the professor, I thank you for your help. Dong said that the Revolutionary Police's website still has his name and photo posted. Is there a way to remove this alert? Otherwise, it will be difficult for him to return home."

"Very well, father. Regarding, Eloisa, I have an acquaintance, who's spent time on the street. She lives in Old Havana and could put Eloisa up for a night. As to removing the professor from the website, I'll speak with a younger colleague to help out. As you're aware, I'm not a fan of the Internet or the World Wide Web.

"Here's my cell number, padre, and my friend's address in old town. If she agrees to host Eloisa, I'll ring to say, 'well received,' OK?"

Observing his lifelong friend, Fr. Sebastian saw Big Man's face etched in worry. He seemed beaten down. Whether from his son's death or Eloisa's beating, the priest was unsure. Big Man was not in a good place. But then again, neither was he.

* * *

"What do you think, Vicente? Three of my flock need to fly the coop. The professor, whom you met, was released from *Villa Marista* this very morning. His namesake son, whom he discovered in Holguin, longs to escape Cuba with him. An Ochoa relative and ex-lover of the General, was badly beaten and put out on the street. She's on the verge of suicide and talks of 'rafting out.'"

"Wow, padre. That's quite a turn of events since we last spoke. Do you know if each of them has a passport?"

"Eloisa had a passport when she went to Brazil with the General. The professor has an American passport but his son has never left Cuban shores. What would you suggest?"

"With *MSC Operetta's* unscheduled visit to repair its boiler, many clients have flown back to Miami or Madrid. The liner has extra space and is taking cargo in the ship's hold today. Modest staterooms are available for passengers below decks. The *Americano* could secure a passage to Miami for $400-500. For the woman's trip to Barcelona, maybe $1,000 plus another $500 for an expedited Spanish visa. As for the prof's son, I'd have to wheel and deal 'off the books,' costing a pretty penny.

"The boiler's repair is almost complete. The MSC liner may be cleared by noon tomorrow. Furthermore, the health inspectors are planning to shut down all cruise liners because of the unfolding pandemic. We'll need your prayers, padre, but time is of the essence. It will be touch and go.

"I'll visit the *Americano* in the hostel at 3 p.m. Please obtain the Cuban woman's passport ASAP. As for the young man, I'll speak with his father about extraordinary options. It'll be the only way out. Nothing's guaranteed."

* * *

Before leaving for the hostel, the priest decided to phone Big Man. He was relieved to hear him say, "Well received." He wondered who was Big Man's friend but was relieved that she took pity on Eloisa. The priest asked if he'd retrieve Eloisa's passport and a small bag from her apartment. If all went well, Big Man should leave the priest a voicemail. Then Vicente would come by the friend's apartment at 9 p.m. and pick up Eloisa's passport. Everything had to go right.

At 5 p.m. Dong called, simply saying, "5:50" and then hung up. As Fr. Sebastian was about to depart, he asked his loyal assistant, "Please keep me in your prayers, Monica. It's been a long day and a longer night lies in wait. Adiós."

She cocked her head. After a couple of seconds, she carefully articulated, "I'll pray for you every hour until I see you next. *Vaya con Diós, padre.*"

How grateful he was for Monica during his wild stint in Havana. She reminded him of St. Peter, the "rock" on which the church had been founded. With two children to raise herself, she had her hands full. He appreciated her faith, her support and her prayers. He needed all the help he could get to survive another 24 hours.

He left the Rectory and aimed for the Cathedral. He climbed its steps and moved silently up the right interior aisle. He slipped out the side entrance, avoiding parishioners. Continuing down the cobblestone street, he bought the last *tamal* from the woman sitting on the bank's stairs with her basket. He savored its spicy, chicken filling. This just might be his last supper.

He turned the corner and didn't perceive anyone following. He went into a narrow alley and set foot into the hostel's back door.

At the reception desk sat the student he'd met last week, absorbed in a Marvel comic book. He nodded the priest toward the French doors. Suddenly, the overhead light flickered and went dark. "Another power outage, padre. They come and go in the afternoon. Here's a candle. The courtyard still has some sunlight."

The padre thanked him and turned to feel a hot wind sweep through the corridor. Was another tempest brewing?

He stopped at the fountain's water and took in its spray. Raised voices escaped from the meeting room: "Your son has no passport, so there's no way he'll walk the ramp past Immigration. The *MSC Operetta* casts off tomorrow on the afternoon tide. We must decide right now."

"Buenas noches, professor and Vicente. Let me share this candle with you. A tropical storm may be coming. Tomorrow may be the last day out. What have you two decided?"

He gave each a light hug despite their tense looks. The professor's shoulders slumped, as he acquiesced. "I guess it's the only way. Vicente says that he can place Junior on a longshoremen team to carry cargo onboard tonight. My role is to finance the purser to look the other way so that my son can stow away. Let's hope that there is still cash in my bag."

"Very well, Lucas. Then the decision is made. The Vietnamese diplomat will arrive shortly. We should not share our plans with him.

"There is another person to bear in mind. The General beat Eloisa up today for being seen at *La Fábrica* with another man. He threw her out on the street. Except for tonight, she has nowhere else to go. Vicente is trying to find her passage on the Spanish cruise liner too."

The professor clenched his fists and rose to his feet. The padre flinched, observing a new side of "Cool Hand Luke." Maybe Eloisa had substituted Ana in Luke's troubled mind. The priest hadn't experienced Luke's Irish temper before. Add his son's uncertain state and the grueling ordeal at *la Villa Marista*, the American vacillated on the razor's edge.

Vicente's plan had many moving parts. If the professor, his son and Eloisa had a chance to escape, there was neither time nor place for a Molotov cocktail of human emotion.

Each had to do their part. If not, they would face the infamous wall, *El Paredón*, as General Ochoa had 30 years ago.

CHAPTER 39

El Malecón to Old Havana, Monday, 5:45 p.m.

H E HATED DRIVING IN HAVANA as much as he did in Saigon. The drivers were not dissimilar as they wove from lane to lane. Dotted lines were mere suggestions. In Cuba, there were always pedicabs, Coco-cabs and horse-drawn carriages that put any driver to the test. One saving grace was the fewer vehicles on Havana's roads than on Saigon's. He closed his window to avoid a wheezing Packard's exhaust. A gas guzzler with fins from a bygone era passed him on the right.

He left the Malecón and headed toward Havana Bay. The MSC ship rocked alone under subdued lights at the passenger terminal. He opened the window of his older-model Mercedes 220 and felt the breeze pick up. On the embassy's satellite TV, the Weather Channel had confirmed that a tropical storm was heading their way.

Overshooting the hostel's street, he drove around the block, dodging pedestrians and roving dogs. Aromas of garlic and onions blew through his window and gusts of wind spun dust devils into the darkening sky.

He pondered his intervention in behalf of the American professor. On the plane, he had appreciated the prof's spontaneous pledge to find help for his sister's immigration problem in Seattle. Family was family. He was willing to help a brother in faith but every action Dong took now would be scrutinized later. He had to watch his step.

Suddenly, the lights went out up and down the narrow street. Dong squinted to find the European hostel. He drove slowly and pulled up at another "Casa" advertising "rooms available." An idea came to him. He went inside and made a reservation for two nights under the name of "Lucas," paying the nun attendant in advance. "Gracias, *madre*."

Outside, a few youths were eyeing his Mercedes. He got in quickly and bumped along the cobblestone lane. The European hostel was in the next block. An adolescent lounged outside and a candle flickered in the lobby. "Amigo, how about a CUC to carry these bags, and another to watch my car? I shouldn't be long." The young man nodded and picked up Luke's Air Force cargo bag and backpack, following Dong inside.

The reception clerk was reading a comic by candlelight but raised his head. "I'm here to meet a resident and a priest." The clerk pointed toward the courtyard and flipped to the next page. Dong saw the priest's profile beyond the fountain in a candlelit room. He paid a CUC to the teen, who returned to the street.

"Fr. Sebastian, good afternoon. Professor, here are your bags." Luke thanked him and walked quickly out the door, checking the bag's pouches.

"Mr. Dong, may I present my friend Vicente. He does his best to make a living as an independent journalist and consultant. Vicente, Mr. Dong is the first commercial secretary of the Embassy of Vietnam."

"Vicente, my pleasure. What type of consulting do you do," asked Dong. He observed a 30-something Eurasian man with an inquisitive look.

"Mr. Dong, the pleasure is mine. I do some reporting and consulting on maritime issues. I am at your service, señor." He deferentially inclined his head.

Dong exchanged cards with the journalist. He heard Luke cry, "Yes!" He seemed happy with whatever he found in his luggage. The American returned with an envelope and removed a scrap of paper with names and addresses.

"Fr. Sebastian, there is a young Catholic in Holguin province who could be the next Cuban star in the U.S. major leagues. He is a home-run hitter. Hercules has no father but keeps the faith. I told him I would pass on his name and points of contact to you. Will you reach out to him, when you have a chance?"

"Of course, Lucas. To keep his faith under hard circumstance shows character. I'll be happy to communicate with him, after things calm down a bit."

Dong looked at his watch and saw that it was after 6:45pm. The Ambassador was expecting him within an hour.

"Gentlemen, I'm sorry to cut this visit short. I have to return to the Embassy right away. Vicente, would you excuse us for a moment?" The reporter nodded and returned to the lobby.

"Gentlemen, I can see that you are making plans. However, I did give my word to the Inspector that the professor would be under my custody. In this regard, I just made him a reservation for two nights down the street at the Casa run by nuns. It's under Lucas' name.

"Professor, check in there tonight. Tomorrow, a little before noon, I will inform the Inspector that I moved you from my home to the Casa. I'll advise him that the change of venue is because of visitors arriving from abroad. By tomorrow afternoon you likely will have another visitor. Do you understand?"

Dong probed the professor's eyes and detected a steely determination. He hoped the American had the stuff to pull off whatever he was intending. The diplomat had to cover all his bases. After all, he was in Cuba.

Luke replied, "Understood," trying to give him a hug. Dong stepped back and simply said. "Be careful, my friend. A new virus has arrived in Cuba. We must take care and maybe give each other fewer hugs for a while.

"Fr. Sebastian, it has been a pleasure. I'm sure the professor will gain much from your counsel. Perhaps we can speak later this week?"

He saw the tired priest incline his head. To both of them, he simply said, "Be safe." With that, he was gone.

CHAPTER 40

Near Havana Bay, Tuesday, 10 a.m.

WHAT A DAY IT HAD BEEN. No, what a week or however long he'd been in Cuba. He'd lost count. But today was the day. The day to live or die.

The window was open, ushering in the humid air. His final drama would likely play out beyond the adjacent warehouse shielding Havana Bay. There, the MSC ship was moored, setting out this afternoon. The salt air gave him a lift, though clouds began crowding the horizon. Could today be any worse than yesterday? He trembled at the thought.

Confidence slowly regained traction within Luke. Last night, he'd made paper effigies of the three devils that had haunted him for years. He burnt them in the Casa's fireplace; only ash remained. There was no turning back now. He and his son were going to make it out of Cuba. Whether dead or alive, he didn't know. Everything had to go right.

His son! How wonderful giving Junior a long hug late last night. Before his son boarded the Spanish ship, Vicente had gifted a quick visit. He'd heard nothing further, which was a positive sign. No news was good news. He presumed that Junior joined the longshoremen carrying crates on board. Later the purser, on the take, would hide him. Luke had paid *muchos dolares* to make that happen. Only one Ben Franklin remained inside his tennis shoe.

Vicente had also promised Luke another surprise once he made it on board. What did that mean? Luke put on his damp trousers, his cheap shades and bucket cap. He'd washed his Levi's in the basin and thought a quick walk in the morning sun should dry them out. He also had one more chore to do before saying *adiós*.

Examining his tourist map, he found that Aguiar street was four short blocks away. He'd have time to go there and return before 11am. He had arranged for the nun's brother to pick him up and drive him to the ship's pier.

He walked down the stairs and nodded to the sister, preoccupied by two German tourists. Turning away from Havana Bay, he strode briskly up to Aguiar street. At the crossroads with O'Reilly, there rose a two-story colonial building, the administrative office of *"El Banco Central de Cuba."* It was the same building in the doorman's photo, the original headquarters of the First National Bank of Boston. He could confirm to his former colleagues that the building remained standing though nationalized decades ago. That is, as long as Luke made it out of Cuba.

He took a quick photo with his old Nikon. A tired vendor sat on the bank's steps with a wicker basket. *"Tamales,* señor?" Luke gave her his last Cuban pesos. "Gracias, señora." He wolfed down the pastry of chicken and olives, flavored with a touch of cilantro.

He retraced his steps, turning down Amargura street toward Havana Bay. Two policemen in gray entered the pedestrian walkway 30 feet away. Luke angled left to an open door. Keeping his cool, he walked into a reception area, which opened to a Spanish courtyard with mosaic tiles.

Luke bumped into a distinguished man in a crisp, blue guayabera, excusing himself. *"Perdón."* It dawned on Luke that he had come face-to-face with Havana's most beloved citizen, the official historian of Old Havana, Señor Eusebio Leal.

"*Americano?*" the older gentleman asked, looking Luke up and down.

Luke removed his shades and hat and wiped his brow. Thinking on his feet, he replied, "Buenos Dias, Señor Eusebio. I admire what you've done to save historic Havana. Like you, Seattle's citizens stood up to preserve our traditional Pike Place Market years ago. You'd be welcome to visit anytime. I am Professor Shannon of Seattle University, at your service. "

The historian's serious look broke into a smile. "I've always wanted to know Seattle. If I visit the Emerald City, I'll be sure to look you up. I'd enjoy hiking in the mountains. But now, I must take leave. I'm expected at the Ministry to do battle. We want to preserve another block of Old Havana. Have a pleasant stay in Cuba," he said, leaving the courtyard in a flourish.

Wow, thought Luke! He'd read about Leal and felt thrilled to have met the famous man—a positive sign. He returned cautiously to the entrance and saw the policemen's retreating backs. He pivoted toward Havana Bay.

He recalled Leal's unique journey. As a 25-year student, he engaged in an open act of civil disobedience early in the Revolution. He laid down before the steamrollers, preventing them to asphalt over the *Plaza d'Armas*, where Havana was founded five centuries ago. As a student of Havana's history, he was appalled and used his body to make his point.

When informed of the youth's defiance, Fidel did not order him shot at *El Paredon*. "He has *cojones*," the Commander remarked. Castro saw an opportunity for tourism as well as money from European NGO's. Old Havana was preserved and both Castro and Leal were proven right.

Enough of reminiscence! It was time to say *adiós* to historical Havana. It was time to get out of Cuba.

He turned the corner and heard the gray Lada groaning at the casa's door. A young man was talking quietly with the nun. "I'll be right down," said Luke, running up to his first-floor room. He hoisted his backpack and hauled his cargo bag down the stairs. The wall clock showed 11:20 a.m. He thanked the sister and gave her his last bar of Neutrogena soap. "Please keep the room reserved for another night, even though I may not return. *Hasta la vista, madre.*"

The nun's brother was a quiet sort, which Luke found comforting. Within 10 minutes, the driver dropped him at the terminal's entrance. Clouds now covered the sun, and white caps bounced off the pier. The *MSC Operetta* rocked just beyond the Immigration booth. The walkway onboard the ship slid back and forth on creaking wheels. The driver took Luke's baggage up to the Immigration line. "*Vaya con Dios, señor.*'"

Luke waited behind five passengers in Bermuda shorts. After a couple minutes, he arrived at the head of the line. "What was your purpose in visiting Cuba? Do you have any currency to declare?"

Luke removed his sunglasses and handed his passport and the copy of the tourist visa to the robust Immigration officer looking bored. "I came for educational purposes. I've just spent my last pesos on a tamale."

The middle-aged official didn't smile but perspired heavily under the blue awning. He glanced briefly at Luke. Humidity did battle with the mushrooming clouds.

"Anything else to declare," probed the official, scanning an old Lenovo PC on his desk.

"No, señor." Luke waited. Eventually, the agent stamped his passport and held it a few seconds before passing it back. He jerked his head toward the gangplank, its side canvas flapping in the stiffened breeze. He gave a quick look at Luke but called out, "Next."

"So far, so good," Luke whispered, trying to reassure himself. He lugged his bag up the footbridge and encountered a red-haired purser on the quarterdeck. This must be the man who garnered Luke's last funds. The robust man with Celtic strains exuded airs of a bon vivant.

"Ah, Señor Shannon. Vicente said to expect you around noon. As the storm worsens and the health inspectors threaten to shut down the passenger terminal, the *MSC Operetta* must depart sooner than scheduled. Last month, the ship had a docking problem in Italy, so we can't allow its bow to jostle against the pier. We're already delayed a week for the boiler repair. We don't want to be quarantined here. We must get away as soon as we can.

"Though your berth is not elegant, it's at sea level. It should have less motion than the upper decks. Once the ship is underway, I'll come by with the other passenger," he confided, lowering his voice.

He scanned Luke's ticket. "Porter, help this passenger to his berth." The purser turned his attention to three pink-faced persons wearing aloha shirts, complaining about the heat, humidity, and the rising wind.

Luke cast a quick look toward the pier. His heart skipped a beat. There stood that teen, gazing at the ship and twirling his red-and-white beads. Luke put on his shades and turned aside. It'd been going so well, until now. What on earth was Johnny doing here?

As he took his last glimpse toward the pier, a black Chevrolet snaked stealthily through pedestrians hurrying on board. The car had people inside, though Luke couldn't ascertain who they might be. He snuck quickly below deck

The ship's roll accentuated, causing Luke to stumble.

CHAPTER 41

On board, MSC Operetta, Havana Bay, Tuesday, 2:50 p.m.

THE SHIP LET LOOSE A LONG BLAST, creating havoc among the gulls. Whitecaps danced above the murky waters of Havana Bay as the 65,000-ton cruise liner headed north by northwest. A gray Cuban patrol boat monitored its departure, its 50-caliber machine guns at the ready. The Cuban sailors braced themselves against the outgoing tide. Could that be a classic Zhuk patrol boat from the days of the USSR?

Tap, tap, tap sounded on the cabin door. Luke opened to the purser's round face. "A present for you, señor," he exclaimed.

Behind him stood his son, shifting from one foot to the other. Though the youth's face looked haggard, his eyes were alive in expectation. He rushed toward his father, brushing the purser aside. Father and son hugged and held on tightly despite the rolling ship.

Like a Cheshire cat, the purser sported a mischievous smile. He touched Luke on his right shoulder, causing him to flinch. "I'm happy to be of service, Professor Shannon, and see you back together again. As we have more room on this leg to Miami, you may find it more comfortable to stay in a larger cabin. Please follow me down the passageway. It's next to Vicente's accommodation."

Luke and Junior grabbed their packs and bag and carefully followed the purser on the shifting deck. The new stateroom was more spacious with two berths and a porthole above sea level.

"It'd be best that you remain in your room right now. As we were lifting up the ramp, some police type arrived and asked to inspect our register. I just saw him wandering the upper decks."

Luke steadied himself by holding the bulkhead, his joy turning to dread. What more would happen to him? One thing he did know: he would never return to the *Villa Marista,* ever again.

"Once the ship gets beyond Cuba's 12-mile limit, I'll circle back. I'll knock three times again. In the meantime, your son looks like he could use some rest. He worked hard last night lifting the cargo for our ship. Please relax but stay in your stateroom. Buenas tardes."

Luke closed the door and locked it. He wanted to hear about his son's adventures, but Junior was barely standing upright. "Son, we each have our own berth. Let's take full advantage—maybe a siesta?"

"That sounds great, father. Last night, I took a cat nap behind the boiler so this soft bed looks good." With that, Junior laid down in his soiled clothes and immediately fell asleep. Luke peered out the porthole and saw rising waves and a threatening sky. The ship heeled 10 degrees but that didn't disturb Junior's sleep. Luke fell into his lower berth and followed suit.

* * *

Knock, knock, knock.

A bare glimmer snuck through the porthole and a faint snore rose from Junior's bunk. Luke opened the door to the purser's florid face. *MSC Operetta* has entered international waters, choppy though they be. Vicente is going above decks to get some air. He invites you to join him. He was able to secure an exit visa for his wife and a Spanish passport for his daughter, so all of his family is on board. He knows how to wheel and deal inside the Cuban system."

"Thanks for the news. My son is dead to the world. I'll join Vicente solo." Luke followed the porter and knocked on Vicente's door.

Vicente looked excited. "This cruise will test my sea legs, professor." He blew his wife and daughter a kiss, securing the bulkhead on the moving deck. He followed Luke up the stairwell heading aft.

"Hold it right there," roared a voice from behind. Though the tall Inspector looked gaunt, he hung onto the ladder and staggered toward them. The Inspector bowled over the purser, who was trying to make his way forward. The heavy-set Catalan bounced around like a bowling ball, slumping against Luke's door. Luke and Vicente quickened their pace in the opposite direction, running up to the main deck.

In the open sea, swells of 15 feet struck the liner's starboard bow. *MSC Operetta* had altered its course to northeast by north, causing the ship to pound the surf. Spray soaked Luke, so he pivoted toward the stern. Vicente was struggling to keep up. No one else was walking on deck. "Vicente. Let's go to the leeward side with less wind."

Today brought back scary memories of Luke's first encounter with a typhoon. As a young ensign and wet behind the ears, he had no idea about the strength of a Pacific storm. He recollected how he had tied the sailor to the helm, to maintain the ship's heading through the long watch. Their destroyer had managed to keep the wind on its bow, surviving the tropical roller coaster. He'd learned that every storm had its signature, ruling everyone and everything caught within. Right now, Luke grabbed the rail and struggled up the port side of the shifting ship.

This is ridiculous, thought Luke. Vicente staggered forward, barely holding on. "There's a hatch dead ahead. Let's find the pursuer, who should have some 'medical cognac' to warm us up, away from that Inspector."

A menacing voice cut through the air. On the deck above skidded the thin man, pulling himself along the guardrails. Swaying back and forth, he managed to descend the ladder, landing on the port walkway with a thud.

As the Inspector tried to gain footing, the ship rolled again to port, causing each person to grab a stanchion for dear life. Out of the mist, his son emerged astern, working his way forward one rail at a time. He wore Luke's red Seattle U. shirt and looked puzzled at the scene.

The Inspector looked like a wild man in the spray. He hung his left arm around a railing so he could pull out his .38-caliber pistol. His Ray-Ban glasses flew off into the tempest below. Revenge was written across his face. "How dare you sneak out of town, without my approval. Think again, professor." The Inspector glanced behind and saw Junior approaching. When the ship rolled to starboard, he lurched at the youth and grabbed him by the collar. He thrust the pistol to his head. The Inspector was stronger than Luke expected.

"So, this is Ochoa's legacy, that you have so desired. Over my dead body, gringo. He was born to a traitor's family and is not for export abroad. He is the property of the Cuban state. Now put your hands in the air and come toward me one step at a time."

Luke saw Junior squirming as the Inspector pressed the gun harder against his temple. "Stay put, anxious youth. You but a half-rate painter. I plan to show off your ugly face in tomorrow's edition of *Granma*. Dead or alive, I could care less." The ship rolled to port and pounded through the crashing swells. A rogue wave hit amidships spraying green water over everyone on deck. Luke grabbed a stanchion and looked down into the abyss.

In a flash, the Inspector's upper body was flung over the rail. The gun escaped his hand as he desperately sought anything to stem his fall. His strong left hand grabbed Junior's long locks flailing in the wind. As the ship rolled 15 degrees, the Inspector and Junior went over the edge. Choreographed before his eyes, Luke witnessed a pas de deux in slow-motion. First the Inspector's right hand flapped in the breeze, as if he wanted to fly. He looked backward at Junior, who was following him down head first. The Inspector released his grip and fell 25 feet backwards through the air. Plunging down, Junior put his hands together, trying to break his fall.

Junior and the Inspector disappeared into the surging sea.

CHAPTER 42

Riding the tropical storm, the Florida Straits, Tuesday at dusk

THIS WAS HIS DEFINING MOMENT. Luke didn't even think about it. He strapped on a life jacket, grabbed another and awaited the ship's next roll to port. He shouted to Vicente, "Pray for us." The Spaniard looked terrified, wrapping his legs around a stanchion and struggling to hang on. The wind shrieked down the deck, causing lines to wriggle like sea snakes on the hunt.

When the ship heeled, Luke jumped in and aimed his toes at the sea. He plunged 25 feet to the Florida Straits and another 20 feet underwater, feeling his ear drums ready to burst. He refused to give in, swallowing his breath over and over again. He stopped falling and began drifting up. He kicked with all his might. Seawater forced its way into his mouth and down his esophagus. Luke feared that he'd drown before reaching the surface. He was on the verge of blacking out.

He finally bobbed to the top, gasping through the ferocious waves. Swells rolled over him as he turned away. The other life jacket tossed about 10 yards ahead. Luke pushed himself to swim and rode the following seas. He grabbed the jacket and saw the *MSC Operetta* sailing away, maintaining its course to Miami.

Luke looked west to the dying sun. He felt so alone. After the blood, sweat and tears he'd shed this week, was this how his life was going to end? The wind cuffed him behind the ears, as if he were a stray dog.

A primal cry surged deep within him, as he screamed, "No . . ." To the heavens, he bellowed, "Help me!" The storm cascaded over him. He looked upward for a break in the clouds. He began reciting the 23rd Psalm.

He kicked half-heartedly, letting the sea carry him wherever it wished. His adrenaline faded and exhaustion overtook Luke. He put his face down in the water and just let go. But something made him lift his head. Just 20 yards away, he heard splashing and saw phosphorescent swells. There was movement nearby. Water was churning but not from the rolling waves. Could it be sharks prowling for prey?

In the twilight, Luke perceived a spot of red. Pushing the other life preserver in front of him, he expected that he'd have to do battle with whatever lay ahead. The trade winds pushed him toward the unusual glow. A head popped up. Could it be?

Then something extraordinary happened. He heard a cackle and detected a graceful mammal push underneath his son's listless body, keeping Junior's head above water. Luke had read about the affinity between dolphins and humans but had not witnessed such a phenomenon. Another dolphin swam up beside Luke, wiggling its bottlenose at him. "Thank you, fellow beings of the sea," he heard himself exclaim.

His son was floating on his back and had lost consciousness. Through the swells, Luke pushed his son's arms through the life jacket and strapped him in tight. He sobbed in gratitude and babbled to him *en español*.

Junior had a light pulse but needed help fast. The bottlenose creatures got closer to these human beings at risk. Luke kept heading toward the last glimmer on the horizon. For a moment, he felt bliss.

At least, he and his son would not die alone, cast adrift in the Atlantic Ocean. Their future lay in someone else's hands. He closed his eyes.

* * *

LUKE AWAKENED. Rather, the more talkative dolphin nudged him under his armpit, as if to say, "No sleeping on my watch." Luke smiled at his maritime companion, wondering how long they could hold on together. There was only a hand flare attached to his lifejacket but no water bottle. Junior needed help ASAP.

He searched the velvet horizon and saw a gleam break through the swells. Luke rubbed his eyes and saw an unsteady white light over red. Luke startled the dolphin by grabbing the hand flare from his jacket pocket. He held the end and twisted off the cap, pulling the tab. Nothing happened. A dud. The oncoming vessel was drifting by.

Frantically, he grabbed the flare attached to Junior's jacket, twisted off the cap and pulled hard on the tab. This time an incandescent red lit their patch of sea, causing the friendly dolphins to dive for cover. Luke treaded water and held the flare high, praying that the crew might spot them.

Little by little, a shaky green and a red light grew brighter below the white masthead beacon. A small trawler was braving the seas to approach them. Two fishermen stood adroitly on the narrow bow, bracing against the seven-foot swells. "Help—*Socorro!*" Luke yelled with all he had left.

A life ring was flung to Luke, who looped one arm through it and wrapped the other around his son. Slowly but surely, the fishermen reeled them in, speaking a strange tongue. Strong, dark arms pulled Luke and his son aboard. Surf slapped the trawler's bow and wind lashed them from behind.

Luke gasped, "My son needs help. Call SOS on the emergency channel. I am a U.S. citizen." Luke then drooped his head onto the gunnels, as a maritime shroud engulfed him and his son. Before closing his eyes, he saw the two dolphins arch gracefully above the waves, as if to say, "*adiós.*"

EPILOGUE

THE COAST GUARD SKIPPER CHUCKLED as Luke made light of their breakfast at Krome, described by sailors and soldiers around the world as "shit on a shingle—a mainstay meal for hungry mouths.

The seasoned captain had rescued Luke and his son from the small Jamaican trawler, awash in the tropical storm. His medical team provided emergency CPR to the unconscious *Cubano*. The corpsmen operated as a tag team, two quick breaths in, followed by 30 chest compressions, constantly checking his pulse and airway. Slowly, Junior showed small signs of life. He moaned and vomited seawater again and again. His breathing was ragged but evened out after an hour. They removed his clothes, wrapped him in a thermal blanket, and administered oxygen. When Junior opened his eyes for the first time, "Booyah" was heard throughout the ship.

As the captain and Luke had previously served on "tin can" destroyers, they forged a common and friendly bond. After Luke related his incredible story about finding his son, the captain volunteered to speak with the Immigration & Customs enforcement director at Krome's detention facility. The captain had known the director for several years. After being medically cleared, Junior, as an undocumented immigrant, was sent to Florida's infamous facility just south of Miami.

Now, one week after their harrowing ordeal, father and son sat with the garrulous captain, trying to figure out their next move. The captain had approved of Luke's own act of civil disobedience. Luke had insisted on being locked up with his Cuban-born son until their attorney sorted things out with the immigration courts. The captain got involved and soothed the director's ruffled feathers to permit Luke's impromptu incarceration.

The captain's ruddy face lit up the grim visitor's room. "Yesterday, I passed your request on to your attorney, Mitch. This has become his *cause célèbre* and don't be surprised if he tips off the press. He should arrive soon. When your son is released into his custody, let's share more tales over mojitos." On board, over medicinal cognac, they had begun comparing past adventures in the Western Pacific.

Junior appeared dazed. It had been a shocking 24 hours. He didn't acknowledge any of their conversation in English. "Tell me more about the Jamaicans, captain? I heard them speaking some sort of Creole but didn't understand a word. I was so out of it. I want to thank them from the bottom of my heart. Because of these fishermen and the friendly dolphins, we are still on planet earth."

"I'll try to get their points of contact in Kingston but doubt they want any attention. Besides being fishermen, they likely run contraband to and from Cuba. They prefer to stay off the grid."

The steel door banged open to admit a uniformed guard, "Your attorney has arrived, Mr. Shannon."

"Great! We'll see you later, lieutenant," declared the captain, referring to Luke's former naval rank, lieutenant (junior grade). "Let's muster up when things settle down. I'll be around for another week." The burly skipper walked forward to give Luke a hug but abruptly refrained himself. "Social distancing' is now the norm, lieutenant." He gave Luke a fist bump instead, while Junior looked warily at the guard.

The captain nodded at Mitch and closed the heavy door. The balding attorney removed his bandana and took in the scene over his half-moon glasses. Luke's son avoided eye contact. They heard inmates raising their voices in adjacent rooms, despite the bulletproof glass.

"Thank you so much, Mitch, for taking my son's case. He is at wit's end. He's never encountered urban gangs, let alone the Salvadoran *maras*. I've had to protect him on more than one occasion against the macho leaders who've targeted him. We were lucky to gain one cell together without another inmate on the floor. As Junior looks like Venezuela's democratic leader, Juan Guaidó, the inmates have dubbed him *'Guaidocito,'* or little *Guaidó*."

Junior jumped when he heard the nickname. Mitch took note, touched Junior's shoulder lightly and spoke in halting Spanish. "It's alright, Lucas. I plan to provide a bail bond to guarantee your presence at Miami's immigration court. Please sign these papers so I can begin the process to get you out of here." The attorney nodded reassuringly to Junior, who looked back at his father. Luke gave him a thumbs up.

"Professor, give me 10 minutes more," Mitch said. He knocked on the door and exited with the burly guard. Other inmates sauntered by in cuffs together; "social distancing" didn't appear to be the norm in detention. One mouthed Junior's nickname, causing him to cringe.

Luke touched his son's shoulder and turned themselves toward the concrete wall. They tried to filter out the curses and the shouts from outside. They weren't successful.

Mitch reappeared 15 minutes later with a signed document and a resplendent smile. "It's time to say, *hasta la vista*. Now, please put out your hands."

Junior stood up quickly but looked askance at the sanitizer in the attorney's hand. "We must take care against this new virus," cautioned Luke, who held out his hand. His son followed his father's example. They joined the attorney and marched briskly down the whitewashed corridor without touching anything. The guard led them through the checkpoints and buzzing doors and eventually released them outside of Krome. They faced flashing bulbs and a setting sun.

Cameramen filmed their departure and local reporters shouted questions from the parking lot. A woman in a serape and a teenager held vigil with the banner, "Free political prisoners." The attorney's driver wove through reporters and photographers and popped the doors to a black Volvo. Before entering the car, Mitch briefly lifted Luke and Junior's arms high, exclaiming, "Father and son!" to the cheering brigade. He put back on his bandana and gave masks to them.

Luke and Junior found refuge in the backseat as Mitch squirted more sanitizers on their hands. The Volvo raced out of the lot heading east on SW 12 Street. A makeshift caravan followed. The rest of the journey was a blur for Luke. The driver's twists and turns on and off freeways made most followers abandon the chase. The Volvo meandered through backstreets, shaded by coconut palms into a neighborhood called "The Grove."

After a sharp turn into an alley, the Volvo stopped at an open door. Mitch did quick introductions to his sister, who whisked them inside. Odors of compost, lime rinds, and cheap rum welcomed Luke to her empty bar. Its jukebox played *Guantanamera* and Junior sighed aloud. Luke saw the suggestion of a smile on his son's lips.

* * *

"JUNTOS!" SCREAMED THE LARGE LETTERS in *el Diario de las Américas*, above a photo of father and son together, their arms raised high. In the *Miami Herald*, a more political headline read "Freed from Krome." Its

Spanish-language counterpart, *el Heraldo*, simply stated, *"Libertados,"* showing Luke and Junior smiling and Mitch wearing his ACLU cap.

Subsequent articles resurrected memories of Ochoa decades ago and how his grandnephew had escaped the Cuban police in 2020. Letters to the editor questioned the fairness of Ochoa's trial causing fiery debates inside and out of the Cuban American communities.

They sorted through the news stories over several *cafés cubanos*. Mitch's sister ran interference for them on the phone. "Today, Marco Rubio's office called and wants a photo op with both of you outside his South Miami office. I told him that would be fine as long as he'd sponsor a private bill in the U.S. Senate to grant citizenship to Luke's Cuban-born son. He agreed with gusto. These private bills are tacked onto others at the end of summer's session. Let's hope that the virus and economic woes don't jinx this tradition. What do you, say?"

Luke translated for Junior, who seemed reluctant to leave the safety of the bar. Mitch came alongside with a toothy grin, "Junior, it will be OK." His son trusted the rotund attorney and tried to give him a hug. Mitch explained "social distancing" again. He orchestrated their day with aplomb through partially opened office buildings, press briefings, and back to his sister's funky bar. The Coast Guard captain stopped by with their luggage, secured from MSC's office at the Port of Miami.

The captain and the lieutenant downed their double mojitos over more war stories in the fading light. Junior drifted toward the juke-box, swaying to the tunes of the Buena Vista Social Club. "Time for the Zoom to Barcelona, lieutenant. Vicente wants to share news with both of you."

Just like that, there was Vicente and his wife on their outdoor balcony overlooking la Rambla, their daughter rocking in a crib. They were nibbling on Spanish ham and Manchego cheese. Skype showed them lifting their glasses of Jerez to father and son 5,000 miles away.

Luke, Junior, Mitch and the bar's modest clientele raised their mojitos high, shouting "*Salud.*"

After the hoopla, they adjourned to a private room and a small TV monitor to share their family news. Luke blurted out, "Vicente, did Eloisa ever make it to Spain?"

"Indeed, she did. On the outbound trip to Barcelona, she met a wine baron from Spain's Rioja region. Together, they were wined and dined at the captain's table. On arrival, she was seen along Madrid's Gran Via in her paramour's trendy shop, serving *Don Ramón* Grenache to aficionados. She made the social page of *el Pais.*

"She even met Ochoa's daughter, known as *La Roja* or 'the red woman' in the Spanish capital. They gave a few interviews and became the talk of the town. They frequented midnight soirees as Spain slowly opened up. As you know, Eloisa makes heads turn wherever she goes.

"As for our little family, we're content in Barcelona despite the lurking virus. Let's hope the sun helps beat it down. My wife, a trained architect, has joined the team to restore Gaudí's *La Sagrada Familia.*" His wife touched him on the lips.

"And our friend, Fr. Sebastian, did he return to his parish in Santiago? I hope that he did not suffer repercussions from helping Eloisa and my son leave Cuba."

"I spoke with him yesterday by WhatsApp. He's returned to his home parish, where he seems at peace. Havana was too fast-paced for him. Apparently, he traveled there with Big Man." Vicente's smile turned down.

"I'm sorry to report that the General dumped his major-domo when he learned that he facilitated Eloisa's escape on the MSC ship. He fired him on the spot. As to the General, he still holds court in Hotel Nacional's garden bar, romancing a special assistant of the Banco Central de Cuba."

Luke was impressed with how Vicente, the constant journalist, followed Cuban news from afar. "What happened to Big Man? Though he had a rough exterior, I sensed that his heart was in the right place."

Vicente continued, "Thanks to the intervention of his boss at the National Revolutionary Police, he secured a detective's post in his hometown of Santiago. Loyal policemen at the Castle lobbied to let him keep his beat-up Chevy. He, Dolores, and the priest departed together last week. Providentially, they secured a scarce gasoline-ration book for the trip. It's hard to find any kind of fuel now in Cuba.

"They stopped in Ochoa's hometown and met up with that young homerun hitter you told the priest about. Big Man and Dolores were so taken by the kid's story that they pleaded to the local magistrate to adopt him. Big Man offered the judge his remaining ration book. The justice signed the adoption papers on the spot. All four are residing happily in Santiago."

"Hallelujah," exclaimed Luke. His son spontaneously gave his father a hug, "Good for Hercules." Tonight, their hearts were full. They waved adiós to their friends in Barcelona and gave Mitch, his wife, his sister, and the captain elbow bumps of thanksgiving. At long last, this evening had the promise of restful sleep.

* * *

It took a couple weeks for Senator Rubio, staffers, and politicos to work their pending bills through D.C.'s shoals. As TV's limelight dimmed and humidity rose above Capitol Hill, the nation's elected representatives faded from the public eye. It was time to show their constituents a little progress before the Labor Day's recess. Late August was the time for private congressional bills. Former Governor Jeb Bush called in a few favors inside the Beltway. The Cuban American National Foundation made its voice heard to help Junior's cause.

Besides granting citizenship to Lucas Junior and select Afghanis who helped U.S. troops, special bills favored an Army German Shepherd with lifetime healthcare and a Wisconsin dairy family with a reprieve from tariffs caused by the Trade War. It was all part of "due process" in the halls of Congress, enticing constituents to pull the pol's levers later in the fall.

As news broke from Washington, D.C., Luke hosted a visit from the exile who had first provided entrée to Fr. Sebastian. He'd seen Luke on local TV and came early to the Coconut Grove bar. "Yes, the padre is a stand-up priest. Cuba needs more people like him. I'm sorry that you weren't able to visit Ana before she passed. How wonderful that you and your son found each other in the countryside. A miracle indeed!"

They were sipping mojitos as Miami's humidity seeped through the morning haze. Luke's son stood by the window, smiling at the parakeets chortling in the palms. Mitch was on the other side of the bar, wearing earbuds and raising his voice to the Amtrak sched- uler. He avoided eye contact with the exile, his arch-rival in Cuban American politics. They let their political animosities subside in order to advance Junior's cause for freedom.

Luke paused to ask, "Was there any sighting of the Inspector or his underlings?"

"No habeas corpus, professor. What I've heard from confidants who frequent the Ministry of Interior is a collective sigh of relief. He had few friends inside or out of official circles. The General has filled the vacuum. As to underlings, I haven't heard much. The young man on the Inspector's payroll is still moping around the Hotel Nacional seeking tourist dollars.

"The Vietnamese diplomat, whom you mentioned, is now quar- antined in his residence. He tested positive for the virus but is on the mend. He remains the embassy's official trade attaché and unofficial spy. He now calls into the *MinInt* gatherings via WhatsApp. His Chinese counterpart was called back to Beijing for consultations."

Mitch approached their table, barely nodding to the Cuban exile. "Luke and Junior, it's time to catch your 11:50 train. My driver just pulled up front, where a few reporters are gathering. One more gauntlet to run, amigos!" They gave the few customers inside the bar elbow bumps and headed for the front door. The attorney gave Luke a bottle of sanitizer and more masks for the long trip ahead.

Milling around outside were a few well-wishers, TV journalists and talk-show hosts from *Radio Mumbí, Actualidad* and *Caracol.* Responding to their questions, Luke simply said, "Thank you, people of Miami for helping free my son." Luke and Junior raised their arms to cheers. They got into the Volvo and sped off through Coconut Grove.

Mitch's driver swung onto Douglas Road and traveled north through the inner city, where Luke had briefly taught at Miami Jackson High School. His former students began a "Go Fund Me" account to finance Luke and Junior's cross-country train trip back to Seattle. Dozens of Miamians donated online and Amtrak made up the shortfall for their 3,300-mile trip.

They arrived at the Miami Station, just south of Hialeah. The clock showed 11:40. Mitch arranged for a porter to take special care of Junior's artwork. "Many thanks, Mitch—how can we possibly repay you?" Luke was about to hug the exuberant attorney, sporting his ubiquitous half-moon glasses.

"Don't forget social distancing, professor. Times have changed since our visit to Cuba. No worry about paying me back. My phone is ringing off the hook. Thanks to you and your son's story, I have many new clients. Enjoy your trip home and here's hoping Amtrak's A/C is working well."

Father, son, attorney and wife rubbed elbows briefly and feigned hugs. The whistle blew, hustling Luke and his son on board. Amtrak was leaving on time, though its cars were half-empty.

Luke and Junior glided into their seats as the train eased forward. Autos stopped at the railroad crossing and Junior pressed his nose against the window. Luke was thrilled to see his son's excitement rising.

Across the aisle one seat forward, a woman in a pink-and-orange Punjabi settled in with her pig-tailed daughter. "Why don't you paint a scene to remind us of our trip?" she coaxed. Junior craned his neck to watch the girl examine the different shades in her watercolor set. She dabbed a little water on reddish-brown and dark orange and began broad strokes. The train hurdled over a bump, flinging her brush to the aisle floor. Junior reached across his father's lap to pick it up.

"Here you are, young lady. You seem to like copper and earthy colors, like me."

She looked at Junior with serious eyes. "Are you an artist? Can you show me something you've painted?"

"With pleasure." Junior swapped seats with his father and took down the painting of his mother, alive in hues of red, brown and orange. The girl was transfixed, staring at the painting and back at Junior. "My mother, señorita," he added quietly.

Luke smiled as his son described how he mixed earthy tones to gain sharper contours on people's faces. He was so earnest and his pupil was so rapt. Luke felt proud, as any father would. As Florida's urban areas gave way to the Everglades and orange groves, the two artists were experimenting with water colors and chatting about special techniques.

When the train went through a tunnel, Ana's portrait mirrored off the darkened window. Luke sighed aloud.

"A promise made is a promise kept," he whispered. Observing her demure look in reflection, he added, "Please forgive me, Ana, for being 30 years late."

The train exited the tunnel and passed the rolling hills of Ocala. Horses ran in the open fields, heading toward the afternoon sun. As the locomotive barreled north to Seattle, Luke eased his head back and closed his eyes, finally at peace.

ACKNOWLEDGEMENTS

L ET ME FIRST THANK THE CUBAN exiles, whom I met late 1989 in Worldnet television's studios in Washington, D.C. Their poignant stories of escaping Castro's regime moved me to the core. Ana Maria Sanchez's lament regarding Ochoa's death by a firing squad has haunted me for years. Thus, I dedicate this book to her.

I acknowledge Jorge Mas Canosa and Tony Navarro for initiating Radio/TV Martí, creating more objective programming for their homeland. Jorge established a foundation bearing his name to advance freedom in Cuba. The Cuban American National Foundation educated this *Norteamericano* about the challenges confronting exiles abroad. Jorge Mas Santos and Francisco Pepe Jose Hernandez are the shakers and movers in this national foundation.

In metro Miami, I so appreciate Herb Levin, author of *Successful Management* and producer of *Cuba: La Generación de Cambio,* for his solid support, advice, and hospitality. Herb's discernment of Cuban-exile history imparted context to my writing. *Gracias, amigo!*

Dr. Jaime Suchlicki, director of the Cuban Studies Institute in Coral Gables, FL, read all 73,700 words of the original manuscript, offering thoughtful critiques. His dedication to shedding light on

Cuba's authoritarian regime is legendary, as are his insights into what may come next.

Pacific Northwest Writer's Association (PNWA) President Pam Binder and Marketing Director Maria Phillips encouraged me to pen my debut novel on Cuba. Pam, an accomplished author, shared her "school of hard knocks" stories with me during her creative writing class. PNWA conference attendee Barbara Davis Kroon, author of *Trap Play*, thoughtfully instructed me on "third-person close."

Editor Oren Ashkenazi reviewed this book's outline, and Shirleann Nold, former editor and book club enthusiast, has read every word, offering "tough love" reviews. Larry and Melissa Coffman of Book House Publishing edited and proofed the manuscript, designed the book's interior and facilitated interface with IngramSpark. Rae Monnet, web designer for many authors around the world, created my author's website. Issaquah librarian Ann Crewdson, *Connections* editor Nina Milligan, and author Stephen Holgate provided moral support during tough times.

Professor José Antonio Echenique of *Universidad Autónoma de México* gave impetus to my initial visit to the University of Havana, when travel was complicated. I am grateful for Seattle University's encouragement to reach out to counterparts at the University of Havana. Vicente Morin Aguado, reporter for the *Havana Times*, I commend your diligence to verify fact, fiction, and folklore inside Cuba.

Alan Gross and Fernando Pruna shared heart-wrenching stories about their confinement at *Villa Marista*. Rosamaria Caballero, Mary Koruga, and Gary Drobnack supplied photos and personal stories about the Cuban people. Norberto Fuentes, author of *Dulces Guerreros Cubanos*, offered historical context about General Ochoa's 1989 "trial."

Persons described in this book are based on real people, whose names have been changed to protect the innocent. Of the

65 Cubanos interviewed, I recognize several by their first names: Angel, Arlen, Ariel, Celia, Collin, Eduardo, Ernesto, Eusebio, Eva, Federica, Fernando, Fidel, Frank, Gerardo, Gilberto, Henry, José, Leah, Manela, Manuel, Marc, Marco, Marelbi, Maria, Marinela, Mary, Mercedes, Miguel, Monica, Norberto, Pablo, Ramón, Raul, Reynier, Roberto, Ronald, Rubert, Sebastian, Sergio, Victor Manuel, Yaima and Yosvany.

To Cuba's clergy and lay men and women, I will pray for your ministries as you continue doing good on shoestring budgets. I am grateful to Fr. Juan Molina, who served as director of the Collection for the Church in Latin America, U.S. Catholic Conference of Bishops, and provided entrée to Catholics during my maiden trip to Cuba. Subsequently, Fr. Richard Vigoa and Raul Panellas of Miami's Archdiocese, kindly introduced me to clergy and lay Catholics in metro Havana and at the San Carlos and San Ambrosio Seminary.

Evangelical pastors and patrons in Havana, Santa Clara, and Holguin, enlightened me about the growing 20,000 home-church movement. I thank Gary and Jim, who support them.

For technical guidance, I am indebted to friendly cognoscenti: Dr. Carl Wyman and Dr. Celia on emergency practices to resuscitate a drowning victim and rustic medicine; Carv Zwindel and his Coast Guard friend on survival at sea; Peter Bradfield on how a ship performs in a tropical storm; Jorge Maezono on Cuban architectural façades; and Tommy Goodman on Cuba's national sport and "baseball diplomacy."

I recognize journalists from the *Miami Herald, Diario de las Américas,* and *the Daily Beast* for in-depth stories on Cuba, Ochoa and Krome Detention. I thank my nephew, Jason, for creating my author's Facebook page, Richard Cruz for jazzing up my LinkedIn profile, and J.D. Fuller for the compelling cover design. Credit is due the authors quoted at the beginning of each Journey in this book—especially King David for the 23rd Psalm.

Thank you, Vicki, brother Terry, family, friends, and Issaquah's Mayor Mary Lou Pauly, for your positive energy during three years of research, writing, and reassessment of current events.

And thank you, readers, for picking up *Havana Odyssey: Chasing Ochoa's Ghost.*

AUTHOR'S NOTE
AND BIO

WHILE THIS IS A WORK OF fiction, the characters are based on real people in Cuba, Miami, Seattle, and Washington, D.C. In the summer of 2018, I returned to "the Pearl of the Antilles," bringing donations to a Cuban seminary, books for the University of Havana, medicine and Neutrogena soap for "friends of friends." I interviewed Cubanos of all walks of life.

Havana Odyssey's almost-final draft was completed late 2019, after Cubans commemorated the 500th anniversary of Havana and the 30th anniversary of Arnaldo Ochoa's death. Since COVID-19 struck in 2020, I rewrote the manuscript to reflect contemporary events and condensed 2019-2020 into one storyline, beginning July 2019 but "melding" into August 2020. Later, I added the subtitle, *"Chasing Ochoa's Ghost,"* to highlight the protagonist's quest.

General Arnaldo Ochoa is still a topic of debate among expatriates and cognoscenti of Cuba. Ochoa's military campaigns in Africa are still taught at the U.S. and Russian War Colleges. He was an extraordinary general who returned to Cuba as the "Hero of the Republic."

A friend of the general speculated that his death warrant was issued when Cubans rose from their seats and offered spontaneous applause wherever he went in 1989. Like Camilo Cienfuegos and Che Guevara from the early days of the Revolution, Ochoa met an untimely demise. The brothers Castro would not share the spotlight —there was no room at the top.

I met Ana Maria in Worldnet television's studios the same year as Ochoa was shot by firing squad. I promised her to tell her "relative's" ("*pariente*") story to the world. Though 30 years late, I pray that I have done her and General Ochoa justice in this book.

May their souls and the souls of all the Cuban martyrs rest in peace.

* * *

Stephen E. Murphy has lived and traveled "south of the border" for decades. He enjoys long lasting friendships in Cuba, Brazil, Mexico, Colombia, Chile, Panama and El Salvador. He has held executive positions in the BankBoston, Paramount Pictures, and the Inter-American Development Bank. For the first Bush administration, he was appointed *Worldnet* Television director, U.S. Information Agency. Under President George W. Bush, he served as Regional Director, Inter-Americas, for the Peace Corps.

As a volunteer, he taught economics at Miami Jackson High School. *The Miami Herald* and the *Wall Street Journal* recognized his efforts to teach inner city students about the stock market and how their picks beat the S&P 500 in 1995. He left Miami for hometown Seattle, where he has taught "Latin America Business" at Seattle University and consulted for firms expanding to the Americas. He has published articles on Cuba and Brazil for the *Puget Sound Business Journal* and for Seattle's Trade Development Alliance *Quarterly*.

Murphy mentors students and young professionals in Miami, Seattle, Havana and Rio de Janeiro and serves as chapter advisor to the Phi Kappa Psi fraternity, University of Washington. He loves swimming in open bodies of water all over the world.

Encouraged by UW alumni, he self-published a 2016 memoir, *On the Edge: An Odyssey*, about "the turning points in life." The author has presented in three countries in 60 different venues, including Books & Books (Coral Gables, FL) and *La Biblioteca Nacional de Cuba*. The book has sold in excess of 1,000 copies and garnered more than 90 Amazon reviews. Murphy is researching a new book, *Brazilian Odyssey*, and is fluent in Spanish, Portuguese, and French.

Three professors in Havana, from left to right: the author, representing Seattle University, then-vice dean, Fidel de la Oliva, University of Havana, and Professor José Antonio Echenique, la Universidad Autónoma de México, with Fidel peering over their shoulders. Photo courtesy of Dr. Maricela Reyes, then-dean, Facultad de Contabilidad y Finanzas, Universidad de la Habana.

CPSIA information can be obtained
at www.ICGtesting.com
Printed in the USA
BVHW041627220922
647764BV00006B/114